TOWN OF LIARS

M. B. WHITEHILL

This one's for my Mom,

Who has been my biggest supporter

From the very beginning.

PROLOGUE

The interview was being conducted in Xander's basement. He kept referring to it as his 'studio,' and while it looked nice, it was still his basement, regardless of what he called it. In fact, it wasn't even his basement, as I knew this was his parents' house. Few people his age could afford their own house, and I knew Xander's podcast wasn't particularly successful. Xander was in his early twenties, and had a long red beard that must have taken years to grow out, as well as an impressive handlebar moustache and comically large glasses that covered almost half of his face. When I had researched his podcast I had noticed that they would constantly slide down his nose and he would have to push them back up at least once a minute.

"Very nice to meet you, Detective," he said when he opened the door at the side of his house that led into his 'studio.'

Despite being taller and much heavier than me, he insisted on squeezing my hand very tightly during our initial handshake, as if to make a statement of how strong he was. If it was meant to impress or intimidate me, it didn't work.

"Pleasure to meet you as well," I said. "And just George is fine."

Xander led me down the narrow stairwell into his 'studio.' The walls were wooden, but it wasn't a cheap wood like many of the houses around here had, this was an aesthetic that he had specifically chosen. On the far wall was a neon sign which I knew read 'Troo Krime,' which was the stupid name they had chosen for this show. I only knew that's what it said because Xander had mentioned the name of the show when he first reached out to me. If I was trying to guess just by reading the squiggly letters flashing in an obnoxious green light, I wouldn't be able to make it out. In the middle of the room was a large table with all of his equipment, including several laptops and a pair of large, expensive microphones.

"So this is where the magic happens," Xander said as we walked over to the table. "Do you want water, or anything?" he asked.

"Water would be nice," I said. "Don't need it now, but I imagine I will later after we've been talking for a few hours."

As Xander walked over to the small fridge in the corner I noticed the small desk off to the side where Xander's cohost was sitting. He must have noticed my eyes wander in that direction.

"Oh, George, this is Julie," he said.

His cohost had been staring at her computer the whole time and didn't even look up to acknowledge me.

"Hi," was all she said.

Julie was the polar opposite of Xander, her hair had four, maybe five different colours in it, and she looked to weigh around 50 pounds. They had different last names, so I figured they weren't siblings, or married. I wondered how they had ended up working together and tried to convince myself that there was no way the two of them were sleeping together, since she would probably die under him. Although she might appear harmless, I knew from my research that she was the one I needed to worry about. Xander had a cheerful demeanour, and would spend the whole interview talking to me like we were just two guys having a fun conversation, and once my guard was down she would be the one to ask difficult questions to try and trip me up.

"Okay..." said Xander as he placed two water bottles on the side of the desk that I was going to be sitting on. "Now, most of this story is public knowledge, so if someone really wanted to, they could just go online and see who died, who survived, who went to prison, but there are a lot of people who listen to this who want to go into it completely blind, no spoilers. So if you can try to just not jump around in the story and go chronologically, that would be appreciated."

"Sounds good to me," I said.

As he spoke I noticed that Xander was doing his best to maintain eye contact with me, but his gaze kept lowering slightly to my nose. I did my best not to laugh. He had just asked me not to jump ahead in the story but I knew he couldn't wait to ask me about it.

The two of them spent the next few minutes setting everything up and finally we were ready to go.

"I am really excited about today's show," Xander said into the microphone. "We are joined today by Detective George Hoffman, who was the lead investigator in the town of Appleton during what has become known among true crime enthusiasts as the Insomniak Incident."

I always felt unfairly overhyped in these introductions, being talked about as though I was some big hero, which never felt earned. But I knew that this praise Xander was giving me might just be part of his plan to later catch me off guard with some question. Over the last six years I had done countless interviews like this. The story about what happened in Appleton in 2009 had developed a cult following over the years, with everyone discussing and analyzing all of the details. There were some who thought the details of the story didn't add up. Xander wouldn't be the first one to try and discover some clue that no one else had and figure out what really happened. They always had some theory that they would try to prove. None had been successful so far. I had listened to a few episodes of Xander's show before agreeing to come on, and truthfully it was far from the worst show I had been on. He was perfectly fine as an interviewer, although in a day when everyone seemed to be starting their own podcasts he did little to stand out from the crowd.

"Before you say anything else," I said. "We're not supposed to call it the 'Insomniak Incident.' I know that's the name that people gave it online, but the company behind Insomniak has been known to take legal action against those they claim are damaging their brand."

"You're right," Xander said, gritting his teeth.

He knew he should have caught that, and I shouldn't have to tell him how to do his job.

"I usually just refer to it as 'That Case,'" I told him. "Because of all the ones I worked this is the one that stands out the most."

"Yeah, I can imagine," said Xander.

He turned over to Julie.

"Might as well just call it the Appleton Case then."

She nodded, not looking up from her screen.

"So I thought we would start with something light," said Xander. "What is the Peacekeeper Pub Crawl?"

I had wondered what the first question would be, and this wasn't what I expected. I couldn't help but start laughing.

"Oh, I haven't thought about that in so long. Peacekeeper Pub Crawl..." I said. "Well, every year right after Christmas our boss would take the whole police department out for drinks. And this wasn't just he buys one round for everyone, no, you drink as much as you want and he pays for everything. If you puke, or get kicked out, or start a fight, well then it's over, but if you can manage to stay on your feet, he's got you covered. Now, the catch was that this event only takes place if our town goes the entire year without any murders."

Xander nodded his head as he processed this, causing his comically large glasses to tilt down his nose. As he adjusted them Julie piped in.

"But isn't that kind of luck?" she asked. "Unless you can somehow prevent murders before they happen?"

"That's true," I said slowly.

I was beginning to understand why they had begun with this question. It seemed innocent enough, they weren't immediately asking me about any grizzly details or about my opinions. They were already trying to find holes. But they wouldn't.

"Eventually the boss changed it, so that if there were murders and we managed to solve them, then he would still take us out. As you say, it is basically luck, so if our luck is bad, we have the chance to make things right."

Julie's expression didn't reveal whether she was satisfied with this answer or not. I was right that in this dynamic she was going to be the 'bad cop,' for lack of a better term. Xander would be the nice one who just wanted to hear me tell my story, while she would be the skeptical one asking questions to see if she could find a crack that no one else had been able to.

"And this boss was Dennis Willard, yes?" Xander asked. "Or did the chief before him start this?"

"No, it was Dennis who started it," I confirmed. "He became chief... I want to say three or four years after I joined."

I could tell that Xander wanted to ask questions about Dennis. Questions about things that happened later.

"So just to give us an idea," Xander continued. "What were the murder rates like in Appleton, in a normal year?"

"In a normal year?" I repeated. "Honestly, often zero. I know everyone says that their town is boring, but I really mean this, nothing ever happened in Appleton. It was a small, quiet town."

"What would have been a bad year?" Xander asked. "Before 2009, I mean."

I exhaled.

"2005... I think we had three? That was probably the worst year I had seen. Two of those were related, if I remember right, but still, three murders in a single year was quite the shocker."

"And then 2009 happened," said Xander.

"And then 2009 happened," I remembered with a sigh. "It was the last Monday before Christmas when we found the first body. And by the end of the year we were up to five."

"Jesus," said Xander.

"And the shitshow didn't even end there," I said.

Then I frowned.

"We can say 'shit' on this show, right? Or do you have advertisers who will get mad?" I asked.

"Oh, the advertisers won't care," Xander assured me. "We talk about dead bodies on this show, it's fine."

He paused and gently tugged on the end of his handlebar moustache, the tip almost touching the bottom of his enormous glasses.

"So when you got called to that first body, had you already met Evan Doherty?"

"No, I had actually been off the week before. I had a bunch of vacation days left over, and Evan had joined the team during that week I was gone. So I didn't meet him until the day we found the first victim, it was actually at that crime scene."

"And what kind of first impression did you get from him?" Xander asked.

I made a slightly exaggerated humming noise and drummed my fingers on the desk to give off the impression that I was thinking. I had been over this story so many times, I had all the details engrained into my brain, but I always made sure to be careful.

"You know how different people deal with personal tragedies in different ways?" I asked. "One person will cry for hours every day, another person just shuts down, doesn't really say much, someone else acts like everything's fine and just goes about their day?"

"Yeah, yeah," said Xander, who was nodding the whole time I spoke.

"So there's no right or wrong way to do this, everyone just processes it in their own way. And this job is the same as that. I don't know if you've ever seen a murder victim, and I don't mean like crime photos or a documentary, no, actually seen it right before your own eyes? There is nothing that prepares you for that, the knowledge that this was a person and then someone did this to them. And everyone in this line of work deals with this in their own way. Some of us are visibly shaken by it, others are shaken but don't allow themselves to show it. The point is that my first interaction with Evan Doherty was watching him step out of his car, approach the crime scene, and react to what he saw."

"And how did he react?" Xander asked.

ONE

On the last Monday before Christmas 2009 I awoke on the couch in our living room to the sound of the front door slamming shut. Even after all this time instinct kicked in that there was some kind of danger, only for me to remember half a second later that Martha was going out for her run. Back in the summer she had told me she was going to start running at the crack of dawn. She had asked me if I wanted to participate as well, but I used the excuse of working inconsistent hours, which wouldn't allow me to have a routine running schedule. I had thought that once it got cold out and the day got much shorter she would give up on this, but she was consistent, and continued to run every morning, never missing a day.

I was immediately filled with that annoyed feeling one always felt on their first day back at work after being off for a while. The past week I had actually managed to spend time with my family. It had been a bad feeling when I realized that I didn't really know that much about my children, beyond their names and physical appearances. Last week when Hope and I had been building a particularly fat snowman I realized that I was still talking to her in that condescending tone people used when talking to a baby, even though she was already four and could understand normal sentences. She didn't seem to mind, however. She was happy that I was spending time with her for once, and wouldn't stop asking me questions about work. From what I gathered she would always ask Martha about my job, but Martha had decided to do her best to shelter our children from the details of police work. I wasn't supposed to talk about crime, or drugs, or dead bodies, or anything like that. But now that it was just the two of us, Hope had figured she could try and get some more exciting answers out of me. On the other hand Carrie, who was eight, didn't seem phased by the fact that I was home all week. She kept in her room, as she always did. Carrie was always reading something and only left her room to eat, and even when she did she still brought whatever she was reading with her. The few attempts I made to have a conversation went nowhere. When I asked her if her favourite singer had released anything new, she muttered that she had grown out of that a couple of years ago. I was glad Martha wasn't around to hear how outdated my notes about my children's interests were.

Yesterday I had been filled with a sense of panic about all of the things I had said I wanted to do during my small vacation, things I knew I had to cram into the last few hours. I ended up coming home very late. In fact, I barely remembered coming home, but I must have been exhausted if I decided to fall asleep on the couch. I saw on my watch that it was already past 6 and I had to be leaving. When I got off the couch I felt a cramp in my legs, likely caused by the fact that the couch was slightly too short for me and I had slept with my legs curled up. I had brought this up to Martha in the past, and her response was that I should just sleep in the bed instead. Since I was already running late I made the decision to just go to work in the clothes I was wearing yesterday. No one would notice, as no one from work had seen me yesterday. Before leaving I walked down the hallway and peered into the two smaller bedrooms in which our kids were still asleep. In the kitchen there was a half-full pot of coffee from the day before, which I poured into a mug and drank in seconds, as I didn't have time to put on a fresh one. Just as I was putting the now empty mug away I noticed that my phone was on the counter. That's right, I had left it at home the night before. When I looked at it I saw that Dennis had called, just ten minutes ago. I must have slept right through it. I listened to the voicemail and found out that someone had reported finding a dead body at the edge of town. I sighed. I had hoped that my first day back would be uneventful so I could ease back into things, but it looked as though this quiet year was about to come to a grim end.

The act of putting shoes on took more energy than I liked. If I told Martha about this her natural response would be that I should be joining her on these runs she was taking at sunrise. Sometimes I wondered whether she was trying to get in better shape so she could leave me. As I straightened up I caught a glimpse of myself in the mirror. Despite having gone through a physical ordeal the night before I was still looking out of shape. And old. By now I had gotten used to my hair turning gray, at least the parts of it that weren't disappearing entirely. I had naively hoped that a few days of not working would restore my youth, but that was a fantasy. I had even gotten rid of the beard to try and look younger but that hadn't done anything either. I knew the real reason I was aging was because I wasn't sleeping much. My green eyes were encircled by bright red veins that were bursting, a clear sign that I wasn't taking care of myself. As I looked for other aspects of myself to hate I noticed that I was frowning.

Hope had asked me about that the other day, she was still at the age where a child is filled with a sense of wonder, and she couldn't understand why I was always frowning. I didn't have a good answer for that question. I wished I could be as blissfully happy as her.

***

As I drove towards the Northeast end of town I ended up stopping to buy an actual warm coffee, as well as a muffin. I had sworn off donuts when I first joined the force because I refused to be what people expected me to be. The road to the edge of town was a narrow path that was technically classified as a highway, even though it was only one lane in each direction. The paint used to indicate where each lane ended had faded years ago, and the road was defiled with long cracks that caused my car to continuously bounce up slightly. Off to the side were flat fields, several miles in each direction, covered by a thin blanket of snow. In the distance were bare trees which did their best to block out the first rays of sunlight on the horizon. As the road turned to the left I hit another bump, which caused me to let go of my muffin as I gripped the steering wheel with both hands. It disintegrated in the air and sprinkled my shirt with crumbs. I tried my best not to get annoyed, as I knew I would have to be focused on the work ahead.

When I arrived at the crime scene I was surprised to see Dennis there. There were two police cars parked at the side of the road, their lights still flashing, illuminating the dark sky with alternating bursts of blue and red. There was also a large truck parked a little further up the road. And then there was the sign. Here, at the edge of the town were two large wooden beams, with a sign nailed to them which read 'Welcome to Appleton: Population-' and then a faded number underneath, which the town had stopped repainting, due to the number always changing.

"There you are," said Dennis as I got out of the car.

Dennis had always looked old, ever since I had first joined ten years ago. He always gave off the impression of an elementary teacher who had given up telling his students to behave, but today he looked particularly defeated. I knew it was probably because of the body. Crimes like this were rare here, and when they happened it was a grim reminder of the kind of job we had signed up for. Dennis was standing with another officer, who I couldn't recognize due to how dark it still was. They were talking to a rather fat man, who I assumed was the driver of the truck. If I had to guess, he was the one who found the body.

"Didn't expect you here," I said.

I realized that I had gotten out of the car with my coffee, and it was too late to hide it. I noticed it at the same time as Dennis did, when his eyes tilted down and his thick eyebrows shot in the opposite direction, causing the snow to fall out of them and landing on his moustache, which itself was already coated in snow.

"Oh, I see you were in a hurry to get here," he said.

I frowned.

"The victim is already dead. They're not going anywhere," I replied.

Dennis looked like he wanted to say something in response, but he stayed quiet. Then he frowned and pointed at my shirt.

"You got something there," he said. "Some kind of stain."

I looked down and saw a small purplish blotch on my shirt.

"Shit," I said as I licked my finger and tried to smear it. "I dropped my muffin while I was driving."

The jam had already dried on the white fabric. Or was that the jam? Maybe this was from yesterday and I hadn't noticed.

"So where is it?" I asked a moment later.

"Come," he said, and motioned me towards the sign.

I should have been prepared for what I saw but I was still taken aback. The welcome sign that I had seen hundreds of times throughout my life and was burned into my brain now had a body nailed to it. It was a woman, she was pinned to the left beam with nails going through her feet and her right hand, which hung by her side. Her left hand had been stretched out across the top of the sign and then nailed in place, her palm hovering over 'Welcome.'

"Jesus," I said.

"Yeah," Dennis said. "It's fucked up."

I looked over at the truck driver who was still being questioned. The officer's voice sounded like Ross.

"That the guy who found her?"

"Yep," Dennis said. "Called it in less than an hour ago, said he almost swerved into the ditch when he saw the sign."

The woman was naked, and it was clear by the blueish tint of her skin that she had frozen to death. I looked around the fields but it was still too dark to see anything.

"How close is the nearest house do you think?" I asked.

Dennis thought.

"Not sure. I think there's that dairy farm a few minutes drive from here. Why?"

I took a step closer to the body and strained my neck up. The woman's mouth was slightly open, but it appeared unblocked.

"Would they have heard her screaming?" I asked before turning back to Dennis. "Or do you think she was already dead when she was put here?"

"From the looks of it, no," said Dennis, as he too stepped closer. "No immediately visible wounds besides the nails. We'll see, maybe Joel will find something."

Before either of us could say anything else there was the sound of tires crunching over gravel. I turned and saw another car slowly pull up to where we were.

"I can take care of this," I said as I began to make my way over.

The last thing we needed was someone showing up right now and getting in the way.

"Wait," said Dennis. "He's one of ours."

Dennis claimed the car belonged to a cop, but the man who stepped out of the driver's seat wasn't anyone I had ever met before.

"One of ours?" I asked Dennis.

"Yeah, he joined the team last week while you were gone. I told you before you left, we're having someone transferred over."

I thought back and vaguely remembered Dennis saying something like this a while ago. But still, seeing this person walking over to us, I thought that there had to be a mistake.

The new officer approaching looked like he was fresh out of school. He couldn't have been older than 20. He was wearing an oversized black coat that contrasted his hair, which was a pale blonde almost the same shade as the snow that was falling and landing in it. I noticed that he too had a coffee, which he could barely hold in the giant fluffy mittens he was wearing, but Dennis didn't seem to mind that he had gotten coffee before work like I had.

"Fuck, it's cold here," he said as he exhaled.

"George, this is Evan," Dennis said, introducing us. "Evan, George."

"Hi," Evan said, but he wasn't looking at me.

He had just noticed the body, and was staring up at it in amazement. And then he started laughing. At first I was confused. I turned to Dennis, but he seemed exhausted, as if he had already gotten used to this kind of behaviour.

"Sorry, is something funny?" I asked.

Evan managed to pull himself together and stopped laughing.

"I'm sorry. I don't mean to make light of this... it's just," and he turned to Dennis. "You told me nothing ever happens in this town. Like, a few days ago you said that."

"Well I'm glad you've managed to prove me wrong," Dennis replied, but Evan had already turned his attention back to the body.

He took a few steps closer and started rummaging through his pocket before pulling out his phone. He raised it up and a flash of light briefly illuminated the scene.

"Are you fucking serious?" I asked.

I turned to Dennis in disbelief but he just shook his head.

"Is he-" I began to ask again.

"Don't," Dennis whispered quietly.

Evan seemed to have not even heard us as he put his phone away. Before he could say or do anything else the other officer came over. I was right, it was Ross, who had begun growing the thinnest whisp of a moustache while I was gone to appear slightly older. Ross was typically the thinnest person in our office, but out here no one would have guessed, as he was bundled in so many layers that it made him the fattest of us.

"Looks like his story checks out," he said in his unusually high voice, looking back at the truck driver who was standing further away. "Says he takes this road a couple times a week."

"That's the guy who found her?" Evan asked, peering over at the driver.

No one answered him.

Do you want to bring him in, just in case?" Ross asked.

"We might as well," said Dennis. "See if you can call the employer, confirm that this is normal. Do we have an alibi for yesterday?"

"Says he was home sleeping," Ross said with a shrug.

"Can anyone confirm that?" Evan asked, before Dennis could give an answer.

Dennis turned to him and looked like he wanted to say something unprofessional, but he managed to restrain himself.

"We'll bring him back to the station. But for what it's worth, I doubt it was him."

"Why, cause he's too fat to lift her up?" Evan asked.

"Okay, that's enough," Dennis said.

While they bickered I walked back over to the sign and stared up at the body again. The victim's hair was a mess, the result of the wind blowing at it for hours.

"Recognize her?"

Evan had somehow materialized right beside me.

"No," I said. "Why?"

He shrugged.

"Figured it's a small town, everyone knows each other."

"I think that's just an expression. We don't literally all know each other."

But he wasn't listening. His eyes narrowed as he stared up at the body.

"Does it look like she's pointing at something?"

The hand which was raised across the sign has one finger extended out, while the others were all curled down.

"I don't know," I said. "Could be that's just how the hand was before she died?"

"Could be," he said. "Or she could be pointing at something."

I looked in the direction that the finger was apparently pointing at. There was nothing. Nothing but empty fields, and even though it was too dark, I knew the city was just on the horizon.

"Maybe," I said.

***

"Where did you find this guy?" I asked.

I was sitting in Dennis' office several hours later. The dead woman had been removed from the sign and was currently being examined by our coroner. Dennis had made a statement to the press and asked anyone who may have information to come forward. As of now we had been unable to identify who the woman was.

"I owed somebody a favour," Dennis replied as he lit a cigarette.

Dennis still smoked indoors, and I had never seen him angrier than when someone made the mistake of telling him he wasn't supposed to do that. I wondered whether Evan had done this last week, or if he thought the idea of Dennis smoking at work was amusing.

"I know he seems a little obnoxious, but I was told that professionalism aside, he is good at the actual job," Dennis continued.

I turned and looked out the window where I could see Evan at his new desk. He appeared to be scribbling something down on a note pad.

"What do you think about what we saw this morning?" he asked.

I turned back to Dennis.

"I don't know what to think," I said.

I was trying my best to put the woman out of my mind.

"We're going to need to solve this one fast," said Dennis, gritting his teeth. "The last thing we need around Christmas is people worrying about a murderer on the loose."

Suddenly there was a knock on the door. Dennis looked up and nodded. Evan walked in and immediately sat down in the chair beside me. I was glad he had left the door slightly ajar, I had never gotten used to Dennis chain-smoking in his office. It was something he seemed to only do when he was stressed, and given what he had just said about Christmas panic, I imagined that this was a bad day for him.

"Wanted to see me?" Evan asked.

"Yes, I wanted to talk to you about your conduct this morning," said Dennis.

"Oh, is this about the picture? Don't worry, I haven't shown that to anyone. That's just for studying."

"Studying?" I asked. "The picture of the dead naked woman crucified, that's for studying?"

"Oh yeah," Evan nodded, as if this were normal.

He lifted one leg up and rested it on his other knee, the tip of his shoe pressing against Dennis' desk. Dennis didn't say anything, but I saw by the way his jaw got tighter that he looked as though he was about to start yelling.

"I'm gonna make one of those boards in my house, you know the one where you connect all of the photos with yarn? Once the next victim shows up, I can start connecting."

"What do you mean, 'the next victim?'" I asked.

Evan looked puzzled, as thought I had just asked a stupid question.

"You think this was his first one?" he asked and shook his head. "Nah, this was done by a professional."

Neither Dennis nor I knew what to say, and Evan looked at each one of us, seemingly still unsure what the problem was.

"Okay, can I ask, just between us," he said. "have either of you ever killed anyone?"

"Oh Jesus Christ," said Dennis, burying his head in his hands while being mindful of the cigarette he was still holding.

I stared at Evan for a moment with my mouth open as I tried to decide whether the entire office had decided to pull a prank on me while I was gone.

"No," I lied. "Have you?"

"Nope," Evan replied quickly... a little too quickly. "But if I did, I wouldn't nail the body to a sign on the highway. Whoever did this wanted us to find her. See, this is what I'm worried about, if they had tried to hide the body and did a shit job and someone ended up finding it, then I'd think okay, we're dealing with an amateur, someone who's probably never done anything like this before. If they've made one mistake, they might make another, we'll get them in no time. But this... we're dealing with someone smart. This guy had to know that we would find the body fast, and he was confident that he hadn't made any mistakes which would help us find him."

"You say 'this guy,'" I repeated, "You're assuming that the killer was male."

Evan tilted his head.

"Come on, man. You saw that shit, that was almost ritualistic. And that's another thing, do you know how long it takes to crucify someone?'"

Again I wasn't sure whether this was a serious question that he wanted me to answer. I looked over at Dennis who just shook his head, indicating that he wasn't in the mood to have this conversation.

"This wasn't a quick bullet to the head or a shove down a flight of stairs," Evan continued. "This shit took time, it's fucking freezing cold outside but this guy was determined to nail her up, and he had to know that all it would have taken was one car to drive past during that whole episode and he would be caught. Unless he was planning on removing any potential witnesses too."

He looked at us, waiting for one of us to answer or pitch our own ideas. When neither of us said anything he clapped his knees and stood up.

"So when was the last time you guys had a murder like this? Actually, is there a map of the town anywhere? I want to see if there were any landmarks nearby that she might have been pointing to."

Oh, this again.

"What is he talking about?" Dennis asked me.

"Just a theory I got," said Evan, and he turned to leave the room.

"We're not done, sit back down," said Dennis.

Once Evan was seated Dennis continued.

"I want the two of you working this case together," he said.

Evan and I both began to explain that this was a terrible idea at the same time.

"Sir, I can handle this on my own-" Evan began.

"I am scared to imagine what your idea of handling this would be," Dennis replied, and he turned to me.

"Please don't do this to me," I exhaled. "I don't want to fucking babysit this guy."

"I'm right here, thanks," Evan said.

"You're going to work it together, because I told you I want this solved fast."

"Why not get Ross to do it? He's already questioning the truck driver," I suggested.

"Truck driver's not our guy," Dennis said. "Plus, I already have him working on other stuff, I want you both on this one."

He leaned in and seemed to relax a little.

"Look, right now your 'theories,'" he emphasized the word, "Are just that, theories. And they are going to stay theories, until you have something concrete. I don't want you shouting your ideas out to just anyone."

Evan opened his mouth to disagree but Dennis lifted a hand.

"But between us, I do think that you're right. Whoever did this, this was not something new to them. They knew what they were doing, and they're taunting us right now."

Once Evan left the office I turned back to Dennis but he was ready.

"I know you don't want to work with him, and I frankly don't care," he said.

I opened my mouth to argue but Dennis wouldn't give me a chance.

"I'm not punishing you, I'm doing this because I trust you to control him and stop him from ripping the town in half to find this person."

I frowned.
"I understand," I said.

INTERLUDE

"I'm already exhausted just listening to you explain what he was like," Julie said.

"I know what you mean," I said.

It felt strange painting such a negative picture of Evan on this podcast, but I had to be honest about our initial interactions.

"And yet it would seem he was right about almost everything," Xander said.

I tried to keep a straight face. There was something about the tone in which he said it, and the wording, 'it would seem.' He didn't believe the story. Over the years there had been countless theories about what really happened in Appleton, and which details were apparently made up. And I understood now that Xander was one of the people that doubted Evan's role in what happened.

"So Dennis had told you that Evan was transferred over, right?" Xander asked me.

"Yeah." I repeated. "He 'owed someone a favour,' I believe were his words. I assumed it was the police chief or mayor or someone like that in the city Evan was from."

"But he didn't mention the reason Evan had been transferred?"

"No," I said. "I didn't really think about it that much at the time. I imagine that if I had given it some thought I would have reached the conclusion that he was probably transferred because people thought he was difficult to work with."

Xander gave a small laugh.

"What was the mood in the town like after that first victim was found?"

I stared down at the table and thought for a moment.

"It was uneasy," I said finally. "There's this weird anticipation, almost. Cause I didn't recognize the victim, none of us did, but you realize that even if you didn't know this person, you probably know someone who did know them, and that someone's about to have the worst day of their life. Someone's about to spend Christmas without a loved one in just a few days, so Dennis really pushed us to find who did this right away."

"Right," Xander agreed. "And despite everything else, I think it's safe to say that Evan was right about this not being done by an amateur."

"Oh, absolutely," I said. "We had never seen anything like this before. You know, we had seen the odd husband killing a wife, or someone getting hit by a drunk driver, but this... this was self-expression. Evan caught on to that immediately."

"Do you think..." Xander began, "And I'm just picking this up from how you've been describing him, do you think he was a little too enthusiastic about this case?"

"I think he really enjoys having a mystery to solve," I said after a moment. "I like when my job is boring, because that typically means that everyone's alive and healthy. But he likes figuring this stuff out. Like I said he was already hyping up the fucking board with all the pictures and string connecting them. He likes doing this."

"Do you think this preference for a boring job comes with age?"

I laughed.

"Yeah, that might be it. I think once you settle down and have a family, you just want things to slow down a bit."

TWO

The rest of the day was uneventful. I didn't have to hear any more of Evan's theorizing and there weren't any developments in the case of our Jane Doe. We still had no idea who she was or who killed her, and no one had come forward with information. When I got home Martha was watching the news. If she looked happy to see me she wasn't showing it. In fact, Martha rarely looked happy these days, her mouth seemed to be permanently frozen in a frown. But that wasn't the only thing that indicated she was miserable. Her hair had begun fading, with new greys popping up weekly where there hadn't been a single one a year ago. And while she kept going on runs in the early hours of the morning, she had recently put on weight, not that I mentioned either of these things. But what really gave it away were her eyes, which I could have sworn had changed colour. Where they had once been blue, it was almost as if they had receded into a lifeless grey.

"So I guess this means you're going to be working long hours again," she said without looking up.

I looked at the TV where I saw the footage of Dennis giving a statement about the body. Thankfully I hadn't been in the shot even though I was standing just behind him.

"Hopefully not too long," I said with a yawn.

That noise was what caused her to look at me.

"Tired?" she asked in a weird tone.

I nodded.

"Maybe you shouldn't have been out so late yesterday."

I could tell that she wanted me to interpret this as a question.

"Maybe," I said.

I wasn't going to elaborate on where I had been.

"I thought the whole point of you taking time off was to spend time with your kids," she said, her voice getting louder.

"I did spend time with them," I said. "But I needed time for myself as well. And keep your voice down."

I knew both of our daughters were probably listening in from behind their doors.

"Make sure they don't see this shit," I said, pointing at the TV. "It's fucked up, what we found today."

***

When I arrived at work on Tuesday, Evan was already at his desk, scribbling notes as usual. He looked up when he heard me approaching.

"Oh, you're here," he said. "Hey, do you know who that guy is?" he asked.

"What guy?"

"The guy in Dennis' office right now," he said, pointing across the room.

The blinds in Dennis' windows were open and I could see that someone was sitting across from him. Even without seeing his face, I recognized the dirty grey hair and the collar of a suit that was obviously too big for him.

"Oh fuck, not him," I said.

"Who is that?" Evan asked again.

"When he comes out of the office don't approach him, don't even look at him. If he comes up to you then say as little as possible," I said.

"But who-"

"I'll explain later," I said as I collapsed in my chair.

Evan frowned but didn't persist.

"Oh, the coroner wanted to talk to us once you got here. About the girl from yesterday."

A few moments later we heard the door to Dennis' office open. Because of the open layout of our office there was no way to hide. The best I could do was put my head down and hope he didn't recognize me. I couldn't even hide behind my computer screen, as the monitor was positioned in a way that wouldn't block my head from view. I did my best to not look up and instead fixated on the sound of footsteps coming from that direction. They got closer and closer and I just hoped he would keep walking but instead he came to an abrupt stop.

"George!"

I tried not to groan at the obviously staged enthusiasm in his voice. But I knew if I played along this would end faster. I looked up and saw the man smiling down at me as an aroma of cigars attacked me. I stared at the decaying teeth smiling at me and did my best to smile back.

"Been so long," he said.

"Uh-huh," I answered.

He turned and noticed Evan, who had thankfully taken my advice and not paid any attention to him. But the man shuffled over.

"Hi, I'm Benjamin. I don't believe we've met," he said, extending a hand.

Evan made the briefest glance over at me as if he were hoping for instructions, but he quickly shook his hand.

"Evan. I just started here."

"Well you chose an exciting week to start," Benjamin said, still shaking Evan's hand for an annoyingly long time. "Horrible what happened to that girl. How could someone do such a thing?"

Evan seemed puzzled as to why Benjamin would find this amusing.

"That's what we're trying to figure out... sir," he seemed unsure whether that last word was necessary.

"What are you doing here?" I asked.

Benjamin pursed his lips.

"Just swung by to talk to the chief, let him know that if there's anything I can do to help, all you guys need to do is call."

"Well thank you," I said.

Benjamin turned back to Evan.

"It's going to be nice working with you," he said and clapped him on the shoulder.

Then he walked out of the building.

"What did he mean by that?" Evan asked.

I knew exactly what he meant but didn't feel like explaining it just yet.

"I'll tell you later," I said.

I could see Dennis standing in his doorway with an expression on his face that showed he was ready to jump off a bridge.

"Come on," I said. "Let's go see what the coroner found out."

***

I had always thought that if Joel had not been our coroner he probably would have ended up being a murderer himself. Not only did he physically look like a corpse, with pale skin thinly stretched over his bones, but he had a strange fascination with death, and talked about it almost as if it were an art form. I dreaded what was about to happen, given that he and Evan were about to have their first conversation together.

"Okey dokey," he began once Evan, Dennis and I were in the room.

The still-unidentified woman was lying on the table in front of us. I tried not to look at her. I had never gotten used to that almost-peaceful expression bodies had. Suddenly my eyes noticed the hole in her hand and I felt a shiver, although I didn't know whether it was from that, or from how cold the room was. I rubbed my arms, trying not to make any noise. The last thing I needed was Evan condescendingly asking me if I wanted a jacket.

"So she froze to death, wasn't the crucifying that killed her, it was the cold," said Joel.

He kept making this weird clicking noise when he talked, as if he had a piece of food stuck between his teeth that he was trying to tongue out.

"Any idea who she was?" Dennis asked.

"Nope. Fingerprints don't match anything. But speaking of fingers, we didn't find anything under her nails, which was disappointing, I had hoped there would be something there."

"Why?" I asked.

"Well, imagine you were being crucified," he said, his eyes widening. "You'd be kicking and screaming the whole time. Sometimes when there's a violent crime you find the killer's hair, or skin, or blood under the victim's nails cause they were putting up a fight. But nope, not here. It's like she got up there voluntarily."

"Maybe he cleaned them for her," said Evan.

"Nah, they weren't super clean, they were... normal, I guess? No worse than yours or mine. Which made me think maybe she was drugged and then crucified but there's no toxins in her system, no marks that would indicate something was injected."

He frowned.

"You said there wasn't anything in her mouth, right?"

"Nothing," said Evan.

"So, in addition to all of this, she didn't bite her tongue off while screaming in pain as she was crucified. Screams which, apparently, no one could hear."

He turned and looked at the body, and all of our eyes followed.

"Yes sir, apart from the nail wounds in her hands and feet, she looks like she's sleeping."

I turned away. I couldn't look at her for more than a few seconds.

***

Once we left the morgue Evan and I decided to go for a drive and grab a coffee. Or rather, he decided for us, and I knew he wanted answers about Benjamin.

"So here's something I was wondering about," Evan began as we left the parking lot. "If you were going to kill someone, not someone specific, but just a random person cause you wanted to feel the experience, who would you target?"

I scoffed.

"Jesus man, like is this a real question? Who the fuck asks something like that?"

"Okay, just hear me out," Evan explained. "You have a family, right? Wife? Kids?"

I was almost afraid to share with him, this man was clearly unstable. But there was no point in lying.

"Yes. And yes. Two."

"Alright," said Evan. "So if somebody killed you, your family would notice pretty fast that you were missing. Right?"

"Okay."

"Me, I don't live with anyone. But I do have a job. And if I suddenly stopped coming to work, people would know something is up. This is why so many killers go after hookers or drug addicts or homeless people. By the time people notice that this person has vanished, it's too late."

I understood the point he was trying to make, but I didn't see how it was relevant.

"Okay," I said again.

"Now does our Jane Doe look like some junkie or prostitute?"

"No," I said. "But you never know."

"I don't think so," Evan said. "And that leads me to my question. Why has no one come forward? Someone knew this person. Someone in this town hasn't seen this person in a few days and knows that the police found a dead body that matches her description. So either she knew no one, or she knew one person and that's the person who killed her, or-"

"She's not from here," I finished.

Evan took his eyes of the road and smiled at me.

"Exactly."

"But there's one part that doesn't add up," I told him. "Even if this person went out of his way to target someone who wouldn't be missed, any advantage they had was thrown out the window when he nailed her to a sign for us to find."

"Yeah, you're right," Evan said.

Then he snapped his fingers as he remembered.

"Oh! I was supposed to ask you. Who was that guy we talked to earlier? Benjamin was his name, I think?"

I sighed.

"Benjamin is sort of our local career criminal," I said, trying to think of how to best describe him. "Long history of arrests, usually things like public intoxication, indecency, DUIs, attempted arson. Shit like that. But he's dabbled in some more serious stuff as well."

"Like what?" Evan asked.

"Benjamin... is good at attracting certain people towards him. Like kids who acted up in school, the kinds who you knew didn't have much of a future, they gravitated towards him. So he'd send them out on assignments, shoplift from a convenience store here, graffiti a building there, but the thing is that certain adults gravitated towards him too. Benjamin ran quite the impressive moonshine operation some years ago, and he had high-stakes poker games in his basement for a while, but we broke that up."

"Anything really serious?" Evan asked. "He ever kill anyone or-"

"No, not that we know of," I said, shaking my head. "Not sure he's the type, either. He might give you a few smacks if you owe him money, but I don't see him as a murderer."

"Why did he say he was looking forward to working with me? And why was he in Dennis' office in the first place?"

I rubbed my temples, thinking about Benjamin for too long gave me a headache.

"Whenever something like yesterday happens, we have a dead body and can't figure it out, he likes to pop by and offer his assistance."

"What kind of assistance?"

"He's trying to aggravate us, he wants to remind us how bad we are at our jobs."

"Do you think he's involved?" Evan asked. "Does he know something?"

We pulled into the parking lot of the coffee chain.

"No," I said. "He's just being an annoyance."

"Okay, but why did he say he was-"

"Looking forward to working with you?" I finished. "He says that to every new cop. And the reason is because years ago one of our guys really was working with him."

I said this right as Evan stopped the car and he ended up breaking a bit too hard, sending my body forward for half a second.

"Seriously?" he asked.

"Yeah. We couldn't prove it, at least we didn't have anything that would hold up in court. But we knew. And he likes to remind us of this every once in a while."

***

Not long after we returned to the station, and just as I was hoping that the rest of the day would be uneventful, I noticed that Dennis was standing in the doorway of his office with an impatient look on his face.

"Everything okay?" I asked.

"We have a name on the victim," he said. "One Vanessa Miles, 26 years old, lives in Albuquerque."

I raised my eyebrows.

"Long way from home."

I could hear Evan make a short humming sound behind me, obviously satisfied that he was right about the victim not being from Appleton.

"Very long way," Dennis said.

"How'd they ID the body?" I asked.

"A friend came forward and says the victim was visiting her over the weekend. We set her up in one of the rooms when she got here, but I wanted to wait for you two to get back before we started asking questions."

The friend, coincidentally, was actually named Jane, which made it confusing for us, as we had been using the typical Jane Doe to refer to the dead woman before we had her actual name. This Jane, the real one, was sitting in one of our interrogation rooms, curled up and shivering, even though the room was being heated. Evan, Dennis, and I were standing on the other side of the glass, looking at her. Her eyes seemed to be fixated on the corner of the room, and I imagined she was wondering whether coming forward was a mistake.

"So which one of us do you want to talk to her?" I asked Dennis. "Or are you going to do it?"

"No, not me," Dennis said. "I'm going to stay back from this one. The girl's parents are actually old friends of mine. I'd rather have one of you handle this."

"Are you worried you'd be biased?" Evan asked.

"No," Dennis replied. "But just to be safe."

"Okay," Evan said and he took a step forward. "I'll take a shot."

"No," said Dennis sharply. "You go," he said, turning to me.

"You don't trust me?" Evan asked, seemingly surprised.

Dennis stared at him for a few seconds.

"Are you serious?" he asked.

"But why not?"

"You know exactly why."

There was something in the way Dennis said it that was strange. Maybe Evan knew the reason, but I didn't. I wondered whether there was something about Evan that I had not been told. But now was not the time to think about that.

She seemed to not even register that I had entered the room. As I walked over, pulled the chair out and sat down, her eyes did not leave the corner she had been staring at. The woman's hair looked greasy, her left eye kept twitching, and she looked like she hadn't eaten or slept in days.

"I'm Detective George Hoffman," I said.

She jumped up, startled, just now realizing that I was in the room. But she still didn't look in my direction. The wall behind me seemed more interesting.

"I understand you were friends with Vanessa Miles," I said.

"I just don't understand why he would do that..." she whispered, without actually answering my question.

I tried not to react too obviously.

"Why who would do that?" I asked.

She finally looked at me.

"The person who killed her. Why would he do that?"

Her fingers started rapidly tapping on the edge of the table. I frowned. I thought we might get something with that 'he,' but she seemed to just be using the word in a general sense.

"Your friend was from out of town. She was visiting you?"

"Should I have a lawyer?" she blurted out, and looked towards the glass where Evan and Dennis were watching us.

"You can, if you choose to," I said, really hoping she wouldn't. "But you're not under arrest. You can get up and leave at any point, should you want to. But if you have something that can help us, we can find the person who did this."

She snapped her head back in my direction.

"Find," she repeated. "And then what? That's not going to bring her back."

She pressed her head down on the table. I wasn't entirely sure, it could just be sleep deprivation, but I felt she might be inebriated. Or maybe it was just the shock of what had happened to her friend.

"When was the last time you saw her?" I asked.

I needed to get something. I knew that behind the glass Evan was already trying to convince Dennis that he would be doing a better job at this than me.

"She arrived on Friday afternoon," Jane said. "We stayed at my house all night. Saturday we went for a hike, and then we went to Hellhole at night."

Hellhole. Well, at least that was a place to start. The club would have been crowded, someone would have seen them.

"And what about Sunday?" I asked.

"We woke up pretty late," she said after thinking for a moment. "Then we went to mass, then back to my house."

A club and then a church. So that was two places.

"When was the last time you saw her?"

Jane shook her head, like she couldn't remember.

"Early evening on Sunday. She had gone to pick up beer and... she never came back."

"Did you think to go looking for her?" I asked.

"I had already been drinking, so I couldn't."

"You could have called someone else to go looking."

"No," she said, and she violently shook her head.

There was something off here.

"When you were at your house on the weekend, was anyone else there, besides the two of you? Any other friends drop by?"

"Nope," and she shook her head again. "Just us."

I tilted back in my chair and tried to look like I was thinking hard about all of this new information.

"Okay," I said.

When I walked out of the room and closed the door behind me I could see Evan shaking his head with a strange smile on his face.

"Well she's definitely hiding something," he said.

"Very perceptive," I said. "She did give us a name, so that's more than we had two hours ago."

"She says the friend drove to get beer, we haven't found a car anywhere," Dennis pointed out.

"That's right," I said. "What do you think, killer's hiding a car in his garage?"

Dennis sighed.

"Who knows? Too many garages to go around and check. But I want you two to look into her alibi. Go to Hellhole and see if they remember her being there."

THREE

Evan and I left a few minutes later. I decided to drive this time, since he wouldn't know directions to where we were going.

"She seemed a bit off, wouldn't you say?" Evan asked as we got into the car.

"Obviously. But is it because she's traumatized or because she's guilty?" I asked.

"Could be both," he replied. "Maybe she killed her friend and is traumatized by that, especially if this was her first."

"I thought we had established that the person who did this had done it before," I reminded him.

"Maybe it was a two person job," Evan shrugged. "I doubt this girl could have lifted her friend up onto the sign. And we hadn't established anything, I just figured this was an expert, but that was before this girl came forward."

"You think she's hiding something?" I asked.

Evan looked confused.

"Yeah, I thought you agreed back at the station."

"I want to hear your thought process," I said as I started the car.

For a moment Evan said nothing. We drove out of the parking lot and began heading in the direction of Hellhole.

"Her friend just leaves and doesn't come back, and she doesn't seem phased by that at all," he said finally.

"You sound unsure," I said.

"I..." Evan said slowly. "I mean, it's weird right?"

"It is weird, and I agreed with you that it feels as though she's not being entirely honest with us. But that doesn't mean that she had anything to do with the murder."

"But then why would she be acting like that?" Evan asked.

I drummed on the steering wheel for a moment as I thought.

"Give you an example," I said. "Imagine a guy is cheating on his wife, okay? He meets up with the girlfriend in a motel, and afterwards they each go home. The next day he's watching the news, finds out the girlfriend was killed in a hit-and-run on the way home. Now, he was most likely the last person who saw her alive, and by knowing where she was the night before, he might have information that can help the police figure this out. But, if he comes forward, then they say 'how did you know this person,' suddenly his secret affair is in a police report. See the problem?"

"Okay..." Evan said. "so she's worried that by coming to us she's indirectly bringing attention to herself?"

"Might be," I said. "Or she might have just been high as shit, and that's why she kept shivering and spacing out. Or maybe the idea of her friend being nailed to a post fucked her up, who knows?"

We drove in silence for a while. Eventually I turned onto a street which had multiple houses with boarded-up windows and doors. Steps leading up to front porches were decaying and collapsing, the wooden planks covering windows were splattered with spray paint that I couldn't read.

"Sorry, where exactly are we going?" Evan asked. "What is Hellhole?"

"Hellhole is a bar at the edge of town, which also functions as the town's only nightclub."

"Ah," he said.

"It's not in a fun part of town. I'd say half of our domestic violence calls are from around here. That-" I said pointing to the house on the corner, "used to be a halfway house."

"And what would two nice girls be doing hanging around here?" Evan asked dryly.

"Honestly, I'd say Hellhole is probably safer on weekends than during the week. At least then there's people here, all of the kids come here to drink and forget that they're never leaving this town. It's during the day that I'm more concerned about what's here."

As we rounded the corner I saw a man in a white undershirt standing on his front porch, staring at us menacingly.

"What's he looking at?" Evan muttered.

"We just keep driving," I said. "We've got places to go, it's just faster this way than going around."

The next intersection had a stop sign which had been knocked over.

"Lovely," Evan said, as his opinion on the neighbourhood continued to deteriorate.

"Almost there," I assured him.

"And if we confirm they were here that night, then what?"

"I don't know," I said. "But maybe they met someone here, someone who took a liking to one of them, someone who didn't take 'no' for an answer, someone who followed them home," I speculated. "It's a start. You think she's hiding something, we start by confirming the few details we already know."

"Thank you for your wisdom, Detective," he said.

I didn't respond.

The building that eventually became Hellhole had been standing here since before I was born, its structure resembling a tavern from the Old West. The pillars lining the front of the building had been reinforced with concrete, and the entire building had been painted black. Bars covered the windows, and the front door was a bright red that stood out from the rest of the miserable scene. The parking lot was just a plain of dirt, with nothing to indicate parking spots aside from the row of boulders at the very edge.

"This is the heart of your town's night life?" Evan asked, raising his eyebrows.

"I'm sure wherever you came from was much nicer than this," I said.

"Can't say that it was."

As we got out of the car, the front door of Hellhole burst open and a middle-aged man in a tracksuit stumbled out, instantly colliding with one of the large pillars in front of the building. He started breathing heavily as he used the pillar to support himself. I rushed over.

"You alright McKinnley?" I asked.

He gave me a thumbs up without looking at me.

"Do you have a way of getting home or do I have to drive you again?" I asked.

He looked up at me and pushed himself off the pillar to show that he could stand up straight.

"I am fine," he said as he squinted, his eyes unadjusted to the daylight.

"I can see that," I said.

"Not causing any trouble officer," he mumbled, as he wiped the beer foam out of his beard. "Just gonna walk this off."

And he began slowly shuffling his feet. I watched him as he walked past us and headed towards the road.

"Quite the colourful group of characters you have living here," Evan said. "Maybe he's the killer?" he added jokingly.

"If he was, and we had not figured it out yet, I would quit this job," I said.

When we walked into Hellhole my ears were filled with the sound of a nasally voice singing to a synth beat that sounded like a zipper being repeatedly tugged on. We walked down a hallway, past a side room that served as a coat room during club nights. At the end of the hallway we reached the main room of the bar. Hellhole had a miserable aesthetic, the walls were all black, but they had been painted so long ago that they had faded to a boring grey. As we had seen from the outside, all of the windows had metal bars on them, which caused what little sunlight came through them to create a striped pattern on the floor. The room was completely empty except for a group of senior citizens sitting at a round table at the far end. Just beside them was a small room with glass windows which was sometimes used as a private booth by the few people in this town delusional enough to call themselves VIPs. The wooden floor squeaked with each step we took as we approached the bar. The frame of the bar was covered with a long wreath, a row of Christmas lights wove through it with about a fifth of the bulbs burned out. Tanner, the owner of this establishment, was busy wiping a mug, and repeatedly shaking his head so that the tip of his Santa hat would stop dangling in front of his eyes.

"Afternoon Tanner," I said as I leaned over the bar.

His eyes widened.

"A bit early in the day, officer," he said.

I smiled.

"I try not to partake anymore. Or at least not as much."

He nodded.

"I can respect that... even if it's bad for business. So what can I do for you?"

Before I could answer Evan walked over and leaned on the bar. He was holding his phone in his hand.

"We're hoping you could confirm whether a few people were here on Saturday night," he said.

I leaned over and saw that he had a picture of Jane on his phone.

"When did you take that?" I asked.

"While you were talking to her," he replied as he flipped the phone to show Tanner.

I realized that he must have taken it from the other side of the glass. I tried to imagine how Dennis had reacted to him to doing that.

"Hmmmm," Tanner said as he leaned forward and squinted at the photo, flicking the tip of his Santa hat out of the way. "Might have," he said. "Can't really tell from that image."

"Name is Jane, if that helps," I said.

Tanner's eyes flickered at the sound of the name. He looked back at the phone.

"Jane... brown hair, about this tall?" he asked, holding his hand up to his chin level.

"Sounds about right," I said.

"Yeah, yeah. She was here."

"What about her?" Evan asked, and he flipped to the picture of Vanessa's body that he had taken at the crime scene when I first met him.

Tanner grew pale when he saw it.

"Oh Jesus, is that-"

"Yeah, that's the dead woman we found yesterday."

He looked away.

"I understand that this may be difficult to look at it, but I would appreciate it if you could help us," Evan said.

Tanner looked back. He leaned forward slightly and squinted.

"She was here with someone, if I remember correctly," he said.

I noticed his eyes darted towards the far corner of the bar where the group of old people were, as if he were worried someone might notice he was talking to the police.

"If you remember correctly?" Evan repeated.

"There were lots of people here that night," Tanner began.

"Yeah, well one of those people is dead now, and another of those people might be behind it," Evan said sternly.

"You think-"

"I think two young women go to a club and one of them ends up dead soon after," Evan said.

"Jane was here," Tanner said. "I know that for sure. And she was with a friend. Was it this person?" he asked, pointing at the picture. "I don't know, the hair looks the same, but she didn't look like a dead body. You're asking me if that," he tapped on the phone screen, "was here, I don't know."

I frowned.

"This friend she was with, was it someone you had seen before?"

Tanner blinked.

"Now that you mention it, no. Not someone who had been here before. Might have been from out of town, but I can't say for certain."

Evan and I looked at each other. It was as close to a confirmation as we would get.

"And did they meet anyone else here? Did anyone approach them? Bother them?" Evan asked.

"Not that I saw," Tanner said.

Apparently this wasn't the answer Evan had been hoping for.

"I wasn't keeping an eye on them in particular," Tanner said, exhausted. "Sure, some guys might have approached them once or twice, but nothing out of the ordinary happened."

He looked to me for assistance.

"Thanks for your help," I told him. "Come on," I said to Evan, and tugged on his elbow before he could argue.

***

"Could you try being a little less aggressive?" I asked Evan a few minutes later as we drove away.

"That wasn't me being aggressive," he said.

"The man was just doing his job, it's not our fault he didn't have all the answers we were looking for," I said.

"He's the second person we've talked to today that hasn't been giving straightforward answers," Evan explained. "We're not going to get anywhere by being gentle."

"I only mean that you would be wise not to start building a bad reputation in this town," I told him sternly. "We've built a good relationship with the people here, the last thing we need is one bad apple ruining that."

"Bad apple?" Evan asked, turning to me. "Is that what you think I am?"

"The first thing I ever saw you do was laugh at a dead body," I said. "So you tell me, are you going to cause problems?"

Evan turned away with a scoff. He didn't answer. In fact, he didn't speak at all until several minutes later when he realized we were taking a different route back.

"You're right," he said suddenly. "We wouldn't want there to be a bad apple in Appleton."

I griped the steering wheel so tightly I thought my knuckles would pierce through my skin. It took all of my energy not to laugh. But then he laughed first, or rather he exhaled loudly through his nose.

"That was so bad," I said, and tried to disguise my laughs as one long sigh.

As we turned onto a side road Evan looked around confused.

"This isn't the way back to the station," he said.

"We're not going to the station yet," I said. "We've got one more stop."

"Where?"

"Girl said they had gone to church Sunday morning, so let's see if that was true."

Not long after that we arrived at our destination. The church was rather modest, with a single bell tower ascending above a small brick building. The bricks were crumbling in several spots, weeds burst out of the long cracks in the stairs leading to the front door, and the sign above the entrance had faded long ago, leaving the letters illegible. I opened the door of the car and noticed that Evan wasn't getting out of his seat.

"Everything okay?" I asked.

"Maybe it's better if I stayed," he answered, staring out the windshield at the church.

I sighed.

"I reprimand you once, and you're just going to stay in the car?"

"I don't know if me talking to the priest is a good idea," he said.

I didn't know what the issue was, but I didn't feel like asking.

"When Dennis asks me later how it went, I'd rather not have to tell him that you stayed in the car. He'll be pissed at you, and he'll also be pissed at me for not doing anything about it. So come do your job."

Evan turned to me, looking annoyed. For a moment I thought he was planning on arguing further, but instead he undid his seatbelt and got out of the car.

Instead of heading to the church I led Evan to the small one-storey house on the side of the property. I rang the doorbell and a few moments later heard loud steps on the other side. When Father Bertrand opened the door he didn't look surprised to see me.

"George," he said.

And then he turned to Evan.

"Oh, hello," he said cautiously.

"Father, this is Evan. We're working a case together," I said. "Evan, this is Father Bertrand."

"Yeah, hi," Evan said as quickly as he could.

Bertrand turned back to me. There was a strange gleam in his eyes. I wondered if Evan could spot the single bead of sweat that had appeared at the edge of his greying hair and was now beginning to flow down his head.

"Of course, please come in," he said with an almost natural smile.

Father Bertrand led us into his living room. Aside from the shrine in the corner which was covered in countless pictures of Christ and Popes both current and former, there was barely anything in the room. Just a long bookshelf on the far wall and a small round table stuck between two armchairs. Bertrand sat down in one of the chairs and motioned for me to sit next to him.

"It's alright, I'll stand," I said.

I noticed behind me that Evan was already leaning against the wall with his arms folded. All I could do was hope he wouldn't say anything that would cause problems.

"Suit yourself," said Bertrand. "So what can I do for you?"

"I'm guessing you've heard about the dead woman we found yesterday?" I asked.

Bertrand blinked.

"That poor girl. Yes, I did hear about that," he lowered his glasses for a moment to wipe what may have been a tear out of his eye.

"We managed to get an ID on her, from a friend, one Jane Brown."

Bertrand twitched just slightly when he heard the name, but quickly smiled.

"Ah, Jane. Yes, she was just here at mass over the weekend. That was her friend?" he asked, his smile vanishing. "Awful."

"So she was at the mass?" I asked.

"Yes," Bertrand replied. "Which was surprising, as I hadn't seen her here in a long time."

"She had stopped going?"

"A few years ago," Bertrand said. "It happens with people her age. More and more often, I find. Some of them eventually come back, most of them don't. Some still show up for Christmas and Easter, although I imagine that's more to keep up appearances for family. But yes, she did come back this past Sunday."

"And did you talk to her?" I asked.

"No."

"Was she there with anyone?" Evan suddenly spoke, straightening up. "Someone you didn't recognize?"

Bertrand frowned.

"No, she was alone."

"You're sure?" Evan asked.

"I see the same people week in and week out, officer," Bertrand explained. "I have their faces memorized, I know what they sound like, I can even predict who they're going to sit next to. If there's someone new, someone I wouldn't have met before, they'll stick out."

"Was there anyone anywhere that you didn't recognize on Sunday?" I asked. "Maybe she sat separately."

"No," Bertrand said shaking his head. "Just the regulars. And one girl who finally came back after being away. I can't imagine what's going through her mind right now."

***

Evan and I left the priest's house shortly after and began driving back to the station.

"See, that wasn't so hard," I said. "You asked the right questions while remaining professional the whole time."

"Thanks," he said quietly.

"No, I mean it," I said, trying to sound friendlier. "I didn't even think to ask about Vanessa, I just assumed that if one girl was there the other one would have been too."

"Here's what I don't get though," said Evan. "She lied to us, but why?"

"Well, we don't know," I said. "But like we had guessed earlier, she must be hiding something."

"No, I mean, why tell a lie that can be obviously disproven? She lied about Vanessa being in the church, a place that is filled with people who, like the priest said, would remember if there was someone new. She had to have known we would follow up on this, and she had to have known how easily this could be disproven."

"Maybe she didn't think we'd follow up," I said.

Evan didn't answer.

***

When we got back to the station Dennis was already waiting for us. We found him sitting on the edge of my desk, tapping the back of his foot against it at a repetitive rhythm.

"Tell me you found something," he said.

"Is the girl still here?" Evan asked.

"No, she's gone," he said. "Left about an hour ago."

He must have noticed the look on my face.

"Why, what's wrong?" he asked.

"She lied. They were both at the club on Saturday night, but she went to church alone the next day, the victim wasn't with her."

Dennis raised his eyebrows.

"And you know this⁻"

"From Bertrand, yes," I said.

I saw Dennis' jaw tighten when I said the name.

"Okay," he said quietly. "I told Ross to follow her, I had a weird feeling we were missing something. I'll call him and let him know to be extra careful."

"Do you want us to go to her, ask her why she lied?" I asked.

"No," said Dennis as he got off the desk. "Right now she doesn't know we know. We wait and see what she does next."

And he walked away.

INTERLUDE

"So that first interaction between Evan and Father Bertrand, did you sense any hostility between them?" Xander asked me.

I pondered this for a moment.

"Hostility isn't the word I would use," I said. "I got the sense that Evan seemed to have a general mistrust of priests, which isn't uncommon in his generation. I didn't know if a specific incident caused this," I said, choosing my words very carefully, "or if it was just an accumulation of things. But Evan knew how to do his job, and Father Bertrand didn't seem to have a problem with him."

Xander nodded.

"And what about the rest of the precinct, did they have a positive impression of Bertrand?"

I smiled.

"You told me at the beginning that you didn't want me to jump ahead in the story."

Xander laughed.

"Yeah, but I just want to get a general feel for how things were in Appleton before everything went to shit. So like, did your coworkers know Bertrand, did they talk about him?"

"No, generally you're not supposed to discuss religion in the workplace," I said. "But it's a small town, so sometimes you see your coworkers at mass."

"Did you go to mass regularly?" Xander asked me.

"Less and less as the years went by."

"And what did you think of Father Bertrand?"

I sat silently for a moment.

"I think he was a good man. He was really engaged with the community. This wasn't just someone who talked at us for an hour a week and collected money, no, he made it his job to know the people, their names, what's going on in their lives, as much as he could."

"So you were on a first name basis with him?"

"Oh, yes," I said. "Yeah, he knew me, he knew my family. He even swung by on Christmas every year, he makes his rounds through the town stopping by to chat."

"What about his relationship with Dennis?" Xander asked.

I sighed very softly.

"To my knowledge Dennis wasn't much of a churchgoer. So I can't say what their relationship was."

"And there was no indication that Dennis had any kind of unethical relationship with the Father?" Xander asked.

There was silence. I knew we would have eventually reached this topic. And I gave Xander the same answer I gave every other person who had challenged the story.

"If there was, we weren't aware of it," I said.

Xander narrowed his eyes slightly, he seemed to be wondering whether he could push me further, but before he could, Julie interjected.

"Can we swing back to Benjamin Nero for a moment?" she asked.

"Of course," I said.

"So, at the beginning when you guys had no leads, no idea who could have done this, were there... for lack of a better term, usual suspects, just a handful of people who you figured, maybe it was one of them?"

I nodded.

"For certain crimes, yes, we would have. There's days where we would show up at the crime scene and go, yeah this was probably Benjamin. But not this, not a woman nailed to a sign. See, with Benjamin you had to look at who the victim was. Back when he was running poker games out of his basement his justification was that it was a victimless crime. Just a bunch of friends hanging out, having a good time, not hurting anyone, right? Now for something more serious, like if he torched a cop car or threw a brick through the window at the courthouse, well now who's the victim? The government. And they deserve it, fuck them."

Julie and Xander were both nodding, they were getting a better understanding of who we were dealing it.

"So Benjamin was a terrible person, no doubt, but we knew how to handle him and what to expect. And just violently murdering a random person like that, that wasn't something he would do."

"So he wasn't on your radar," Xander asked.

"No," I said. "Him coming into the office that first time and taunting us, that was normal. Wasn't something new. For those first few days we were at a loss, apart from Jane there weren't really any leads. Of course, at this point we also only had the one body," I sighed. "We had no idea how bad it was going to get."

"Cause from my research you guys seemed to just watch Jane for a few days and hoped to learn something from that," Julie added.

"Right," I said. "But the thing is that it was almost Christmas and the idea of there being a murderer on the loose was understandably scary to a lot of people. Dennis had thought that we should wait and see what Jane does on Christmas, see if someone else visits her. I remember we had been theorizing about whether there was someone who helped her. I'm sure you can imagine that lifting that body up and putting nails in place, that's a lot of physical work."

"And it was cold too," Xander added.

"Right. But on Christmas Eve morning we all agreed that we needed to have something. We couldn't just go on camera and say 'Merry Christmas Everyone, we have no idea who the killer is, don't worry about a thing.' And Evan had... one of his bright ideas, to use this to our advantage, as a scare tactic."

FOUR

"We scare her," Evan said.

We were in Dennis' office on Christmas Eve morning. Combined we had gotten about 7 hours of sleep. There had been no new developments. Even Ross, who Dennis was forcing to watch Jane's house every day, was getting irritated.

"She just stays at home," he had told us that morning. "All day, every day, no one visits her. If she didn't open the blinds in the morning or shut them at night I would be convinced she was probably dead."

"I'm worried about your idea of 'scaring,'" said Dennis with a frown.

"Okay, later today you give a press release," Evan said. "No, just listen for a second," he added hastily as Dennis opened his mouth to argue. "You give a press release, and you will have to say that we have no idea who did this and there's a killer on the loose. You don't want to say that, you want people to enjoy their holidays. So you tell the truth, that we have one suspect. And you give the name. That's what we tell her. We tell her that we know she lied to us, and we will be naming her as our only suspect, unless she can point us to someone else."

Dennis had a look on his face that I had become increasingly familiar with over the past few days. It was a look he gave when he didn't want to admit that Evan had a good idea. Despite his odd personality, our newest team member had proven to be quite capable at his job.

"Okay," he said, standing up from his chair and leaning over his desk. "When Ross gets back, I want you two to go."

***

Ross was back within the hour, relieved that he no longer had to sit in his parked car for hours a day.

"Anything we should know?" I asked.

"Nothing!" he said exasperated, as he rubbed his eyes. "She's so boring, does nothing all day."

Evan was already at the front door but before I could follow him Dennis grabbed me by my elbow.

"Are you sure you can control him?" he asked.

"Yes. It'll be fine," I said. "I'll do the talking."

Dennis frowned and looked over at Ross, who had stumbled over to the coffee machine.

"Be ready for anything," he said. "It's possible Ross wasn't as subtle as he thinks, the girl could know we've been watching her."

"I think we can handle it," I said, but he was right.

She might have noticed the black car parked on her street for several days.

"What did the boss want?" Evan said when I finally came outside and saw him standing at the edge of the sidewalk, waiting.

"Just wants us to be on our toes in case the girl is expecting us."

"Oh man, can you imagine?" he said with a short laugh. "First she crucified her friend, now she's luring cops to the house. What will she do next?"

We got into the car and started driving in the direction of Jane's house.

"So you got any Christmas plans?" Evan asked me eventually.

"Me? Just staying home with the family. You?" I replied.

"Nothing really," he said. "Probably going to stay in."

There was a long silence. I waited to see whether he would continue, but he obviously wasn't going to.

"You can come over and have dinner with us," I said.

"Oh no, that's okay, thank you but-" he immediately recited.

"That's why you asked," I said. "You asked me what I was doing because you didn't have any plans of your own."

"That's not why-"

"Yes it was," I said.

I had my eyes on the road but I could still sense that Evan looked embarrassed.

"Is that okay? Like, will your wife mind-"

"She'll be fine," I said. "Don't worry about it, it's nothing."

Again, Evan sat silently for a moment before adding a quick "Thanks."

***

Jane lived at the end of a quiet street. We parked on the other side of the road a few houses down. Most of the driveways were still empty, as people were at work. There was no car in Jane's driveway, but Ross had mentioned the other day that she didn't seem to have one, as he could still see through the window that she was home.

"So what's the plan?" Evan asked. "You want to interrogate her here or back at the station?"

"Back at the station," I said. "We don't want to cause a scene. And in the event that someone else is watching her, someone else who might be behind all of this, the last thing we want is for them to see that there were cops in her house."

"And what if she doesn't come with us?" Evan asked.

"Worst comes to worst, we can arrest her. She is a suspect. But I'd rather not."

"Why not?" Evan asked.

"I've never been crazy about arresting people who might be guilty. I prefer saving it for people who I know are," I said. "I don't know, I can't really explain it."

"No, I get it," Evan said. "Alright, let's go."

When we knocked on the door there was no response.

"Ms. Brown, please open up," I shouted after a few seconds.

"Please?" Evan asked. "And what if she says 'no?'"

I turned to him, annoyed, but I saw his eyes widen.

"Curtain just moved," he said, pointing behind me.

I turned back around and looked at the large living room window close to the front door, and sure enough, the curtain closest to me was swaying ever so slightly.

"Ms. Brown, we'd like to talk to you," I said, but before I could even finish my sentence Evan decided to improvise.

"We know you killed her!" he yelled.

I spun around.

"Are you fucking-"

But then the door opened. I turned back around and did my best to instantly compose myself. Jane looked as though she hadn't slept since the last time we saw her.

"What do you want?" she asked, leaning one hand against the door.

"Can we come in and talk?" I asked.

If she even let us into the house now it would be a miracle, there was no way we'd convince her to come back to the station. She looked over my shoulder at Evan.

"What did you yell right before I opened the door?" she asked.

I clenched my fist. If Evan managed to fuck this up I didn't know what I would do.

"I yelled what I needed to so you'd open the door," he said.

She looked back at me.

"You can come in. He can't," she said and turned around.

I looked at Evan. There was something in his eyes that almost resembled embarrassment.

"Go sit in the car."

Evan opened his mouth to argue.

"No. Get in the fucking car, and stay there," I said.

I went into the house and shut the door behind me. Jane's house might have once been tidy, but that seemed to have changed once her friend was murdered. The couch had several pillows that didn't match at all, which made me think that Jane had been spending most of her time here, likely trying and failing to sleep. The table in the middle of the room had four pizza boxes, three of which were stacked in a pile, while the fourth was on its own. This fourth box had empty beer bottles in it, arranged in uniform rows.

"Have a seat," she said, motioning to the one spot on the couch that wasn't occupied by a mountain of blankets that looked like they had been vomited up.

I sat down and noticed something else on the table. There were three empty pill bottles. I noticed that the label on one of them read 'INSOMNIAK.'

"I'm sorry about him," I said. "He gets a little carried away sometimes. I think he might like the job a bit too much."

"He said he knew I killed her," Jane said.

She hadn't bothered taking a seat, and was standing on the other side of the table with her arms folded. I wondered whether she was contemplating running. She couldn't run out front, Evan would be there waiting. I glanced over at the patio door at the far end of the room.

"He said that so you'd panic and do something stupid so he'd have an excuse to arrest you," I said. "He doesn't 'know' you killed her, but you are the main suspect right now."

She blinked.

"What are you talking about?" she stammered.

"See, we followed up on your story and it turns out that Vanessa didn't go with you to mass on Sunday morning."

Jane's face started to turn slightly red.

"I went by myself."

"That's not what you told us," I said.

Her eyes darted to the back door.

"Running isn't going to help," I said. "It's Christmas, so people naturally want to spend time with their families peacefully and not worry about there being a killer on the loose. We're not going to tell the public that we have no idea what happened, we're going to tell them that we have one suspect. And that's you."

"No, you misheard me, I never said she went with me-"

"Let's say that's true," I interrupted. "Let's say that all three of us misheard what you said. Why don't you help me clear up my memory and tell me what Vanessa did on Sunday morning while you went to church?"

I could see that her hands were starting to shake.

"Okay," I said, and I stood up. "I'll be heading out then."

I took two steps towards the door.

"Wait!" she said.

I turned and saw that she was starting to breathe heavily. She collapsed on the couch and buried her head in her hands.

"I know you didn't kill your friend," I said. "But you're going to point me towards who did."

I walked over and sat down beside her.

"I went to church by myself," she said, staring at the empty beer bottles. "Vanessa went to the Hole."

"She went to the Hole by herself?" I asked.

"We were supposed to go together, we were..."

And then she stopped. She turned towards me.

"If I say anything-"

"What are you so afraid of?" I asked.

"I'm not afraid of anything!" she said with wide eyes. "I went to church, Vanessa went to the Hole."

"Why did she go there?" I asked loudly.

She shrugged.

"That's not good enough."

"What do you want from me?" she shrieked.

I frowned.

"You know what I think?" I asked. "I think you know exactly what happened to your friend. And I think you're worried that something similar might happen to you."

I could see her bottom lip was starting to quiver.

"Now you can either help me figure out what happened, or I'm going to eventually be called to a second murder scene, and I'll have just as little information as I did at the first one."

She opened her mouth and tried to speak but only a weird noise came out. Finally after a moment she was able to talk properly.

"W... what kind of protection can you offer?"

I raised an eyebrow.

"To you?" I asked.

She nodded.

"We can have someone watch your house. We can move you somewhere safer. But who exactly are we protecting you from?"

She took a deep breath to try and relax but she was still shaking, and her teeth clattered as she began to speak.

"I don't know who killed Vanessa," she clarified. "We were supposed to meet someone on Sunday morning at the Hole, but I didn't want to, I went to church instead. Vanessa went by herself."

"Who were you meeting?"

She looked at me and I could see genuine fear in her eyes.

"I don't think he killed her, but if you start asking him questions, he's going to know I told you."

"Who was it?" I asked again.

"Martin Nero."

INTERLUDE

"You mentioned already that at the time you hadn't considered Benjamin Nero a suspect," Xander recalled.

"That's right," I said.

"What about his son?"

I took a long sip of water as I thought about the question.

"I mean..." I said, unsure of what we had thought back then. "if you told me one of the Neros killed someone and asked me to guess which one, I'd probably say Martin, I guess?"

"But it's still a bit of a stretch?" Xander asked.

"Yeah, especially once you remember the kind of crime we were talking about. Could Martin Nero have angrily pushed someone down a flight of stairs and they cracked their skull open? Sure, I guess? Not the most improbable scenario, but this kind of slow, methodical murder, no, wasn't like him."

"And was he similar in character to Benjamin?" Xander asked.

He laughed when he heard me exhale.

"His father's son," I said, shaking my head. "The same kind of petty criminal, but this extra layer of arrogance. See, over the years we arrested

Benjamin countless times, and there was one thing that always bothered me. Regardless of whether he was innocent or guilty, or even when he knew that we knew he was guilty, he never once asked for a lawyer. He was that confident that he could talk his way out of it. Now Martin, when he sensed that he was in trouble, the very first thing he would say is-"

"I'd like to speak to a lawyer?" Xander asked.

"Nope," I said, "My dad's gonna hear about this."

"Jesus," Xander groaned and started laughing again.

"So he's just the worst type of person," Julie piped in.

"The worst," I said and suddenly felt bold. "Fuck Martin Nero."

"Oh my God." Xander's laughs got louder. "Oh man. Should you be speaking that way of the dead?"

I did my best to ignore the horrified look that had been on Martin's face when I last saw him.

"I'm past caring about that," I said.

I drank some more water as Xander slowly composed himself. By the end he been almost lying down on the table but now he had straightened up.

"Okay. Shit, what was the other thing I was going to ask?" he said, catching his breath.

"Evan's outburst at the door," Julie said as she checked her notes.

"Right!" said Xander. "So, Evan yelling that you knew she killed Jane."

"Honestly man, it worked," I said. "At the end of the day, yes, it was unprofessional, but we did get results."

"Now, I know I had asked this earlier when we were discussing the first time you had met him, but you still at this point didn't know why he was transferred?"

"No, I didn't," I said. "And I hadn't even asked. See, someone being transferred isn't necessarily because of a scandal or some kind of misconduct, it's often something as boring as budget constraints."

"Right, right," said Xander. "When did you find out?"

I looked up and furrowed my brow.

"It would have been after New Year's. Yeah, I don't remember the exact date, but it was after... that incident, which we'll get to soon," I said.

"And that's when he told you?" Xander asked.

"Oh no, Evan and I never talked about this. Dennis told me. When he presented his theory, and he saw that I wasn't convinced, this was the evidence he provided."

"And had you known earlier, would you still have invited him to your house for Christmas, do you think?" Xander asked.

I didn't tell him what I actually thought about that question.

"Maybe not," I said with a weak smile.

What Evan had or had not done wasn't a concern to me. I could take care of my family.

FIVE

I left Jane's house shortly after and walked over to the car. Evan was standing outside, leaning on the car and drumming his fingers impatiently.

"Get in the car," I said.

Evan didn't respond. Once we started driving he finally spoke up.

"Did you find out anything?" he said quietly.

"I found out quite a bit, despite your actions."

"You wouldn't have even gotten through the front door without my help," he said.

"Your help," I repeated. "You know, I'm debating whether I should tell Dennis about-"

"Oh no," he said dryly. "Please don't tell my boss, I'll do anything."

I suddenly swerved the car onto the side of the road and parked it at the edge.

"What are you doing?" he asked, his mood suddenly shifting.

I turned to him.

"What the fuck is wrong with you?" I asked.

"Jesus, it was a joke-"

"Everything seems to be a joke to you here," I snapped. "From the moment you showed up, you haven't taken any of this seriously, it's all just a game. I can already see that Dennis is just looking for an excuse to get rid of you. You're testing his patience, just like you're testing mine."

"I'm trying to get results," he interjected, but I wasn't done.

"You know I'm starting to see why you were transferred. Dennis said he owed someone a favour, must have been a pretty big one."

The moment I mentioned the transfer something changed in Evan's expression.

"You don't know a goddamn thing about why I'm in this town," he said.

His voice was quiet, but I could hear anger in it. And there was something else. It almost sounded like shame.

"I know you think you're really good at reading people because you've been a cop for 40 or however many years and you're best friends with everyone in this town, but you don't know me. You don't know what I did to end up in this place."

I hadn't been expecting this so I wasn't even sure what to say.

"Why don't you enlighten me then?" I said.

"Why?" he scoffed. "So you can judge me?"

We sat quietly for a minute and I realized that Evan wasn't going to continue this conversation, so I started the car again and continued to the station.

***

When we got back I noticed that the door to Dennis' office was closed. Through the window I could see that Ross was inside and they seemed to be arguing about something. I walked over and knocked on the door. Dennis peered out the window at me and looked relieved that someone had come to interrupt whatever conversation he was having.

"Please tell me you have something," he said as he took his feet off the table.

I turned to Ross.

"You're going to have to go back and watch Vanessa's house again," I said.

That looked like the last thing he wanted to hear.

"Why?" Dennis asked.

"Because she asked us if we can protect her."

"From what?" Dennis asked.

"Yeah, from what?" Evan asked, suddenly appearing behind me. "You didn't mention this in the car."

Dennis turned to Evan.

"Why weren't you there with him?" he asked.

"Long story," I said.

I didn't want to derail this with an argument about Evan's lack of professionalism.

"Bertrand was telling the truth. Our victim wasn't at the church on Sunday. She was meeting up with Martin Nero. At the Hole."

Dennis stared at me for a few seconds and then immediately opened a drawer in his desk and pulled out a pack of cigarettes.

"Jesus," Ross sighed.

"Sorry, is that name supposed to mean something?" Evan asked, looking around the room. "What's the Hole?"

Dennis looked at me as he lit his cigarette.

"You want to explain that one?" he asked.

"The Hole..." I said. "It's a sort of cave out in the woods, it's a popular place where kids go if they want to have their first smoke or jerk each other off or play with a Ouija board, anything they're not supposed to do at home," I explained. "And Martin Nero is Benjamin's son."

"What, that clown who came in the other day and said he wanted us to work together? His kid's involved in this?"

"We don't know if he's involved," I said, remembering what Jane had told me. "Jane said the three of them were supposed to meet that morning, but she went to church instead. That does not mean that Martin is our guy."

"No, but we're going to have to question him," said Dennis with a sigh.

"She was worried he might get angry at her if we do that," I said.

"Well, we have to do our job," Dennis shrugged. "But we can have Ross watch the house."

"Do I have to?" Ross asked. "Can't someone else do it? It's so boring."

"No," Dennis said. "In fact, go now."

Ross looked at me as if there was something I could say to change Dennis' mind but I said nothing. Once he had left Dennis stood up.

"What are you thinking?" Evan asked. "We arrest this guy now? Tell everyone we have a suspect right before Christmas?"

"No," said Dennis. "We don't know how involved Martin is in this, if he's even involved at all, but we're only going to get one shot. So for now we say we have a person of interest, but we don't release a name."

Eventually we decided that after Christmas we would go to the Nero house and try to figure out if Martin knew anything. Even if he was innocent, there was the fact that he knew the victim and had seen her the day before she died, and didn't come forward with that information. As I was preparing to head home at the end of the day, Evan came over to my desk.

"Listen, do you want to grab a drink after work?" he asked.

His voice sounded uneasy.

"I try not to drink too much anymore," I said. "But if you want to sit and talk, we can go somewhere."

Evan nodded slowly.

"Sure," he said.

"Is everything alright?" I asked him, noticing that he seemed off.

"Yeah," he said, as he slowly turned to head back to his desk. "Everything's fine."

I headed out towards the parking lot and called Martha to let her know that Evan would be joining us for dinner later. After his outburst earlier today I wasn't too keen on spending more time with him, but uninviting him now would have seemed mean-spirited.

***

We ended up going to a small coffee shop that was a few blocks away from the station. The proximity meant that cops were frequent customers, but I figured that today we'd be the only ones there. Once we had our coffees we sat down in a pair of large armchairs in the corner that were a little too low to the ground, causing me to have to stretch my legs out under the table. Evan sat down across from me and exhaled as he wrapped his hands around his mug.

"What did you want to talk about?" I asked, louder than normal, since the jazz music playing over the radio had been turned up to an unreasonable level.

"Just please... don't yell," he said, and he looked out the window to our side, scanning the street as if he were worried that someone would recognize him.

"What?" I asked, as I turned my head to see if there was anyone there.

"I'm sorry about this morning," he said quietly. "And I'm sorry I laughed at the dead body the first time you met me."

"You don't have to apologize to me," I said. "I just know you can be better. So be better."

"You don't know that," he replied. "You don't actually know me. Like, at all."

"That's fair," I said.

There was an awkward pause and Evan lifted up his coffee to take a long sip. The only sound was the obnoxiously upbeat rendition of Jingle Bells that had started playing on the radio, so I hoped Evan would start talking again soon to drown it out. He was jittery, I could see why he had maybe wanted to go for an actual drink.

"You wanted to know what I did to get transferred," he said.

"You don't have to tell me that story if you don't want to," I said.

"No, I think I should. It's only fair that you know," he sighed. "Back at my old precinct... we had spent years trying to get this guy, he was sort of in the same line of work as Benjamin here, just on a bigger scale, real piece of shit, just lived to commit crimes. He called himself Moses, which wasn't his real name, but you get the sense of how he viewed himself."

"Okay," I said as I sipped my coffee.

"Eventually, after years of us having no success, one of his guys decided to flip, I guess he had a change of heart. He was willing to give us everything, the whole operation would collapse. The thing is... this guy's testimony was the only thing we had. Without him it falls apart."

"Right," I said.

Evan sighed again, louder this time. He stared down at his coffee. I could see that he really didn't like talking about this.

"So we arrest Moses and about a dozen of his closest guys, we nab them all at the same time so none of them could warn the others. Of course, we had to also 'arrest' our guy to keep up appearances. Went off perfectly."

By now Evan's hands were shaking as if he were about to have a seizure. I was sure that if the music in the shop was turned off I'd be able to hear his heart pounding.

"What happened?" I asked.

"The day before the trial was supposed to begin our guy died in his cell."

"They figured out it was him?" I asked. "Or did he kill himself?"

"No. Some journalist found out who the traitor was and published his name. She wanted to have a big breaking story."

There was raw hatred in his voice as he explained it.

"I'm sorry," I said.

"We were supposed to protect him," Evan said, rather loudly. "I was supposed to protect him, and we let them get to him!"

I briefly glanced over Evan's shoulder. There were other people in the shop, but they were all the way on the other side, and didn't seem to notice that Evan was yelling.

"And that's why you were transferred?" I asked.

Evan gave a short laugh.

"Oh no. That's not why. I... I decided to pay the journalist a visit," he said.

I looked down and saw that his hands were squeezed into fists so tightly that his knuckles had gone completely white.

"And then I was the one in jail," he said.

"When was this?" I asked.

"Just a few months ago," he said. "I was only locked up for a few days... before Moses bailed me out."

"He bailed you out?" I asked. "Why?"

Evan laughed again, or rather made a noise that sounded like a laugh, but there was no humour in it.

"He said that he was a free man because of my fuck-ups, so he felt he owed me this."

"Jesus Christ," I said.

"Yeah. So I went on temporary leave without pay."

"How did I not hear about this?" I said. "A cop assaulting a journalist, that would have made the news all around the country."

"Because Moses paid off as many people as he could to stay quiet. That and I imagine some journalists were afraid to report on it, now that they had seen what happened to one of their own. The official reason for my absence was stress leave, which isn't that big of a lie. Then eventually I find out I'm being transferred to some town in buttfuck nowhere, the most boring place on earth,

I was told. And here we are, in the middle of our own murder mystery."

For a while neither of us said anything. For the first time I saw who Evan really was. The brash, loose-cannon persona I had gotten to know was just a facade he was putting on. I decided not to push this issue further, I imagined that if I kept asking for more details he might have a mental breakdown. In fact, I wouldn't doubt that I was the first person he had had an honest conversation about this with.

"If you don't want me to come to your house today-" he blurted out.

"No, no, no," I said. "You can still join us."

He looked embarrassed.

"Thanks."

"You don't have to justify what you did. Not to me," I said. "That man's death was not your fault."

"I know it wasn't," Evan said. "But I still crossed a line. I took the law into my own hands."

I finished my coffee.

"This Moses, he ended up walking free?" I asked.

"Yep."

"And the journalist, did she face any legal repercussions for what she did?"

Evan shook his head.

I stood up.

"Then what you did was the closest thing that dead man will ever get to justice."

SIX

After I dropped Evan off back at the station I drove home to help Martha prepare for Christmas Eve.

"Can't remember the last time you brought home a friend from work," she said as we were setting the table.

I placed the first set of cutlery down by the plate at the head of the table. I stared down and frowned, forgetting which side the spoon was supposed to be on.

"He's not a friend," I said.

I meant that. The conversation we had over coffee was eye-opening, and not one I was intent on sharing with my family.

"No?" she asked as she looked up.

I noticed a strange sadness in Martha's eyes that I had first seen last week when I had been off work. It had all been her idea. I had lost track of the amount of times she had told me that I barely interact with my own children, although there was not much I could do about that. I had hoped that our week at home would have fixed that, and the kids had seemed happy, but I could tell that Martha was still dissatisfied with something.

"He sounds a lot like you," she said.

"What's that supposed to mean?" I asked.

All I had told her was that Evan was loud and seemed to always act like he was in a movie. I had conveniently left out him laughing at a corpse and taking pictures of it, as well as being prone to witness intimidation.

"He sounds rather frustrated that he can't do things his way and has to do what others say."

"I'm not frustrated by that," I said. "I always follow the rules at my job."

"I wasn't talking about your job," she said.

I frowned. I thought of something clever I could respond with, but it would just end with her getting upset and not speaking to me for a day or so. Martha then walked over, looked down at the cutlery I had set down on the table in front of me, and adjusted the fork, which apparently was crooked.

There was a series of loud thumps coming from the hallway as Hope ran into the room. I bent down and grabbed her just as she was running past me and lifted her up, immediately feeling my back strain from the process.

"Now," I said. "Dad's got a work friend coming over for dinner."

I noticed Martha roll her eyes as I suddenly did refer to Evan as a 'friend.'

"What are we not going to ask him?" I asked Hope.

She blinked and shrugged.

"I dunno," she said and laughed, knowing that I knew she was lying.

"What are we not going to ask him?" I repeated.

"If he's ever shot anyone," she mumbled, tilting her head to the side so she wouldn't have to look at me.

Hope had done this once. Somehow Martha had found a way to blame me for it. I put her down and she immediately ran off again. I didn't need to worry about repeating these instructions to Carrie. She was probably nose-deep in a book right now and would likely bring it with her to the dinner table and continue reading there while everyone else was having a conversation. She would gladly ask Evan about the most disturbing crime scenes he had ever seen, the more mutilated the body, the better, but Martha would shut that down in an instant.

I walked into the kitchen just as Martha was shutting the oven door. The turkey that had been in there for four hours now sat on the counter.

"Mom called this morning while you were gone," she said.

"Oh?"

"Think I might take the kids and visit her over the break," she added.

I noticed that she had said 'kids', but not me. I wouldn't have been able to go anyway due to work, but I could tell what she meant. Before I could say anything else there were voices in the living room as Hope had turned the TV on. Immediately I heard the familiar sound of Dennis' voice fill the air.

"Baby, turn that off," Martha said immediately.

I think she wished I had any other job in the world. Any reference to crime was always met with disdain, as if it were my fault that there were fucked up people out there.

"We think we might have found who killed that girl," I said quietly.

This wasn't true, and even if we knew that it was Martin, I couldn't disclose that, as Dennis had only mentioned a 'person of interest' in his statement, but I hoped that this would calm Martha down a bit.

A few minutes later the doorbell rang and Martha immediately put on a rehearsed smile.

"Are you going to get that?" she asked me, with a hint of annoyance in her tone.

I walked over and opened the door and saw Evan. He looked visibly uncomfortable, like someone who wasn't accustomed to social gatherings.

"Hi," he said.

I let him in and took his coat, which was covered in snow that had just recently begun to rapidly fall. I was glad we had tomorrow off, as I could already tell we were going to be snowed in.

"So this is Evan," Martha said as she entered the hallway, looking happier than I had seen her in years. "I've heard so much about you."

"Oh dear," Evan said, glancing at me.

He said it like it was a joke but I knew he was genuinely wondering how much I had said. I walked him over to the dining room while Martha went to Carrie's room to convince her to spend time with other people for a little bit. Sure enough, Carrie came down the hallway with a book tucked under her arm, all the while making sure that her footsteps were slightly louder than normal, but not loud enough to be obvious how annoyed she was.

"George says you've lived here your whole lives," Evan said once we had begun eating.

"Not in this house, but this town, yes," she said with a hint of bitterness.

Martha was already on her second glass of wine of the night, although she had finished the first one long before Evan had arrived.

"How are you liking it here?" she asked.

Evan's eyes quickly darted to me as he reminded himself that he probably shouldn't mention how exciting he found the murder puzzle we'd been working on. I wondered whether in that brief moment he had noticed my hand hovering over my knife.

"It's pretty cold," was the first thing he managed to say. "But it's beautiful," he hastily added. "Nice and quiet."

Evan and Martha continued with icebreaker questions. I didn't say much, as most of what they said were things I already knew. But eventually they reached something I hadn't heard about.

"So are you living here alone, or do you have family?" Martha asked.

"Alone," he said. "I do have family but... yeah, I'm alone."

There was silence. Martha realized that she must have touched a sensitive topic because she turned red and immediately grabbed her wine glass to hide it.

"Why are you living by yourself if you have family?" Hope asked, her small face scrunched up as she tried to figure it out.

"Because he's divorced."

Carrie had spoken for the first time since sitting down with us. She didn't even look up when she spoke, her eyes were fixated on the enormous piece of turkey she was trying to cut through.

"Carrie!" I snapped.

"What?" she asked, looking up and seeming unsure what the problem was.

"It's okay," Evan said with a light smile.

I noticed that Martha was emptying her whole glass trying to hide her embarrassment.

"And no, actually, I'm not divorced. I'm separated," he told Carrie, but he still seemed impressed that she had figured it out.

"I'm so sorry," I said. "We don't have to talk about that."

"I said it's fine," he said again.

There was a strange contrast between how he was acting while talking about this and how he acted just hours earlier when he was telling me about why he was transferred. The separation didn't seem to bother him.

"I had no idea you were married," I said. "You're still a kid!"

Evan laughed.

"I'm 26, but thanks."

He glanced at the wine bottle in the middle of the table.

"May I?" he gestured.

"Help yourself," Martha said as she waved her hand in front of her face.

The temperature had apparently gotten hotter due to the awkwardness. Evan poured himself a glass and raised it to his mouth, but before he drank he looked back at Carrie.

"Actually you weren't technically wrong, kid. I am divorced... and separated."

Now everyone was confused.

"I don't-" I began.

"Divorced from one wife, separated from another," he said, and that's when he started drinking.

I looked over at Martha and she seemed to realize that I hadn't known any of this. Somehow she thought that was funny.

"But I thought you could only get married once," Hope piped in, again sounding extremely confused.

"That's enough," Martha hissed.

"No, it's fine," Evan said. "Well, if you make the right decision the first time, then you'll only have to do it once," he told Hope.

That seemed to clear things up for her.

"Might as well get it all out there," he said with a sigh. "Divorced twice, separated once."

"Jesus Christ, you're 26 and you've been married three times?" I said.

"I know, right?" Evan said as if he were just hearing this for the first time. "I still can't believe it sometimes."

We all sat quietly as Evan waited to see which one of us inevitably asked him for more details. It was possible that this wouldn't be a story that Martha wanted our children hearing, so I didn't want to be the one to ask. Besides, it could be a sensitive topic. And then Carrie turned to Hope and gave her opinion.

"I told you marriage was a waste of time," she said.

"That's enough," Martha snapped at her.

Before we could continue learning even more about him the doorbell rang.

"Oh, are you expecting someone else?" Evan asked.

"No, that's probably Bertrand," I said.

Evan's smile faltered for just a second but he recovered. I stood up and went to open the door. Bertrand's smile was even more rehearsed than Martha's had been. That wasn't normal. Bertrand enjoyed going door to door on Christmas, and I knew he would be happy to visit all of the other families on his list, but he wasn't happy to see me. I knew why. But I didn't care.

"Merry Christmas Father," I said.

"And to you," he recited. "May I come in?" he asked.

"Of course."

Father Bertrand brushed the snow out of his hair before walking in. It was snowing much more rapidly now.

"Quite cold out," he said as he took off his glasses and rubbed them against his jacket.

He walked over to the dining room and peaked his head in.

"Merry Christmas to all of you," he said.

That was when he noticed that Evan was there.

"Ah, Evan. Good to see you."

"Yeah, thanks, you too," Evan said as fast as he could, not looking up from his food.

I wasn't sure if Bertrand had gotten the impression yet that Evan distrusted him, but he didn't show any sign of it.

"Hi Father Bertrand," Hope said, frantically waving her hand.

"Hello!" he said enthusiastically. "My, you're getting big, I haven't seen you in a while."

I knew what that meant. That was him chastising Martha and I for not having been at mass the past few weeks. Carrie had taken Bertrand's arrival as an opportunity to start reading again, and she made a huffing sound when her own growth hadn't been acknowledged.

"Well, I won't take up much of your time," Bertrand said, clapping his hands together. "Just wanted to wish you all the best and hopefully I'll see you again soon."

Maybe he thought we didn't get the hint the first time.

"I did want to talk to you for a moment though," he said, lightly jabbing his finger into my arm.

"Right, of course. I'll walk you out," I said.

I led Bertrand over to the door and grabbed my jacket from the closet. We walked onto the front porch. I quickly glanced over at the front yards of each of our neighbouring houses. There didn't seem to be anyone standing outside, and both houses had light shining from their respective living rooms as the families were enjoying Christmas.

"What was that the other day?" Bertrand asked me angrily.

"Keep your voice down," I said.

"You could have warned me that you were coming with someone! You show up at my house with another cop and-" he said, his eyes wide with disbelief.

"We were following up on a lead. It would have been strange if you knew we were coming ahead of time," I said.

"But I didn't know what to think! What if I had panicked and ran?" he asked.

"Then we would have had a problem," I told him.

Bertrand was being irrational.

"I'm sorry," he said. "I just... I didn't know what to expect, I didn't know if you maybe had told him-"

"I haven't told him," I said. "I haven't told any of them. Now, is that all you wanted to talk about, or do you actually have something to report?"

Bertrand exhaled, trying to calm himself.

"McKinnley's been hitting his wife again," Bertrand said.

I sighed.

"Jesus," I put my head in my hands. "He told you this?"

"No, his wife did."

I frowned.

"Why did she go to you and not to the cops?" I asked.

Bertrand gave a weird laugh that showed he didn't actually think this was funny.

"She came to the confession booth and said she's been having bad thoughts. I asked her what she meant and she said she's been seriously considering killing her husband before he kills her."

"Do you think he will?" I asked.

"On purpose? Probably not," said Bertrand. "But if he keeps hitting her one day he will hit too hard."

"Fuck," I said.

I leaned over the railing and looked out into the darkness of the street.

"Are you going to do something about it?" he asked.

"I'll look into it," I said.

That apparently wasn't good enough.

"Look into it? I need more than that, George," he said. "That's the whole point of us having this arrangement, to stop things like this."

"I am well aware of the purpose of this arrangement," I said.

All of a sudden there was a loud snap off to the side of the house. We both turned to look but there was nothing there.

"I'll keep an eye out on McKinnley," I said. "And I will handle it."

I tried to sound confident, and that seemed to ease Bertrand's misgivings.

"Alright," he said finally.

He turned and walked towards the stairs that led into our front yard.

"Is there anything else about Jane?" I asked. "Anything you didn't share before?"

Bertrand turned back.

"I already told you everything."

I waited out on the porch for another minute as I watched Bertrand cross the street and knock on the door of another house. Then I turned and went back inside. When I entered the dining room I noticed that Evan was gone. I turned my head and saw that the bathroom door was ajar, so he wasn't there.

"What happened to Evan?" I asked.

"He went outside for a smoke," Martha said disapprovingly. "I imagine him and Dennis get along well."

I sat back down and a minute later the patio door opened and Evan walked back in, his arms glued to his sides as he shivered. We all sat back down and continued eating.

"What did the father want?" Martha asked me.

"Just wanted to remind me that he hadn't seen us at mass in a long time," I lied. "As if I didn't get the message the first time."

There was something off about the expression on Evan's face as I said this. I had already gotten the impression that he wasn't crazy about the priest, but he almost looked suspicious right now. But then Carrie chimed in with more tasteless questions.

"So if you're 26, that means you've been married three times in eight years," she started.

"Carrie..." Martha warned but our daughter ignored her.

"...that means on average each relationship lasted two years and eight months, which if including a one year engagement and at least six months of dating before-"

"I'll stop you right there, cause your math is going to be off," Evan interjected.

Martha's face was now the same shade as her wine, but if Evan was bothered by any of this he didn't show it.

"The first one was my girlfriend from high school, we got engaged as soon as we became adults because we thought we'd be together forever," he said. "The marriage barely lasted a year."

"I'm so sorry," Martha said. "We don't have to talk about it if you don't want."

"Oh, it's fine, it was a long time ago," Evan smiled. "But at the time I was very upset, so my friends decided to cheer me up by taking me to Vegas for a weekend... where I got married and divorced a second time."

The look of confusion on Hope's face was adorable as she tried to wrap her mind around the idea of an entire marriage happening so fast.

"How-" she began.

"You'll understand when you're older," I said, and I gave Evan a look that indicated this second marriage did not require details.

"It was a long time before the third," he said. "I wanted to be sure I got this one right. But I didn't."

***

The rest of the evening was uneventful and Evan went home within an hour.

"I'll do the dishes, I don't feel like sleeping yet," I told Martha.

She didn't argue and went off to bed. I walked into the kitchen and noticed the pile of plates balancing on each other in the sink. Before I got to them I walked over to the patio door and opened it. A round hill of snow was already forming on the table in front of me, and the deck was also covered in a blanket of snow that sagged slightly in between the planks. However, I could see where Evan had been standing when he went out for his cigarette. The snow had been disturbed there, and then more snow had unevenly covered it afterwards. But Evan hadn't been standing in one place the whole time. I had gotten a strange feeling when Martha had told me he went out for a cigarette, as I hadn't seen him smoke once in the time we had been working together. And I was right to be suspicious. Because the uneven snow indicated he had walked off the patio and around the side of the house.

INTERLUDE

"Can I just get you to clarify something, because I feel like some people listening might not be understanding the full picture?" Xander asked me. "The way Dennis and the other officers seem to talk about Benjamin Nero it almost feels like... I don't want to use the wrong word, but were you scared of him?"

I pondered for a moment.

"Scared isn't the right word, but I do understand what you mean," I said. "How do I explain this properly? Okay, as I've already established, Benjamin Nero: career criminal? Yes. Violent murderer? Probably not. And we have to be clear that even though Martin was now our main suspect, that didn't necessarily mean Benjamin was also involved, in fact it was more likely that he wasn't."

Xander seemed intrigued by that last point.

"What makes you say that?"

"Remember how I said that Martin's first line of defense was always 'my father' this, 'my father' that?"

Xander nodded.

"Well... and I didn't know this at the time for sure, but I had my suspicions, Benjamin seemed to really dislike that. He didn't have a problem with his son being a criminal, that part almost filled him with pride, but he HATED that his son would always use him as a literal get-out-of-jail-free card. The fact that Martin couldn't be a successful criminal on his own disappointed him as a parent."

"Wow," Xander said.

"But at the same time, if we take a swing at his son, we can't miss," I continued.

"So basically, if I'm understanding it right, if you accuse Martin of something and your evidence is flimsy, Benjamin will shut that down, but if you can prove that he did it, then Benjamin says 'sorry kid, you're on your own?'"

"That's exactly it," I said. "You described that perfectly."

"Can I ask..." Julie spoke up. "and this doesn't ultimately affect the story, I don't think, but what was the town's opinion on him?"

I sighed.

"I don't know how to say this without coming off really posh and arrogant, but... there were certain types of people that were attracted to him. As I've said before, troubled kids seemed to gravitate towards him, people who dropped out of school, didn't really have much ambition, already had a criminal record, but also a lot of older people, who honestly should have known better. Like middle-aged men who were unemployed and suffered from alcoholism and had nothing to do all day and hated the sound of their wives complaining, they all weirdly idolized him."

"Interesting," said Julie.

"And even though Benjamin was predictable, to an extent, I always in the back of my mind kept telling myself that it was possible that he was way smarter than he was letting on. Because let's not forget this man had once gotten a police officer to flip and become an informant. That's not something that just anyone can pull off. When he met Evan for the first time and he said he was looking forward to working together, he said that where all of us could hear it, because he wanted us to always remember what he was capable of."

SEVEN

The day after Christmas we reconvened in Dennis' office. When I arrived in the morning he already looked to be in a bad mood.

"Have a good holiday?" I asked.

The office was a cloud of cigarette smoke. I glanced over at Evan to see if he was irritated by that.

"Barely slept," Dennis said. "I've been thinking of how we're going to solve this. Close the door," he said.

I turned and just as I reached the handle Dennis yelled.

"Hey!"

Ross had been walking past the doorway and he froze and turned.

"Why aren't you outside the girl's house?" he asked.

Ross' face looked as though he had just died and come back to life.

"Jesus, again? Why, I thought we were moving onto-"

"Go!" Dennis yelled.

Ross dipped his head down in resentment and walked away. I closed the door.

"I want you guys to bring in Martin for questioning. Go to the house, see if he's there, but, and this is the important part," Dennis said. "I want you to talk to them, alone," he said to Evan.

Both Evan and I seemed equally surprised.

"Actually?" Evan asked.

"Sir, if I may-" I began.

"I know what you're going to say," Dennis said to me. "And I understand. But I want Evan to do it because to Benjamin he's an unknown variable. If you go, or even worse, if I go, he'll know how to get under our skin. Evan is a complete wild card here. You stay in the car."

I understood the plan but it still seemed risky. I wasn't sure about leaving Evan alone with Benjamin and Martin, even for a few minutes, especially after what I had heard Evan tell me a few days before about why he was transferred.

"You guys can go now," Dennis added. "While the sun's shining."

We walked out of the building but I stopped just at the edge of the sidewalk and pulled out a pack of cigarettes. Evan began walking across the parking lot, unaware that I had stopped, but a few seconds later he paused and turned back.

"Just gonna have a smoke," I said. "You want one?" I asked, motioning the pack at him.

"No, I don't smoke. Thanks," he said.

And I had him.

We got into my car a minute later and began driving towards the house at the edge of town where Benjamin lived.

"So you got any notes on how I should deal with him?" Evan asked.

"The son or the father?" I asked.

"Both."

I drummed on the steering wheel as I thought.

"Benjamin will welcome you like an old friend. We're all buds, him and the cops. Now, when you tell him why you're there, he might take a step back and see how things unfold, he's gonna want to know just what you have on Martin before he weighs in. Do not, do NOT accuse Martin of being a murderer."

"I wasn't going to-"

"Well, I saw you do it to Jane the other day," I said.

"Oh, Jesus Christ, are we back to this again?" Evan exclaimed.

"Yes, we're back to this, because if you fuck up this investigation, I swear to God-"

"I won't do anything," he said firmly.

I exhaled.

"Okay, the reason we want to talk to him is because we were told that he had spent time with the victim the day before she died. We don't know if it's true or not, that's why we're following up and asking him questions," I said very clearly.

"Got it," said Evan.

"Now, at some point Benjamin will point out that Dennis sent you instead of anyone else. And he will ask you why you think that is."

"Do I tell him the truth?" Evan asked.

"Um... tell him the truth, tell him Dennis sent you in because Benjamin doesn't know how to push your buttons yet... that might work, although he'll probably think that's the excuse we told you to give. But what if you admitted that, and then you said you suspect the real reason is Dennis is worried we can't figure out who the killer is, so he's sending you, hoping you'll fail and he can pin everything on you."

"That..." said Evan. "that's kind of insane, but it might work."

We were only a few minutes away from the house but I pulled over to the side of the road.

"Why are we stopping?" Evan asked.

I parked the car and turned to him. Evan leaned back when he saw the look on my face.

"What, did I say something?" he asked, alarmed.

"You told me you didn't smoke," I said.

"What?"

129

"In the parking lot before we left, you said you didn't smoke."

"Yeah..." said Evan, unsure what the problem was.

"Then why did you tell Martha you went out for a smoke? When you were at our house, you went out for a smoke while I was talking to Father Bertrand."

Evan looked confused.

"No, I went out for some fresh air."

"So you're telling me the truth right now, and my wife was lying to me, yes?" I asked.

"No, she didn't lie, she probably just misunderstood me-"

"You said you were getting fresh air, and she understood that as you going out for a cigarette. Fuck, she must be stupid."

"No, George, listen-"

"You walked all the way around the side of the house," I said sternly. "What were you looking for?"

I realized now that I had leaned forward a good foot and Evan's head was now pressed against the passenger window. His eyes were wide and he was panicking, but suddenly he composed himself.

"What is your arrangement with Father Bertrand?" he asked quietly.

"What?" I asked.

My heart was pounding. I had hoped he hadn't heard anything, but now my fears were realized.

"You two have an arrangement. That's what you called it. What is it?"

"That's not your concern," I said.

I needed to find a way to divert this. I didn't know how much he had heard, but I needed to figure out how to turn this back around on him.

"I couldn't figure out where I had heard the name 'McKinnley' before, and then finally this morning I remembered," he said. "That was the guy we bumped into outside Hellhole, the one who was stumbling across the parking lot. So he's been beating his wife and she's thinking of killing him?"

I could feel my face getting hotter.

"So if she does, do I tell Dennis that you knew she might? And what if he asks who you heard it from?"

"That's enough!" I snapped.

There was a long silence in the car. I turned away from Evan and stared out the windshield. Part of me hoped that Benjamin might just kill him when he tried to bring Martin in for questioning. That would give me the perfect excuse.

"George..." he said finally. "I told you the reason I'm here. I told you the mistakes I made, how I fucked up. I'm not proud of it, and it certainly wasn't easy for me to talk about, especially to you."

"Why especially to me?" I asked.

"Because I thought you were boring. I thought you had a stick up your ass, I could fucking hear you groaning every time I did the smallest thing that you disapproved of. And then when I told you what I had done to end up here, you not only understood, you commended me for it, like it was the right thing to do."

I finally turned to him and I was surprised to see that he looked concerned.

"I'm starting to think that we're not quite that different," he said.

I did my best to prevent my chin from wobbling in anger, I didn't want to him to know how uncertain I was feeling right now. The next thing I said or did could prove disastrous. Then I realized that I hadn't taken a breath in about a solid minute. So I finally exhaled slowly.

"Father Bertrand and I have an arrangement, you're right. If Bertrand hears a confession from someone and they admit that they have committed a crime, or have been thinking of committing one, which depending on who you ask is also sinful, then he passes that information on to me."

Evan looked confused.

"But don't confession booths have that little wall between you, isn't the whole point that it's anonymous?"

"They do. And they are. But if you've been listening to the same people tell you all of their secrets for twenty years then you become very familiar with their voices," I explained.

"He can tell who's confessing just by the sound of their voice?" Evan exclaimed. "For like a hundred different voices?"

For the first time I allowed myself to smile.

"Well, he says he can, and I think that for some people he's able to, but I imagine that the security cameras he has on his property are helpful. He can keep track of who's coming and going from the church. But I don't question how he does it, just as long as I get results."

"Jesus Christ," Evan said.

"Yes," I agreed.

I started the car. It appeared I was safe for now. Maybe Evan's dislike of priests could come in handy here. A more pious cop would have turned me in for what they saw as unethical practices.

"Isn't that like, severely frowned upon in the church? Spreading confession gossip?" Evan asked me as I pulled back onto the road.

"Oh, it's very frowned upon. The people here would fucking kill him if they knew he was doing this," I said and laughed.

There was a part of me that almost felt relieved that I had someone I could share this with.

"Does Dennis know about this?" Evan asked.

"He does," I said. "When I first flipped Bertrand I told Dennis almost immediately."

"And he's okay with this?"

"He told me to do what I believed was right. And he told me he never wanted to hear about it."

Evan didn't say anything else for the next few minutes, evidently he needed time to process what he had learned. Thankfully he didn't seem angry at me. Or mistrustful. I thought back to what he had said about us being more similar than he had first thought. Funnily I had the same thought when we were in the coffee shop.

"How did you flip him?" Evan asked suddenly. "How did you convince him to break a rule so important to him?"

"Wasn't the first important rule he had been breaking," I said. "I had found out that Bertrand had been breaking the rule about priests keeping their dicks in their pants."

"Wait," Evan said. "Was he molesting-"

"No! No, no, no, no!" I said, realizing how that had sounded. "No, nothing like that. As far as I know, Bertrand has never touched a child. If he had I certainly wouldn't have been letting him into my house."

"Right," said Evan. "That makes sense."

"What I meant was, there is a pretty big rule about not coveting your neighbour's wife."

It took Evan a few seconds to realize what I was saying.

"Oh Jesus, are you serious?" he asked and started laughing.

"Oh yeah. And it wasn't just one neighbour, it was quite a few."

Evan didn't stop laughing until we had finally reached Benjamin Nero's house.

The Nero house wasn't quite a villa, but it was noticeably larger than most of the other houses in Appleton. It was a two-storey grey building that stood in the middle of a large plot of land. There was a strange contrast of both splendor and decay. The property had a large metal fence around the perimeter, but some of the beams had cardboard signs attached with zip ties that read 'KEEP OUT.' The snow from a few days ago had melted, so we could see the yellow grass that existed in patches all around the property. Off to the left was what could generously be described as a small pond. In reality it was just a large hole with muddy water. Past the open gate was a long path leading to the house. This wasn't a proper driveway, or even a long strip of gravel. It looked like it had once also been grass but so many cars had driven on it that the grass had been stripped away, leaving only dry, cracked mud behind.

"This is it?" Evan asked.

"Yeah," I said. "I should probably leave the car here, I'm not in the mood to listen to Benjamin complain about trespassing. So it looks like you're on your own from here."

Evan didn't move.

"Don't tell me you're nervous," I said.

"Should I be?" he asked me, suddenly sounding uncertain.

"I don't know. If I hear gunshots, should I assume it's you?" I asked.

Evan looked puzzled, he seemed to be trying to figure out of I was joking or not.

"I can handle it," he said finally.

He got out of the car and I watched him walk down the dirt path to the house. Eventually he reached the front door, and shortly after I could see it open. I squinted and recognized Benjamin. They stood in place for a few seconds, likely talking and then Benjamin shifted to the side, allowing Evan to enter the house. Then his head turned and he stared out across the field directly at me. He waved. It was far, but I think I saw him smile.

Now that I was alone I had time with my thoughts. I didn't know how long Evan would be in the house, but I needed to think about what my next move was going to be. Father Bertrand and I had been so careful for so many years but recent events had caused him to slip up. And now Evan knew. Evan knew because Bertrand just couldn't keep his mouth shut. Fortunately, Evan didn't seem to mind what I was doing, just that I had kept it a secret. I wondered how likely he would be to tell someone about this. If word got out that Bertrand was passing information onto me he'd probably get excommunicated, and he'd be lucky if the people in this town didn't crucify him. They might come after me too, although I doubted I would lose my job. I wasn't sure whether Dennis would defend me. He had seemed to disapprove of my arrangement with the Father when I first told him, although I'm sure if I ever solved a case thanks to information I got from a confession booth then he suddenly wouldn't mind. Whatever the case, I realized that the best thing for me to do would be to find out something about Evan that I could use to control him if he decided to talk. I wondered whether Dennis was aware that Evan had been in jail shortly before he came here. Dennis owed someone a 'favour,' but did he know the details of it? But no, I decided against it. Evan had told me that story in a moment of weakness, and I refused to exploit that unless I absolutely had to. The other option would be to prove to him that my arrangement with Bertrand was actually useful. Maybe I would have to look into McKinnley and see if he really was close to murdering his wife.

My thoughts were interrupted when I saw the front door of the Nero house open. Evan came out. Then Martin. And finally Benjamin. I groaned. It looked like Benjamin had a thing or two to say about his son being taken in for questioning. When they reached the car Evan opened the back door and waited for Martin to slide in.

"Morning George!" Benjamin said with his usual condescending smile.

"Morning," I replied.

"Would you look at that? I told this young man that we'd be working together soon, and a few days later he comes knocking on my door!" he gave an annoying laugh. "Seriously though, I'm counting on you to make sure my son comes back in one piece," he said as he stared down at me.

"You have nothing to worry about," I said.

"I always worry when Martin's in trouble. I'm a parent. Surely you can understand," he said.

I wondered whether Benjamin really thought he was being subtle right now.

"I do," I said.

He gave a short nod and clapped the top of the car with his hand before backing away. We drove off and I gazed at Benjamin through the rearview mirror, half expecting him to pull out a gun and start shooting at us.

"Have a good Christmas, George?" Martin's voice suddenly piped up from the back seat.

I looked back and saw him slouched with his arms spread across the headrests, as though we were out for a fun ride.

"Was nice," I said shortly.

"Must have been good to spend time with your family," he added.

I wasn't sure whether he realized that his father had just made the same thinly veiled threat a minute ago. They really were exactly the same, the two of them. I didn't respond to him. I didn't say much at all. I had no idea how much or how little Evan had explained in the house, so I didn't want to give anything away.

EIGHT

"Hey boss, good to see you!" was the first thing that Martin said when he saw Dennis at the station.

Dennis frowned.

"Any problems?" he asked.

"Nope, everything was fine," said Evan.

Dennis turned to me as though he wanted me to confirm whether that was true. I just nodded.

"Set him up in the room," Dennis said.

Once Martin was in the interrogation room we gathered outside to discuss our next move.

"What happened when you went to the house?" Dennis asked.

"Benjamin opened the door, let me walk in as though we'd been friends for years."

"Of course," I said.

"I told him we needed to ask Martin some questions, he asked why, I said we were investigating a murder and Martin may have seen the victim the day before. Then he asked why we drove all the way out to his house when you could have just called him."

Dennis pressed his fingers into his forehead.

"I'm so fucking done with both of them."

"So I told him that you sent me because you thought he wouldn't know how to annoy me as easily as he would you two."

"Oh, you actually did say that?" I asked.

Dennis turned to me.

"I imagine that was your idea," he muttered.

"Benjamin seemed to think that was funny, so then he called Martin down. Martin didn't want to come in, but Benjamin convinced him that it would be okay."

"So Martin seemed nervous?" Dennis asked.

"A little," said Evan. "But was it because he's guilty or just a general nervousness that cops are asking about him?"

"But if he's nervous and Benjamin wasn't, that could mean that Benjamin doesn't know of his involvement," said Dennis.

"We won't know until we ask him," I said. "How do you want to handle this?"

We all turned to the window. Martin was leaning back in his chair at a concerning angle. I wondered what Benjamin would do if his son tipped his chair and cracked his skull on the floor.

"You go first," Dennis said to Evan. "We're going to break him."

"You think he killed her?" I asked.

Dennis hadn't seemed this confident before.

"Look at him," he said.

Evan walked into the room and sat down across from Martin Nero. The boy was a younger version of his father, the same grey eyes, the same punchable face curved into an arrogant smile. Beneath all of the gel his hair was black, which matched the leather jacket and pants he was wearing. He seemed not to share his father's preference for suits that weren't the right size. Whereas Benjamin seemed to always dress to look like a bum, whether intentionally or not, Martin instead dressed to convince people that he was wealthy. While Benjamin had a patchy beard, Martin's face was smooth like a baby's. His voice matched his face, it was a high-pitched whining noise that sounded like his mouth was full of food.

"So they sent you in?" he asked, tilting his chair back so that he could stare down his chin at Evan. "Are the old men too scared to talk to me?"

I frowned. This was all just a game to Martin. He couldn't wait to find out how quickly he could annoy us. But Evan didn't seemed to be phased by anything he said.

"Do you know why you're here?" he asked.

Martin shrugged.

"You said you had questions for me. Questions about some dead girl."

"Some dead girl," Evan repeated.

Martin likely didn't care about Vanessa or that she was dead, but he wouldn't go out of his way to appear so indifferent... unless he wanted us to think that he had nothing to do with it.

"This dead girl has been causing us some problems, we can't seem to figure out what happened."

Martin said nothing.

"You know it's interesting, your father showed up within a few hours, wanting us to know that he's here to help if we need him."

"Is that why I'm here?" Martin said with a scoff. "Because of something my father said?"

"No. But it was interesting, he was the only person who came forward offering help. No one else did. We didn't have a name for this person, nothing. And it was strange, cause if a person dies or goes missing, well, they had family, they had friends. Someone would come forward and say something, right?"

"Can you not do that thing where you're asking questions that you clearly already know the answer to, but you want me to say it out loud? It's really condescending," Martin said.

"You want me to be straightforward with you?" Evan asked.

"Yeah, that would be cool," Martin said loudly. "You guys want to ask me stuff, cool, but can you get to the point and stop bullshitting around?"

"Where were you on Saturday night?" Evan asked.

For half a second I could see that Martin looked confused but his expression became neutral again.

"Saturday?"

"Yes."

"Went to Hellhole with the guys," he said. "Left the house at 9, got there at 9:30, left at around 1."

Good thing that he remembered those details. I knew exactly which guys he was talking about, all of his dipshit friends who had no future other than doing what he and his father said. I could reach out to them if I needed any details confirmed, but I wouldn't have to. Evan reached into his pocket and pulled out his phone, showing Martin the picture of Vanessa he had taken.

"Did you see her there?" he asked.

Martin tilted his chair forward so he could see what Evan was showing him but the moment he realized it was a photo of a corpse he immediately turned his head sideways, averting his eyes. I could hear him exhale slowly.

"This the kind of picture you carry around with you?" he said.

"Answer my question," Evan said, not in the mood for his wisecracks.

"You're asking me if I saw this specific person at a packed bar, on a weekend, in the dark?" he asked.

"Yes."

He sat quietly for a moment. I could see he was starting to get slightly annoyed.

"I don't know. Maybe, maybe not. I see a lot of girls there. Not like there's anything else to do in this shithole of a town on the weekend."

"So you didn't see her there?" Evan asked.

Martin raised his arms in exasperation.

"How the fuck should I know? It was packed, there were strobe lights dancing everywhere, couldn't see or hear anything."

"Have you ever seen her anywhere else?" Evan asked.

"I don't know."

"Well why don't you look again?" Evan said, sliding the picture towards him.

"If I had ever seen this person she wouldn't have looked all fucked up like she does in that picture, okay? I have no idea who that is."

"Does the name Vanessa Miles mean anything to you?" Evan asked.

Martin's eye twitched slightly.

"I know a few Vanessa's," he said.

"Oh this is bullshit," Dennis whispered beside me.

"But none with that last name?" Evan continued.

"I don't know all of their last names."

"And none who look like this picture?"

"Again, that's a dead body, they always look fucked up after they die."

"Okay, so you came back from Hellhole that night and just went to bed?" Evan asked.

"I don't even remember much, I got really fucked up, I just woke up in the morning."

"Just gaps in your memory?"

"Yeah."

"But you knew what time you came home, cause you specifically said you left at 1."

Martin rolled his eyes.

"Our cameras have a timer on them, it showed I got home at 1:30."

"Fair enough," Evan said with a nod.

Martin seemed to relax slightly.

"What happened next morning, did you go anywhere, see anyone?"

"I was so fucking hungover, I could barely get out of bed," he said, rolling his eyes.

"You didn't go to church that morning?" Evan asked.

Martin let out a laugh.

"Are you serious?" he asked.

He saw that Evan wasn't smiling.

"I haven't been to church in years. If I were there on Sunday, George would have seen me."

He shook his head and turned towards the glass.

"Unless you weren't there either," he added and smiled strangely.

I didn't have to explain myself to him.

"So you just stayed home and recovered?" Evan asked.

"Yes," he said.

"And those security cameras that you have so much faith in, they can confirm that, right? They won't show you leaving the house that morning?"

"Yes," he said again.

But there had been a slight pause this time. He had hesitated. I turned to Dennis, whose smile mirrored my own.

"I'm on it," he said, and immediately walked out of the room and headed back to his office.

If Martin was lying and realized his mistake, all that he would need to do right now is request his phone call. Then he'd ask Benjamin to 'accidentally' delete any footage from that morning.

"Okay," Evan said. "Need your expertise on something else, since as you proudly mentioned, you know a lot of girls around here. The reason no one recognized our victim is because she's not actually from around here."

Martin raised an eyebrow.

"Really? So what, someone came out to the middle of nowhere and dumped a body?"

"Well, 'dumped' isn't the word I would use, given that she was nailed to a sign. But she was actually here visiting a friend. Tell me, are you close to Jane Brown, by any chance?"

His eye did that weird twitch again. Now he was wondering whether Jane had said anything, whether she was the reason he was here.

"I wouldn't say close," he said. "I mean, I know her, we went to school together, I don't know if you'd say we were friends."

"Did you ever spend time together?" Evan asked.

He shrugged.

"Bump into her at a bar sometimes, you know how it is here, same people all the time, you see them every once in a while."

"So not friends?" Evan asked.

Martin let out a sigh.

"Not really?" he said. "I don't know, maybe she'd say we were, but I don't really think so."

"You ever try to fuck her?"

"Jesus Christ," I whispered, glad that Dennis wasn't here to witness what had just happened.

That must have been the last thing Martin suspected because he burst out laughing.

"Wow," he said a minute later when he composed himself. "Um, I don't think I need to answer that, officer."

"Why not? Harmless question," Evan said.

"Not relevant though," Martin said.

"What about her?" Evan asked, tapping on the picture that was still on the table. "Would you? I mean, if she was alive, that is?"

Martin's eyes were so wide I was worried they might fall out of their sockets. I debated whether I should walk into the interrogation room myself and pull Evan out before he asked anything even worse.

"What is this? Like, why am I actually here?" he asked.

"Just trying to solve a puzzle, that's all," Evan said.

Then he stood up.

"I'm going to grab myself a coffee. Do you want water, or something? I know it gets a little hot in this room."

149

"Water. Sure," he said.

Evan stepped out of the room.

"What the fuck was that?" I asked him when he closed the door behind him.

"What?"

"You asked him whether he'd fuck the witness? I am thankful Dennis didn't hear that, I'd be genuinely shocked if he didn't lay an egg if he heard."

"Where is Dennis?" Evan asked, looking around.

"Went to make some calls," I explained. "He wants that security footage."

"Oh good, I hoped one of you would get on that," Evan said. "Thankfully he didn't ask for his phone call. Or his lawyer."

"They never ask for lawyers," I said. "Neither of them. The most we get is him complaining 'my father.'"

"So what do you think?" Evan asked. "Kid's fucking guilty."

"Right now it's his word against Jane's," I said. "Nothing we can prove."

We stood quietly, staring through the window at Martin, who was back to tilting his chair.

"Okay, the reason I asked," Evan said, peering over his shoulder in case Dennis came back. "is why were they at the Hole? You said that was a place where kids went to like smoke and drink and fool around, well this dipshit looks like he peaked back in high school, maybe he took Vanessa out into the woods to have his way."

"It's possible," I said. "But that doesn't explain why Jane seems afraid of him. And it doesn't explain why he'd kill Vanessa."

The door opened and Dennis walked back into the room. He looked agitated.

"Everything okay?" I asked.

That's when I noticed he was wearing his coat.

"I'm heading over to Benjamin's house," he said.

"Why?" I asked.

"We need to see that footage, but he has no reason to let us see it. If he turns us away and then destroys it, we have nothing."

"You think you can convince him to show it?" I asked.

"I can," Dennis said. "This is already turning into a shitshow. If the boy is innocent Benjamin will want to prove it, that way he can let everyone know just how incompetent we are."

Dennis peered through the glass.

"Did you get anything else from him?" he asked.

"Nope. But he seems to barely know either of the girls," I said.

I looked back and could see that Martin was staring at his nails intently. He seemed bored. But he didn't seem worried.

"Alright," said Dennis. "I'm going."

He left the room and I turned to Evan.

"You should go get that coffee you told him about."

Once Evan left I went over to the window. I knew how this would all end. Martin would be arrested for the murder. There was something that could definitively connect him to everything. We just had to find what it was.

Eventually Evan returned with his coffee and the cup of water that Martin had asked for.

"So from what I understand, you and your father seem to have a bit of a reputation in this town," he said as he sat back down.

"What's that supposed to mean?" Martin asked.

"Well, I looked over your files, looks like you can't go more than a few months without getting arrested for something."

"Someone has to make it look like the cops are busy," Martin said with a smile. "Arrested, yes, but it's just small stuff."

"Small stuff?" Evan repeated. "I wouldn't call drug manufacturing 'small stuff.'"

Martin laughed.

"Oh, you read about that, did you? Tell me, did the file mention how that case was resolved?"

"No," Evan said. "Now that you mention it, no it didn't."

Martin took a sip of his water.

"Your friend Dennis 'knew'" Martin raised his fingers in quotation marks "that I was involved, but he couldn't prove that. So you know what he did? He told my father."

Martin laughed.

"See, my father is very strict about 'his town' not having a drug epidemic. That's what makes us different from big cities, we're supposed to be better than that. If people in the cities want to slowly deteriorate and die by the thousands, that's fine, but my father would not have it here. So he snapped his fingers and suddenly it all vanished. There was not a trace of it."

Evan gave a faint chuckle.

"Something funny?" Martin asked.

"No, it's just I had heard one of your father's many hobbies was moonshine production."

"Ah! I'm glad you're beginning to see the hypocrisy here," Martin said. "You may have seen it already as you've been driving around, and if not you will see it soon, but this town has no shortage of middle-aged men who have nothing to do other than drink their life savings away day in

153

and day out, without actually ever contributing anything to society. But it's allowed to happen, because my father allows it."

Martin leaned in across the table.

"Make no mistake, officer. My father is the one running the show in this town. When he offered his help the day you found that dead girl, he meant it. You will not find the person who did this without my father's help."

"You think he knows?" Evan asked.

"No. But he could easily find out, if he wanted to," said Martin.

Evan came out of the room shortly after.

"That was interesting," Evan said.

"I told you, he can't go a few seconds without mentioning his dad."

"Yeah, but did you get the feeling that they don't like each other?"

"Oh yes," I said. "Benjamin hates being used as a crutch. If your evidence is flimsy Benjamin will protect his son, but if you actually have proof of wrongdoing he'll toss the kid to the wolves without a second thought."

Evan was going to say something but then I heard my phone ring.

"Hoffman," I answered.

"Is Martin still there?" I heard Dennis' voice on the other end.

He sounded alarmed.

"Yeah, we still have him."

"Do not let him leave," said Dennis.

"What is it?" Evan asked.

"Did he leave the house that morning?" I asked.

"Oh, he left alright," said Dennis.

"What about the footage from later that night?" I asked.

There was silence but I could almost feel Dennis' anger coming through the phone.

"There was a power outage that night so the footage is missing," he said.

***

Dennis came back from the Nero house and immediately arrested Martin. So now he was still in the interrogation room, but he couldn't leave. He still hadn't asked for a lawyer, but had reminded us several times that his father would hear about this. The look on his face when Dennis said his father already knew was something I would cherish for a long time.

"Are you sure Benjamin's not going to be a problem?" Evan asked later in Dennis' office.

"No," said Dennis. "As soon as Benjamin saw the footage that directly contradicted what his son had said, he was willing to stand back and see what would happen."

"And are we sure the power was out?" Evan asked. "They didn't just delete the footage and blame it on the weather?"

"No," said Dennis. "If there was evidence that Martin hadn't gone that night, then Benjamin would show it."

"If it even was Martin himself," I said. "Would he have done that himself, or would he have gotten one of his lackeys to do it for him?"

"Not sure," said Dennis. "It's possible. In any case, we're going to leave him in that room until tomorrow morning, see if he's up to talking then. Right now he might still be deluding himself into thinking his father will come save him as he always does. I want to shatter that."

It was late in the afternoon and we were getting ready to leave. All I wanted to do was get a good night's sleep. Maybe tomorrow this would be over. If we could prove Martin's involvement and go public, I could finally rest easy. I knew that once this was done I would have to spend more time with the kids, maybe leave somewhere for New Year's so we weren't stuck at home again.

"One thing I can't figure out though," said Evan. "And something I don't think we've really paid much attention to. What's the motive? Like, why would Martin do this?"

Dennis shrugged.

"Why do people kill other people? I don't know, you tell me."

There was a knock on the door. We all turned and saw Ross standing on the other side of the glass.

"Let him in," Dennis sighed.

I opened the door. Ross' eye was twitching. It looked as though he had a little too much coffee.

"I'm going to blow my brains out," he said with a smile.

"What?" Dennis asked.

"Nothing. There's nothing going on. She just sits on the couch and watches TV. No one has come by the house, fuck, there hasn't been a single car driving down that street. Nothing! Either Martin hasn't figured out she talked, or he doesn't care!"

"Keep your voice down," said Dennis.

"Go home and get some sleep," I said to Ross. "You look like shit."

Ross turned to Dennis, as if he wanted to be sure that him resting would be okay.

"Fine. Whatever," said Dennis. "If they haven't gotten to the girl now, they probably aren't planning to."

Before leaving for the day I walked past the room where Martin was being held. He was busy trying to flip his empty water cup so that it landed on the table upside down. I wondered whether he was actually this calm on the inside, or if he was just putting on an act, knowing that we could see him from the other side. I decided not to worry about him for now. We would come back tomorrow and get to work on him. After he spent the night here he might be more willing to cooperate.

INTERLUDE

"With everything that was going on, maybe it was easy to miss, but did you get the feeling that Dennis was acting a bit strange during all of this?" Xander asked.

"I know," I said with a sigh. "It is fairly obvious now, and I know there are people who are listening to this who are very smugly saying that they could have cracked this case much faster than we did. But they don't know what they're talking about."

"Have you had people reach out to you about this?" Xander asked. "Do people think you weren't doing your job properly?"

"Oh, you know how the internet is," I told him. "Everyone's the smartest person in the room. I'm sure you've gotten it too, some fat fuck in a basement yelling about how much more successful they'd be in your position."

"Every day," Xander said, rolling his eyes.

"Yeah. In hindsight all of it seems simple. And who knows, maybe if I had taken a step back and looked at the big picture then it would have made more sense. You know, I used to laugh at Evan cause he would have one of those crime boards in his house, you know like they have in movies with all the pictures and the string connecting them together?"

"Yeah, yeah," Xander nodded.

"So he had one of those, like I said, the puzzle aspect of this job is something he seemed to actually view as fun. And maybe that would have been helpful, maybe if I had just set this all up, visualized it, seen what we know, what makes sense, what doesn't add up, this could have been solved faster."

NINE

The next morning I woke up feeling terrible. I looked over to see if Martha was next to me, but then I remembered I was on the couch. That's right, I had come home late, didn't want to wake her. I sat up and massaged my hand, which was sore from having been in an awkward position under my body for a few hours. I looked out the window and saw that it was still dark out. I heard a loud stomp and jerked my head in the opposite direction. The lights were on in the kitchen, I could hear Martha walking around. I slowly got up and walked into the kitchen.

"Morning," I said.

She didn't answer. I walked over to the counter and grabbed a mug. The coffee pot was still half-full from the day before.

"That's cold," she said as I poured it into the mug.

"It's fine," I mumbled.

She was waiting for me to mention why I had been out late. She didn't want to have to ask me, she wanted to me to say it of my own will. But I didn't. I didn't have to explain anything. Sometimes you just had to get away from everything. I realized that something felt off in the house, then I figured out that it was quieter than usual.

"Shouldn't the kids be getting ready for school?" I asked.

Martha turned to me and gave a strange look. She didn't seem disappointed, it was as though she expected something like this.

"The kids are asleep," she said. "It's Christmas break, they don't have school today."

Right. That's what it was.

"Sorry," I sighed. "It's been a rough week."

She didn't reply. I put down the empty coffee mug and went over to the front door. As I was putting my coat on she approached me.

"You're wearing the same clothes as yesterday," she said, folding her arms. "You look like shit, you shouldn't be going to work like this."

"It'll be fine," I said.

I might look terrible, but Martin likely looked much worse, given that he had been in that room all night. There was a strange part of me that was looking forward to this. Martin and his father had been nuisances for years, but one of them had finally crossed a line. And now we would throw everything we had at them. As I was walking down the stairs in front of our porch my phone rang. I saw it was Dennis.

"I'm just leaving the house, what is it?"

"We have a problem," he said.

His voice sounded strange, like he was doing everything he could not to appear angry.

"What happened?" I asked as I approached my car.

"Ross went by Jane's house this morning. She's dead."

"What?" I asked. "How, he was locked up, he couldn't-"

"Suicide," said Dennis.

I groaned.

"Jesus."

"You need to come by her house," said Dennis. "There's something here you're going to want to see."

INTERLUDE

"Alright," said Xander. "I know a lot of people listening to this were probably confused, cause we had said at the beginning that there were a lot of bodies in this story, but so far we had only seen one. Well now we get to the second one, and believe me, this story starts rolling down the hill really fast."

"Yeah," I said, trying not to think of what happened next.

Sometimes I would still see flashes of it in my mind. The looks on their faces when they realized what was happening. I thought of Evan and the last time I saw him. What would he think if he could see me sitting here, telling our story?

"Do you want to take a quick break?" Xander asked. "We haven't run an ad in a while. This looks like a good spot to pause."

"Sure," I said. "However you usually do it."

For a minute we'd be able to speak freely, without fear of being on the air. But I had to assume everything I said was still being recorded. I didn't trust either of them.

"You good?" Xander asked me, his eyebrows curving at an amusing angle. "You want a drink or something? Or a smoke, you can smoke in the studio, doesn't bother me."

I chuckled.

"Thanks, but no. I don't smoke much anymore. And I never drink when I'm working."

"Really? You should try it, it's fun, really brings out my creative side," he said.

"Yes, well I'm a cop, so me drinking while working would be heavily frowned upon."

Xander sighed and shook his head.

"Right, sorry. That was stupid, I was thinking of my job."

"No, it's fine," I said. "Whatever helps you be the best at what you can do. But even still I'd rather not get fucked up while telling stories like this, maybe if we were talking about something light, but this... no, I'd rather have a clear head. It would almost feel... disrespectful to do otherwise."

Xander nodded.

"Can I ask though... and you don't have to answer if this is too personal, but like, you've obviously seen some crazy shit in your job, did you ever get tempted to just get blackout drunk to forget about it?"

"A long time ago," I said. "When you first start that's what you think is the solution, just burn those memories away. But I think that's a dangerous precedent to set for yourself.

Eventually you're going to have to face the reality. World's a messed up place. You gotta find your own way of handling it. I found mine."

Before Xander could ask me to elaborate Julie walked back into the room holding three coke cans, passing one to each of us.

"We good to keep going?" Xander asked, giving me a thumbs up.

"Of course," I said.

"So you get the call from Dennis, Jane had apparently committed suicide. What was it at her house that he wanted you to see?" he asked.

"That would be the letter she had left for her parents."

TEN

It was strange seeing yellow tape in front of Jane's house. When I arrived, there were already two police cars outside, as well as a third, unmarked car, which I knew was the one Ross had spent so much time in the past few days. The front door was shut and the blinds covered the windows. I imagined that Dennis didn't want any of the neighbours peering through to see what had happened. When I walked in, the living room looked much the same as the last time I had been here. Dirty dishes and empty pizza boxes littered the coffee table. The TV was on, silently playing static, I guessed this was how it had been when they had found her. Jane was lying on the couch. She looked as though she could have been asleep. One arm was drooping off the couch, her fingers an inch away from the carpet. Just out of reach was an empty wine bottle. There were also several pill bottles on the table, which looked similar to the ones I had seen last time.

There were two forensic photographers taking pictures of various angles of the room. The only other person in the room was Dennis, who was standing behind the couch with his arms folded. He was fixated on the body, I didn't think he had even noticed me enter the house. His eyes were wide and he looked as though a vein in his forehead was about to pop.

"My condolences," I said as I approached him.

Dennis blinked and looked at me.

"What?" he asked.

"You had mentioned you were close with her parents," I said, remembering what Dennis had mentioned a few days earlier.

"Yeah," he said. "I was. Not as much anymore, but still... fuck, I need to call them and tell them."

"Do you want me to do it?" I asked.

"No," he said. "And no, I shouldn't call them, I should go see them in person. I'll go in a bit."

There was a flash across the room as one of the forensics took another photo. I looked back down at the body.

"How did Ross know she was dead?" I asked.

"What do you mean?"

"I mean, she looks like she's sleeping."

"He thought so too. He had shown up when it was still dark and he had noticed that the blinds had been left open, which he thought was odd, so he approached the window. He thought she was sleeping but when he saw all the booze and meds he decided to knock on the door. She didn't move."

I looked around the room.

"Where is he?" I asked.

"He was in the bathroom, curled up on the floor, last I saw him," said Dennis. "I guess some of us haven't gotten used to this kind of shit."

I peered down the hallway. The bathroom door was slightly ajar and light was pouring through the crack. I walked down the hallway and opened the door to find Ross sitting on the floor, his back against the bathtub. He didn't realize I was there.

"Are you alright?" I said quietly.

He didn't look up.

"All I did was complain about how boring it was here," he said. "If I had just stayed in the car that night, I might have seen... something..."

I sat down on the floor opposite him.

"This wasn't your fault," I said.

He finally looked up at me. Ross had always been the youngest person in our department, but right now he looked older than I did, and even thinner than he usually was. And pale. I almost wanted to say he looked like he had seen a ghost, but I figured this wasn't the time.

"I know," he said. "It's not any of our faults. But that doesn't mean we couldn't have done more."

I stood up and reached down with my hand towards him.

"Get up," I said.

Ross hesitated, but then he stood without my help.

"Go home, stay there for a day or so," I told him.

"You think the boss will be-"

"I'll handle it," I told him.

I led Ross back into the living room. Dennis was now standing by the front window, staring outside through the gap in the blinds. I could see his fingers twitching. He likely felt like going for a smoke, but he couldn't do that inside. I remembered that there was something he had wanted to show me. I looked around the room and that's when I noticed Evan standing in the backyard.

"Go," I said to Ross.

He nodded but still walked over to Dennis, I assumed to ask for permission. I went out to the back and found Evan pacing back and forth.

"Hey," I said.

If I had thought Ross looked like a mess, Evan was even worse. When he turned in my direction I could see anger. If Martin had been standing with us right now I had no doubt that Evan would have beaten him to death.

"Hi," he said.

"How are you feeling?" I asked, even though I could clearly see what the answer was.

"She told you this would happen," Evan said.

"What?"

"She was worried that Martin would come after her if she told us anything," he explained. "She asked you if we could protect her, and now she's dead."

"We couldn't protect her from herself," I said, wondering whether I was trying to convince myself or Evan.

"Herself," he repeated. "This is Martin's fault."

He spoke quietly, but there was no mistaking the anger in his voice. I looked around the backyard. I imagined the neighbours were already aware of the multiple police cars out front, so I had to be careful. They might be standing in their own yards, trying to hear what we were saying.

"Martin is locked up," I said. "He couldn't have done anything."

"Then his father did," said Evan. "Or someone who works for them. We thought just cause we had Martin in a room that we were in control. We let our guard down and let this happen."

Now I understood why he was acting this way. He was remembering his last case in the city, where his witness had been murdered. Evan had blamed himself for that, and now he was doing it again here.

"There is nothing you could have done to stop this," I said firmly. "And you need to stop blaming yourself for things that are out of your control."

Evan opened his mouth to argue but I didn't let him.

"No," I said, raising a hand. "Just take a moment, collect yourself, and come back inside."

I went back into the room. Dennis was still by the front window. I walked over to him, hoping that this wasn't yet another person I needed to convince not to feel guilty.

"You wanted to show me something?" I asked.

Dennis blinked, as if he had forgotten about it.

"Right," he said.

He turned to the forensics.

"Can you guys give us the room for a minute?" he asked.

They nodded and went out into the front yard. A moment later Evan came into the house.

"He's already seen it," Dennis said.

Dennis walked over to the fireplace. On the mantle there was a wide envelope which he grabbed and handed to me.

"Put gloves on first, this is evidence," he said.

Once I had gloves on I took the envelope. It read 'Mom and Dad.' I flipped it around and saw that it was open.

"Was it like this, or did you open it?" I asked.

"I opened it," he said. "It was on the floor next to her."

I frowned. That didn't feel right. What was in here wasn't for our eyes.

"You shouldn't have," I said.

But Dennis wasn't about to get emotional.

"Jane was a key witness in an unsolved murder. I was going to treat this as a crime scene until I knew otherwise, so this was evidence."

I didn't say anything.

"Read it," Dennis said.

I didn't know why my hands were shaking. It was just an envelope, there was nothing in here but words on a piece of paper. But I could hear my heart pounding, as if I were afraid of what was in here. I had to relax. I couldn't let them see how nervous I was. I took out the single piece of paper that had been folded into the envelope and gazed at it.

'Dear Mom and Dad,

By the time you read this I'll probably be dead. It is strange knowing that these are the last words I say to you. Maybe I should have gone to see you, say all of this in person, but I know then you would have tried to help me, despite me telling you that there is nothing you can do.

I do this not because it is easy, but because it is easier than what he will do to me.

When he first came to me he said that my job would be easy. All I had to do was get a hold of Insomniak. Then I would hand it off to Vanessa, who would take it from there. She knew people in the city, people who could help us make a fortune. Now Vanessa is dead. I heard what he did to her. I saw the pictures of her body. And at first I was confused as to why. Why did he do this to her? She was doing her job, I was the one who was beginning to have doubts. But now I understood he killed her to send a message to me.

I knew Insomniak was dangerous. I knew what it could do to people. What it could make them do. But I didn't let it bother me. This would be in a city somewhere far away. That's what I used to justify what I've done. I just pretended it wasn't happening. Like bombs being dropped on children in a country half a world away.

What he offered us was protection. If the police ever found out, he would have a way to get us out. He had connections. That's what he called them, but I knew what he really meant. The amount of times I have had to hear the phrase 'My Father.' So it seemed easy. After all, I'd be using a fake name, and he assured me that he had the right people in place so that none of this ever came back to me.

You might be wondering why? And I don't have a good excuse. Money. That's the reason, nothing else. I won't try to defend myself or justify what happened. But then he had the idea of expanding. He wanted to sell Insomniak here. He thought we could make more, just the two of us, cut out Vanessa and whoever she had on her end. But I said no. It would draw too much attention. That's the reason I gave him, but in truth I was scared of seeing the effects of it here, with people I knew. And yet somehow it did. Despite my efforts, I've seen people using Insomniak here in our town. I could hear them when I was trying to sleep.

I invited Vanessa to come visit me before Christmas. That's when I was going to tell her everything. Tell her I no longer wanted to do this. Tell her that I felt terrible, knowing the lives we had destroyed. Tell her that he was planning to cut her out. She wasn't happy. She didn't believe he would betray her, and she was angry at me for backing out. We met up with him at Hellhole that night and he told us to come out to the Hole in the morning. But I didn't. I went to mass, where I knew I would be safe. I didn't know for sure, but I think if I had gone to the Hole he would have killed me. And a day later Vanessa was dead. I don't know why he killed her, what might have happened at the Hole to convince him to do this. But now I was trapped, without a friend in the world.

I don't know if this letter can be used as evidence. I've already told the police I was scared for my life. But they didn't seem to listen. I told them if they arrested Martin Nero he would know that I talked, but they did it anyway. I think about Vanessa nailed to that sign, slowly freezing to death in the winter night. I could not allow him to do that to me.

I'm sorry for the pain I have caused you. Know that there is nothing you could have done to save me.

Jane'

I reached the end of the letter and stared at that last word for another minute.
"What the fuck," I finally said.

"Yeah," Dennis sighed.

"What do we do with this?" I asked. "Are you giving this to her parents, or are we holding onto it until we know more?"

Dennis frowned, as if he hadn't even considered that.

"You can't be serious," said Evan. "You're going to hide this from them?"

"Let me see it," Dennis said, sticking his hand out.

I gave the letter back to him. He spent the next minute reading it over again silently. Evan had an incredulous look on his face.

"We go back to the station and we break Martin," Dennis said. "This," he waved the letter. "This is evidence."

"Is it?" I asked. "Isn't this just 'he said,' 'she said?'"

Dennis seemed puzzled.

"You're saying this girl lied in her suicide note?"

"No," I said. "But all it takes is for Martin to say she's lying, we can't ask her any follow up questions."

"What was the name of that thing they were selling?" Evan asked. "Insomniac?"

"There," I said, pointing to the bottles on the floor. "She had those the last time I was here too."

Evan walked over and picked one up, turning it so he could read the label.

"Insomniak," he read. "With a 'K.' I feel like I've heard of this before."

He kept reading and then sighed.

"Jesus. Look at who this is prescribed to," he said as he tossed the bottle to me.

I turned it and saw the name read 'Jane Doe.'

"So this is fake," I said.

Evan was already picking up the other bottles.

"Yep, they're all the same," he said. "All a fake name."

I turned to Dennis. His eyes looked like they were going to shoot out of his skull in anger.

"Okay," he said quietly. "We're going back to the station, and I want to break Martin. We're going to get to the bottom of this today."

Dennis let the forensics back in and we left the house. As we walked across the front yard I could see Jane's neighbour standing in her driveway. She looked familiar.

"Did something happen?" she asked.

That's when I recognized her. I had forgotten they lived here.

"Sorry Mrs. McKinnley," I said. "Can't talk about it."

I strained my eyes. I didn't want to get too close, cause then I would have to admit what I was looking for, but I thought the skin near her eye looked a bit darker. Once we had dealt with Martin, I would have to look into McKinnley further. I knew if anything happened to the wife, Bertrand would be furious that I hadn't done anything in time.

ELEVEN

I had woken up that morning feeling like absolute shit, and I had then seen both Ross and Evan look much worse than me. But they still didn't compare to Martin. Spending the whole night locked in an interrogation room seemed to have finally convinced him how serious we were.

"And he's still not asking for a lawyer?" I asked as we approached the room.

"Who needs a lawyer when you have 'my father?'" Dennis asked.

Evan was already inside. Dennis had decided to let him continue instead of switching it up, and I was curious to see him go from bad cop to even worse cop.

"I hope you're comfortable," Evan said.

Martin didn't answer. He was no longer arrogantly tilting his chair backwards, instead he was leaning over on the table, barely able to hold his eyes open.

"I was wondering if you could tell me about this?" Evan said, pulling the bottle of Insomniak out of his pocket.

He placed it on the table and slid it across.

"Have you told the parents yet?" I asked Dennis.

"No," he said. "I will though. I'll do it myself."

"What am I looking at?" Martin asked, picking up the bottle.

"We found this in Jane's living room. Quite a few of them."

Martin put the bottle down and shrugged.

"I don't know. I mean, it's not surprising that she was kind of fucked up, but I don't know what this has to do with me."

"So you don't know what this is?" Evan asked.

"Well, I'm assuming there were some kind of pills in here, but I have no idea what they're for," he said.

"See, the thing is..." Evan leaned in. "Jane said that you've been selling these."

"Selling them?" he repeated.

"Yeah. See, when I first looked at this, I thought the name sounded familiar. And that's because I've seen this before. Rather, I've seen the effects of it. This... this shit can kill you if taken wrong, especially if you've mixed it with alcohol, which by the state of Jane's house, she had been doing a lot."

Martin blinked. The implications of that sentence seemed to have hit him.

"What do you mean, the state of Jane's house?" he asked.

"Oh, didn't I mention?" Evan asked. "Jane's dead."

Given that the previous day Martin had said that he knew Jane but that the two of them weren't particularly close, he seemed very upset to learn that she was dead.

"What are you talking about?" he said.

Confusion? Worry? His face was a mixture of emotions. But they all led to one thing.

"He's lost control of this," I said.

Oddly, it seemed satisfying, watching Martin be afraid and powerless for the first time.

"Do you want to hear her suicide note?" Evan asked cheerfully.

He reached into his pocket and pulled out the letter.

"No, no, no," Martin said as he began to push his chair back. "This is bullshit, you're making this up. Dennis!" he yelled as he looked out the window.

"Oh he's there," Evan said as he unfolded the letter. "He's not going to stop me reading this. So, how about you listen to what's on this page, and you tell me whether you still think I'm making this up, or if there are details here that I couldn't possibly know?"

Evan began to read.

"Dear Mom and Dad," he said in a dry tone.

The way Evan read the letter it was almost as though he found it amusing. Or maybe it was Martin's reactions that were amusing. I didn't think Martin breathed a single time during the whole letter. By the end his face was almost turning purple.

"Jesus," said Dennis. "He's a sick fuck. Look how much he's enjoying this."

"Anything you want to contribute?" Evan asked.

Martin finally exhaled and straightened up in his seat.

"That doesn't prove anything," he said.

He tried to sound confident, but he didn't.

"Sorry?" Evan asked.

"That's all made up," he said.

He was starting to shiver.

"You can't prove any of that."

"Told you," I said to Dennis.

"You're right," Evan said. "I can't. This is just her word. The one thing we do know for a fact is that she killed herself, because that seemed preferable to getting crucified, something she was convinced you did to her friend and were going to do to her too."

Evan got up and left the room.

"Let him sit there for a while and think about this," he said to us once he closed the door behind him.

As we were leaving I took one last look through the glass at Martin. The expression on his face was one that I had seen many times. It was the look of someone who was realizing that they were out of options.

***

"Insomniak! Very interesting stuff."

We were in the morgue for the second time this month. Jane looked even more peacefully asleep than Vanessa had. This time there were no physical wounds. I felt as though there should be something though. Something that indicated the damage that had been done. Maybe she should have looked scared.

"It does have a long sciencey name that I won't bore you with."

Creepy Joel was delighted when we had brought him another body that he could examine and talk about. Dennis was standing beside me with his arms folded, clearly wanting to get out of this cold room as quickly as possible.

"See, the 'proper'" he waved his fingers to show quotation marks, "use of this is for insomnia, hence the name. You pop a few before bed and you're fast asleep. However," he said and he gave a strange smile. "if you mix it with alcohol then you won't sleep. You'll be wide awake and you'll be hallucinating the whole time."

His enthusiasm was strange. I wanted him to get to the point.

"So she was taking this to go on a trip?" I asked.

"No, no. See, you have no idea how powerful this is," said Joel. "One pill, crushed up, mixed with the right amount of scotch, that could send all four of us to the moon and back for a whole day. Just one pill. So if this girl was smuggling out entire bottles-"

"Then you could make a fortune off it," Evan finished.

"Exactly!" said Joel, waving his finger in the air. "But there is a catch, as there often is. See, you mix a little and you get really fucked up, you mix too much and you die. Case in point, here. If she had been drinking as much as you said then it's amazing her heart didn't explode."

We thanked Joel for his valuable contributions and left the room.

"So what's our next move?" I asked Dennis.

Dennis was about to share what he was thinking but Evan immediately walked away from us.

"Where are you going?" I asked.

"I'll get this resolved in two minutes," he said without stopping.

I was confused for a second and then I realized what he was about to do. He was heading back to the interrogation room. I turned to Dennis, whose horrified expression mirrored my own. We began to run after him. As Evan heard our footsteps he began to move faster. When we arrived at the interrogation room the door was already wide open. The chair Martin had been sitting in for the better part of two days was on the floor. Martin himself was pinned against the wall. For the first time he looked like a kid. He was at the complete mercy of Evan, who was standing an inch away from his face, yelling incoherently. I had no idea what he was thinking, all I knew was that if Evan killed him then there would never be an end to this. I sprinted into the room and grabbed Evan by the arms, pulling him away. Martin collapsed to the floor, breathing heavily.

"Get the fuck off of me!" Evan yelled as I dragged him away, his feet kicking the floor repeatedly.

Finally I managed to get him out of the room and Dennis slammed the door behind us. I let go of him.

"What the fuck is wrong with you?" Dennis said, his face purple with rage.

"Why are we going so easy on him?" Evan asked. "This piece of shit is guilty. You know it, I know it, but we're dancing around this because you're scared of his dad."

This was the wrong thing to say. I was worried that now Evan was the one who was a few seconds away from being murdered.

"Get the fuck out of my building," Dennis said quietly, pointing his finger to the exit. "I don't want to see you for the rest of the day. Or tomorrow. In fact, don't come back until you've done some reflecting, and if you ever speak to me like that again, I will fuck you up, do you understand?"

Evan didn't say anything. I stood between them, waiting, expecting anything. Then we all jumped as we heard a loud slam behind us. We turned to see Martin pounding on the window of the room. He couldn't see us through the glass, but he knew we were there.

"Keep him on a shorter leash Dennis! You know what he's like! You want me to end up like the last one did? You know what my father would do to you?!"

"Go," said Dennis again. "Fuck off, now."

Evan didn't argue. He left the room and then Dennis finally addressed me once Evan was far away.

"Come on," he said. "I can't listen to this asshole either."

Martin was still standing by the glass. I didn't like the way he was looking at us.

"Dennis!" he yelled. "Come in here, I want to talk."

Dennis sighed. He didn't want to, but he knew we were in the wrong here, and the last thing he wanted was to escalate this even further. He opened the door.

"I have to apologize for that," he began, but Martin cut him off.

"I think it's time I get a lawyer," Martin said.

INTERLUDE

"So Benjamin did have a lawyer?" Xander confirmed.

I shrugged.

"It's possible they always had one on retainer and never bothered to use him. Or maybe Martin panicked and Benjamin had to go looking for one. Either case, Evan's behaviour had put us in a difficult spot."

"Why do you think he lashed out like that?" Xander asked.

I knew the answer. It had been obvious, even back then when I hadn't know everything about Evan's past yet.

"I think it reminded him of that last case back in his hometown. See, Jane wasn't a witness we were protecting-"

"Even though she had asked for protection," Xander cut in.

I frowned.

"Yes, she had. But it was more complicated than Evan's last case. Jane had been a suspect, however briefly. And she was complicit in this. She might not have killed Vanessa, but she was a part of this little operation they were running. And yet Evan still felt guilty. He thought maybe if we had done things differently she wouldn't have killed herself. I mean, there was nothing we could have done. The signs were all pointing to Martin being our guy, we had to act on this."

TWELVE

There was nothing we could do while we waited for Martin's lawyer to arrive. He sat in the room, smugly staring out the glass. He thought he had beaten us, and it was possible that he had. I worried that he would walk out of here free the moment he told his lawyer that one of us had laid a hand on him. Meanwhile, Dennis had the unfortunate task of having to tell Jane's parents that their daughter was dead.

"What do you want me to do?" I said.

I didn't feel like waiting around for Martin's lawyer to show up.

"Follow up on those pills. See if the doctor knew they were prescribed under a fake name," Dennis said as we both left the building.

I got into my car alone and went on my way. While the name on the bottles wasn't real, the place Jane had gotten them definitely was. There were a handful of drug marts in Appleton, but the one I was headed to was one I had never visited, owing to it being on the complete other end of town.

***

Dr. Rah's Variety was located in a part of town where half the buildings had boarded up windows. The building had an odd shape, with a curved dome and arches over the front door. That and the enormous pillar in the parking lot indicated that this building was once a fast food place, and sure enough the wall above the entrance still had that restaurant's logo imprinted on it, as the paint colour behind where the old sign had been was much less faded. The parking lot itself was a mess, with weeds growing through the cracks every few feet. A sign on the front door showed that they were open, with each letter of the word 'OPEN' lighting up one at a time, followed by all of them flashing rapidly enough to give someone a seizure. As I pulled into the parking lot I saw something large lying in the handicapped spot. My eyes widened as I realized it was a person. I parked a few spots away and got out, cautiously approaching the body. Then it stirred. The man was wearing a grey tracksuit and his face was completely red. He squinted as he looked up at me.

"Jesus, McKinnley, what are you doing here?" I asked as I relaxed and moved my hand away from my holster.

"Just resting for a moment," he mumbled, turning his head while talking and not even looking in my direction.

"Do you need me to drive you home?" I asked.

He shook his head violently.

"Be fine," he said.

I frowned. I'd be back for him later, might even give me a chance to settle this thing with his wife. I had enough going on with the Martin case now without adding McKinnley on top of that. I could almost hear Father Bertrand's condescending voice in my head.

'You wanted me to share information with you,' he would say 'now you have it. So do something about it.'

I walked into the store and heard an annoying bell ring the moment the door opened. There were a handful of aisles before me, and I saw a counter on the other end of the building. There was another counter over to the left, but there was no one standing behind it. I heard a shuffle at the back so I approached it.

"Hello!"

At the back of the counter, behind a layer of thick glass, was a small bald man with round glasses and a benign smile.

"Hi," I said.

As I smiled back at him I got a strange feeling, I was almost excited to see his expression change when he found out why I was here.

"I'm looking for Dr. Rah," I said.

"That would be me," he said and he tilted his body slightly so that the tiny nametag on his shirt would stick out more.

"Fantastic," I said as I reached into my pocket to take out the empty bottle. "I was hoping to refill this."

His eyes narrowed suddenly as he realized that something was off. This man had never met me before, so if I was refilling something I would have already been here at least once. And I would have known him by sight without having to ask for his name. He probably should have listened to his instincts and ran.

"There," I said as I placed it on the table.

He picked it up and lifted it to see what was written on the label. I watched a part of him die inside as he read the name 'Jane Doe.'

"Umm..." he said a split second later when he composed himself. "This doesn't appear to be yours," he said.

"Right," I said. "See, the problem is that the person who this belonged to is dead."

Dr. Rah did his best to look confused but I could see the sweat begin to trickle down his head.

"I'm sorry?" he asked.

"Yes. Dead. Of course, when I say it belonged to her, that's not entirely true, because this wasn't her real name."

"I..." he stammered. "I don't understand-"

"The name isn't hers," I repeated calmly. "And there were several of these in her house, all with this name, and all from here. Now, either you weren't doing your job properly, and you actually thought that 'Jane Doe' was a real name, or you knew that something was wrong but you decided to go along with it anyway."

I had to start speaking louder because his hand had started shaking, causing the bottle to repeatedly tap against the counter.

"Sir, I..." he said, his eyes darting around the store to see if there was anyone else here. "I'm going to have to ask you to-"

"Leave?" I finished.

That's when I took my badge out, and any remaining calm evaporated from Dr. Rah as he let out a low moan.

"Now as I continue trying to figure out whether you're incompetent or guilty, I would like to mention that our Jane Doe, the dead one, was very afraid of a particular person harming her. And if that same person drove by here and saw my car parked out front, they might have some unpleasant plans for you. So it is in your best interest to tell me what I would like to know as quickly as possible. The sooner you tell me, the sooner I leave, and no one will find out I was here."

By now his eyes had widened to the point they were larger than his glasses.

"So, this woman comes in and... what? You don't see any problems with this name, you don't verify it in any way?"

"I... I can't recall..." he said.

Now he was staring down, as if afraid I could see the truth in his eyes.

"No, I think you're too smart to not see a problem. So you just gave her Insomniak, no questions asked. Do you know what Insomniak does to a person when misused?" I asked. "Of course you do, you're a doctor. So knowing that large quantities of this are being misused must have weighed heavy on your conscience, no?"

He didn't reply. He was still staring at the counter, and he was muttering something rapidly. I slammed my fist down and he jumped.

"Look at me when I'm talking to you," I said angrily.

"I'm sorry," he whispered as he nodded quickly to show he understood.

"It must have weighed on your conscience... unless you were given something to soothe that."

"No.. no, no, no, nothing like that," he said, shaking his head so fast that I thought it would fly off his neck.

"No? They didn't give you any money to turn the other way?" I asked.

"Didn't take money. 'Money leaves trail,' he told me. This way no one would find out."

"He?" I repeated.

Dr. Rah shuddered.

"He," I said. "I have a feeling I know who this 'he' is. Problem is the last person who was afraid of this 'he' ended up dead, and I'd rather not go through that again."

That's when I spotted something on the wall behind the counter.

"Can I come around back?" I asked. "Don't worry, I'm not going to hurt you. Unless you run, of course."

"I... yes, of course," Dr. Rah said.

I walked over to the opening at the side of the counter. Dr. Rah backed into the wall as far away from me as possible and slid down.

"Relax," I said. "You don't have to say anything. A simple nod will do."

On the wall was an eye test chart, with letters starting off large at the top and getting smaller towards the bottom. I scanned it until I found an 'N.'

"Hey!"

I snapped my fingers at Dr. Rah, whose eyes were fixated on the floor. His attention shot in my direction.

"I need you to focus," I said.

I pointed at the 'N' and kept my finger there long enough to be sure that he registered what I was doing. Then I slid my finger to an 'E' near the top, slowly so that I could watch his eyes track my movement. I lingered over the 'E' for a moment, then went down to an 'R,' and finally an 'O.' Then I lowered my finger. I stared at Dr. Rah, who had tears forming in his eyes. He closed them, causing the tears to trickle down his face. And then he nodded.

"Excellent," I said. "That's all I needed to know. Now, if he or anyone else should ask if I was here, what are we going to say?"

"No," said Dr. Rah quietly.

"Good," I walked around to the front of the counter. "One more thing."

I turned towards him. He was still sitting on the ground.

"I'm willing to believe that you were a less than willing accomplice in this mess. I'm giving you the benefit of the doubt. But if you run, if you skip town, if you try to start a new life somewhere, I will fucking find you, you understand?"

I didn't wait to see him nod, I turned around and left the building. When I got outside I noticed that McKinnley had managed to sit up straight and was now lazily tossing pieces of gravel across the parking lot.

"Get up," I said.

He didn't acknowledge me.

"I said get up, McKinnley. That's not a request."

He finally looked up. His dried up, cracked lips were arched into an exaggerated frown. Finally he decided to plant his feet on the ground and then slowly straightened up, his arms waving madly as he did so, as if he were afraid he would topple back over. I put him in the back of the car and began driving towards his house.

"You don't look so good, McKinnley," I said. "You been drinking again?"

"Not your concern," he said, raising his chin up proudly. "I ain't done nothing wrong."

That was a lie.

"How's your wife been?" I asked.

"What do you care?" he asked suspiciously. "She been saying something?"

No, but the priest has. I wondered if I just dumped McKinnley on the side of the road and let him freeze to death, would anyone even suspect there was foul play?

"Just making sure everyone's okay," I said.

"Everything's fine," McKinnley slurred his words. "Mind your own business."

I didn't press the issue. Neither of us spoke for the rest of the trip. When we finally arrived, I parked on the side of the road between the McKinnley house and the now abandoned house of Jane, which still had scraps of yellow police tape flapping in the wind. McKinnley got out of the car and began to stumble towards his house, which was impressive, as the driveway had a steep incline. The whole time he was muttering to himself incoherently and it seemed that his wife heard him because she opened the front door before he even got to it. She didn't say a word as he pushed past her into the house, but before she closed the door she looked out and made eye contact with me. Neither of us said anything but I could see in her eyes that she was afraid.

INTERLUDE

"By the time I had come back to the station, Martin was already gone. Whatever lawyer they found had done quick work. Just as I had worried, the written confession and accusation of someone who was now dead wasn't enough to put Martin away," I told Xander.

The can of coke they had brought me was now empty, and I was in the middle of crunching it up to the point where one edge of the can snapped open and I began to carefully rip the can apart.

"Are you alright?" Xander asked, noticing what I was doing.

"Sorry?" I asked, blinking.

"You just seem a little aggravated," he said, looking down at the now destroyed can.

A single drop of leftover coke had spilled out on to the table.

"Sorry about that," I said, hastily trying to wipe it up.

"Don't worry," he said.

Nevertheless I licked my finger and tried to wipe up the drop.

"I guess I just felt bad for the girl," I said. "As she wrote that note she probably thought we'd at least be able to get Martin. But it turned out to not be enough."

Xander nodded.

"And were you worried about the doctor at all?" he asked. "Did you think he would talk?"

"I didn't know what he would be like until I talked to him. Once I did, I got the impression that he could be scared into silence. And of course, I didn't realize that the lawyer would be as quick as he was."

"Right," said Xander. "Now from what I've gathered you didn't see Evan for the next day or two?"

"The next day," I said, closing my eyes as I tried to remember the details correctly. "He had that outburst where he almost killed Martin, he was gone that entire day, and the day after that. I did call him to let him know about the doctor, but other than that I didn't see him at all. And then the day after was Jane's funeral, and that's where I saw him. I had gone to pick him up that morning, and that's when I saw his crime board for the first time."

Xander smiled, he seemed to be excited for this part of the story.

"I can draw it for you, if you want," I said. "I still have it memorized."

"That would actually be great," Xander said. "I mean the listeners can't really see it, but it'll be cool to have."

I heard Julie shuffling behind me, likely looking to see if they had a pen and paper in any of their drawers.

"Now while this had all been happening, that's when Dennis went to visit the parents?" Xander confirmed.

"Yeah, he had gone to see them the day we found the body. They lived out of town, but they came back for the funeral."

"And had Dennis mentioned anything about his visit to them?" Xander asked.

He wasn't going to ask me about the suicide note. Not yet.

"I know what you're referring to," I said grimly. "And no. Now that I think back he did look a bit preoccupied during the funeral, but I figured he was just overwhelmed with the case. We all were at that time."

THIRTEEN

The morning of Jane's funeral Evan didn't show up for work.

"He probably thinks I'm still angry at him," Dennis said. "I am, but I need him back. I tried calling his house and nothing. Mind swinging by and seeing if he's okay?"

I had never visited Evan's home before but Dennis gave me the address so I drove across town. Evan's house was small, a plain, one storey building made of brown bricks, with two identical bushes in front of the living room window. I walked up to the front door and knocked. I thought back to when we had visited Jane's house for the first time and the slight movement of the living room blinds had given her away. I had no such luck here.

"Evan!" I yelled. "I know you're home, your car's parked outside."

Silence.

"Don't make me kick the-"

And the door opened, as if on queue. Evan looked absolutely terrible. He was leaning against the door as if that were the only thing holding him up. His eyes were red and his hair was sticking out in a thousand directions. He was wearing a buttoned up shirt and black pants, an outfit identical to what he had been wearing at work when I last saw him, and I seriously doubted that he had just changed into that this morning for fun. He had clearly not been getting ready for work and had been planning on staying home again.

"Morning," he mumbled.

The air inside the house was hot, a shocking contrast to outside.

"I guess you should come on in," he said, turning around and stumbling into his living room.

I walked in and closed the door behind me.

If I hadn't been told that this was Evan's address I would have assumed that nobody lived here. The living room was completely empty. No couch, no chair, no table, no carpet. Just a hardwood floor and bare white walls. There was a fireplace, but the mantle was completely empty. He didn't even have a TV. The only actual thing that Evan had seemingly purchased with money were the blinds that blocked out any sunlight.

"You want food or something?" he muttered from the kitchen.

I was shocked that he even asked this question, as it implied that not only did he have a fridge, but it wasn't empty.

"No," I said. "Thanks. We really need to get going."

"Right, just a moment," he said. "Hey, come here, I want to show you something."

I followed the sound of his voice. As I looked around the house it appeared that there were only four rooms. Evan had found a house with as little space as possible, which it seemed was all he needed. Aside from the barebones living room and kitchen there were two doors in the hallway. I assumed one of them led to a bathroom. The other door was slightly ajar and there was light coming from it. I entered and found myself in what was apparently Evan's bedroom. The room was small, and just like the rest of the house the windows were covered to block out the sun. There was a small bed in the corner that looked like a bed from a military camp. It was so thin that I was amazed Evan didn't fall off it every night. I was sure there were prisons that had better sleeping conditions. To my right was a desk about the same size as the bed with dozens of pages scattered on top. Some of them looked like handwritten notes, while others were printed out documents.

"What do you think?" Evan asked.

Finally I noticed what he had wanted me to see. On the floor were two large lamps pointing towards the far wall, illuminating a giant board.

Evan had been hard at work. In the middle of the board was a piece of paper that read 'MARTIN NERO.' There were other notes similar to this one. 'JANE BROWN/DOE,' 'VANESSA MILES,' all attached together with string. A note that read 'FRIENDS?' was positioned between Jane and Vanessa. Each of the three main names also had one string leading away from them. Jane lead to 'DR. RAH,' Martin to 'BENJAMIN,' and Vanessa to 'UNKNOWN ABQ CONTACT.'

At the bottom of the board there were even more notes, arranged in a long line from left to right, which I saw was a timeline.

'Jane tries to quit' -> 'Martin and Vanessa meet at the Hole' -> 'Martin kills Vanessa?' -> 'Martin Arrested' -> 'Jane kills self?' -> 'Martin released.'

"Impressive," I said.

Then I noticed something.

"Why does 'Jane kills self' have a question mark at the end?" I asked.

"Because we don't know for sure," he answered.

I was confused.

"We're unsure about whether she's dead? Cause she looked pretty dead to me."

"No," he said, shaking his head. "I don't know if it was suicide."

"Why?"

"That note," said Evan. "It's a little too perfect."

"Too perfect? What does a perfect suicide note look like?" I asked.

"One that gives us all of the information we need," said Evan. "The note was what pushed us towards Martin. Now he wasn't just someone who met with the victims before they died. Now they were actually involved in criminal activities with him, AND they were scared of him."

I didn't know what to say to that.

"Have you shared this theory with anyone else?" I asked.

Evan shook his head.

"Well do me a favour and don't bring this up at the funeral. I'm sure Jane's parents are upset enough without the thought that someone else might have done this to her," I said.

"Of course, Jesus, what kind of person do you think I am?"

I didn't answer that.

***

After pumping Evan full of coffee and convincing him to change outfits we headed to the church for Jane's funeral. By the time we got there

the service had already started. We walked into
the chapel and stood near the back. I was worried
that Evan would fall over or start throwing up and
I didn't want to bring any attention to us. Besides,
we hadn't actually known Jane, aside from when
we had questioned her, so I wanted to have the
people who were close to her stand near the front.
When we entered Father Bertrand was in the
middle of his eulogy. His eyes briefly flickered in
my direction but his expression didn't change and
he didn't stop speaking for even a second. The
pews were about half full, a surprising amount of
people had shown up. About half of them were
older, which I assumed meant they knew Jane's
parents. I didn't remember what they looked like,
but there was an older couple in the front row
which I guessed was them. I glanced around to see
who else I could recognize from the back of their
heads. I spotted Dennis about halfway down the
aisle, his grey hair glistening from all the gel in it.
Off to the side I also saw McKinnley, who looked
strange in a tuxedo. At least he was able to stand
up straight. I imagined that his wife had forbade
him from drinking that morning. But I noticed his
wife wasn't there. That was strange. McKinnley
likely wasn't here from the goodness of his heart.
His wife probably forced him to go since Jane had

been their neighbour, but then why wouldn't she be there as well?

"Quite the turnout, huh?" said a voice beside me suddenly.

I turned and saw Benjamin Nero standing next to me. His expression was neutral, he didn't seem particularly upset that Jane was dead, but if he was just here to taunt us he didn't want it to look too obvious.

"What are you doing here?" I asked.

I slowly moved my left hand out a little. I realized I was standing directly between Evan and Benjamin and I needed to be ready for anything. If Evan was going to take a swing at him, I had to stop him.

"I'm here to pay my respects," Benjamin said, raising his eyebrows as if this were the obvious answer.

"Right," I said, nodding. "I forgot, your son was close to her, yes? Speaking of which, I don't see your son anywhere," I added, glancing around the room.

"My son is very upset. It's always horrifying to lose a friend, especially one so young. I'm afraid he wasn't feeling strong enough to attend."

"Oh, fuck you," Evan whispered behind me.

Benjamin tilted his head to the side to look around me.

"Sorry?" he asked, his mouth forming into a faint smile.

"Your son's not here because he has a guilty conscience," Evan said.

"Evan, stop," I said, but Benjamin's smile was only getting wider.

"Is that so? You think guilt stops people from attending funerals? That never stopped you," he said.

I immediately spun around just as Evan took a step forward. I lifted my hands to block him.

"Stop," I hissed angrily. "Not here."

"Go ahead, kid," I heard Benjamin behind me. "Why don't you take a swing at me, like you did at my son. You really are living up to your reputation."

The look in Evan's eyes was starting to become dangerous. I reached for his hand, which was clenched into a fist so tightly I knew his nails were probably digging into his palm.

"Relax," I said. "There will be a time for this."

That seemed to relax him a little. I turned back to Benjamin.

"I'm sorry for your son's loss," I said through gritted teeth.

Benjamin clapped me on the arm.

"Thank you, officer," he said condescendingly. "I only hope that you find the person who did this."

"What do you mean?" I asked.

"Oh, come on," he said. "You don't really believe this was a suicide, do you?"

I didn't even want to imagine the look on Evan's face behind me. Benjamin laughed quietly.

"George... I thought you were smarter than this. Anyways, I won't take up more of your time. Best of luck to you both. You now have two murders and nothing to show for it."

And he left the chapel.

FOURTEEN

"One day someone is going to blow that man's brains out," Evan said a while later as we descended the steps outside the chapel. "Him and his son. Fuck them."

"Easy," I said.

When the service had ended we had joined the line of people waiting to pay their respects to Jane's family. We had shaken the hands of both parents and said how sorry we were for their loss. Jane's mother had been sobbing the whole time, but her father didn't shed a single tear. It's not that he wasn't upset, but he seemed mainly angry. As he shook my hand, he squeezed it, as if to indicate he blamed me for not stopping this in time. Thankfully, Evan didn't say anything he wasn't supposed to, and we left the church without incident. When we were outside we bumped into Dennis. I stood awkwardly, hoping the first conversation between him and Evan since Evan's temporary dismissal wouldn't turn into a fight.

"You look like shit," said Dennis.

Off to a great start.

"Thank you, sir," Evan said.

"He looked worse when I found him," I told Dennis.

"Alright, come back to the station, we have lots to talk about."

He walked over to his car, leaving us alone. I turned to Evan.

"Listen," I said. "We're going to have to tell him about our conversation with Benjamin in the church. When we tell him that Benjamin said Jane was murdered, do not say that you had the same idea this morning."

Evan was confused.

"But why? It makes sense that-"

"I don't want it to look like we're connecting dots where there aren't any. We have no idea if Benjamin really believed what he said, for all we know he just said this to rile us up. We tell Dennis what happened in the church, and we see what he thinks of this first."

***

When we were back in the office I told Dennis what had happened.

"Jesus," he said, burying his head in one hand while the other held a cigarette up high.

"But why would he say that?" Evan asked. "If she was killed, it's probably the same person who killed Vanessa."

"Probably," Dennis repeated. "But probably isn't good enough."

"Why would it be someone different?" Evan asked. "This is obviously Martin cleaning out the house."

"Martin was in a cell when Jane died, so there's no way he could have done anything," Dennis pointed out.

"So it's his father cleaning up his mistakes," Evan said, getting louder.

"No," said Dennis. "If Martin fucked up then Benjamin would make him fix it himself."

"Do we actually know that, or is this just what Benjamin has said?" Evan asked.

"Stop," I said.

They both turned to me as I spoke for the first time.

"If Jane was killed, and if Benjamin was behind it, why would he bring attention to it?" I asked. "If they killed her and staged it as a suicide, why would they reveal it was staged after we had already bought it?" I asked. "And let's not forget the note."

"That note is bullshit," said Evan. "That note gave us everything we needed on a silver platter."

"And you think Benjamin did that? Not only does he frame this as a suicide, but he forges a note that implicates his son in Vanessa's murder?

Now we're going from Benjamin not helping his son out, to actively trying to get him arrested."

Evan didn't say anything. He didn't have a good answer for it.

"Until we have more evidence, we can't do anything," said Dennis.

"What about the doctor?" Evan asked me. "We could bring him in."

Dennis was about to answer when there was commotion outside.

"What is that?" Dennis asked, standing up from his chair.

I opened the office door just as Ross was sprinting past.

"What is it?" I asked him.

"McKinnley called," said Ross.

"Oh Christ, what does he want?" Dennis sighed.

Ross was pale.

"His wife is dead. Fell down a flight of stairs and smashed her head into the corner of a wall."

***

All I could think about was the look of fear I had seen on Mrs. McKinnley's face just days ago. Now her face was unrecognizable. At the bottom of the stairs in their house there was a doorway just off to the left that led to their dining room. The corner of this door was where she had landed, and now her blood, brains, and bones were scattered across three different rooms. I was standing at the base of the stairs, trying to avoid the parts of the carpet with blood on them, which was difficult, as the design on it was a mixture of greens, browns, and reds, and I couldn't tell what was carpet and what was person. I could faintly hear Evan's voice somewhere far away, he was interviewing McKinnley, who claimed that he had come back from the funeral and found her like this. Bertrand had warned me something like this would happen. He was going to scream at me when he found out about this.

"I don't know..." McKinnley whispered. "She said she wasn't feeling well. And I came back and found her like this."

Evan didn't say anything, he was busy writing down notes.

"She wasn't feeling well. Was she on any kind of medication?" I asked.

McKinnley made a strange face, as if this was a difficult question for him to figure out.

"Not sure. I don't think so, maybe something for headaches?"

We weren't getting anything out of him. This was beyond frustrating. There's no way that the wife had just fallen down the stairs, not after what Bertrand had told me. I thought about when I had driven McKinnley home just days ago, and how suspicious he had gotten when I asked if his wife was okay. No, he definitely killed her, whether intentionally or if he was in a blind, drunk rage, I didn't know. But there was no way I could prove any of this. My only evidence was a confession to Bertrand, and I couldn't give him up as a source.

***

After we finished taking his statement we were getting ready to leave but Evan stopped by the stairs. He gingerly stepped over Mrs. McKinnley's foot and walked up a few stairs. He stared at the wall where she had died and stuck his arm out straight, pointing it directly at the point of impact.

"What are you doing?" I asked.

"Trying to find the right angle," he said. "I'll explain it later."

We left the house and drove back to the station.

"I think he killed her," Evan said after a few minutes of silence in the car.

Somehow this didn't surprise me. But I was glad he brought this up first.

"Wow, you're seeing murderers everywhere today," I said.

"No, what he said makes no sense," said Evan. "To reach the wall she must have fallen from the bottom few stairs, four from the bottom at most."

"Okay," I said.

"But that kind of impact, that's like a full flight, as if she jumped from the very top. Plus the actual point of impact is too high for those bottom stairs, the trail of blood is all the way from like halfway up the doorframe."

"So what?" I asked. "You think McKinnley threw her into the door, then went to the funeral, and then came back and said 'oh no, look what I found?'"

"That's exactly what I think," Evan replied.

What do I tell him? That I believe him?

"But can you prove it beyond just a feeling?" I asked.

He grimaced.

"No."

FIFTEEN

Little happened for the rest of the day, but just as I was about to leave Evan approached my desk.

"Can we go somewhere?" he asked. "I feel like getting a drink."

I looked up from my chair.

"Didn't you have one this morning?" I asked, but then I realized that something was bothering him. "Fine," I said. "Sure, we can go."

***

We ended up at Hellhole, which was rather busy for a weekday. Evan and I managed to get a booth in the far corner. He seemed to want to be as far away from people as possible.

"Can I just get your opinion?" Evan asked as we sat down with the first beers of the night.

"Of course."

"Do you think Martin is guilty?" he asked me.

"Guilty of what?"

"The murders."

I noticed he was still using the plural of murder.

"Well," I said, taking my first sip. "Let's look at what we know for sure."

"No, I don't care about evidence, do you think he's guilty?"

"See, that's your problem," I said. "What I think is irrelevant. Now, once again, what do we know for sure? We know that Insomniak is being illegally smuggled out of Appleton and into bigger cities. We know this. Jane's suicide note confirms it, and so did the doctor. What we also know is that this operation includes at least five people, two of whom are now dead."

"Five?" Evan asked, confused. "Martin, Jane, Vanessa, Dr. Rah,-"

"And whoever Vanessa's connections in the city were," I said. "I doubt that she was selling it on her own. Now we know for a fact Martin was involved because again, the note and the doctor confirmed this, and I don't think Dr. Rah would have just made this up. Bringing Martin into this if he was innocent would be a bad idea for everyone involved. Now the questions we have are: Did Martin kill Vanessa, and what role did he play in the operation?"

"What do you mean what role?" Evan asked.

"It seems that he was just running security here, making sure that everyone else involved would never get arrested. Everyone else is taking risks, Dr. Rah is smuggling drugs out of his own store, Jane is purchasing them under a fake name,

Vanessa is transporting them out of Appleton. Everyone is taking risks. Meanwhile, Martin is likely taking a percentage of the money made and in return, should anything go wrong he starts yelling 'my father' at anyone who will listen. Now, from what Jane told us Martin had the brilliant idea of expanding their business in this very town, which would likely result in a higher profit margin for everyone involved."

"But Jane had a change of heart," Evan said.

"Exactly," I said. "Now I don't know what exactly happened when they went to the Hole. Maybe Vanessa also wanted out of this game, but it is actually possible that by killing Vanessa, Martin cuts off their access to the city, so if they want to make money they have to sell in Appleton now. And also, by killing her, he sends a message to Jane and Dr. Rah about what happens to people who want to retire early."

"You still haven't answered my question," Evan said.

I sighed.

"We have nothing concrete to suggest that Martin killed her. There is a lot of circumstantial evidence, and based on the suicide note we have a motive, but we don't know for sure."

Evan lowered his head and lightly smacked it against the table.

"I know that's not what you want to hear," I said. "And I'm sorry. But that's the reality. In fact, I honestly doubt that Martin or Benjamin will ever receive a prison sentence."

"And that doesn't bother you?" Evan asked desperately.

"Of course it bothers me," I said quietly. "I've been here a lot longer than you, Evan. I know what kind of people they are, and I have been waiting for years for one of them to make a mistake. But they haven't."

Evan downed his entire beer. It was warm in the bar, at least as warm as it could be in the middle of winter, but I could see his face turning red as though he were in a sauna.

"Do you want to tell me what's really bothering you?" I asked.

He sighed.

"I... I keep thinking about her. About that note. About the fact that she asked you, asked us, to protect her. And we didn't do a thing."

I frowned. He was still feeling guilty about Jane.

"People depend on us," Evan said, and I saw he was beginning to sweat. "We're in a position of power, and people rely on us to help them, and I keep fucking up and letting them die."

"Jane's death was not your fault," I said. "You didn't force her to overdose, and if she were really that afraid of Martin, well... we had him locked in a room. And to be honest, maybe she should have thought about the risks of this lifestyle before she decided to partner up with people like him."

Evan didn't say anything. I saw he was avoiding my gaze.

"But this isn't really about Jane, is it?" I asked. "You're thinking about that last witness. The one they killed before the trial. I'm sorry about that, but you didn't kill them either. It wasn't your fault."

"It was," Evan said quietly.

"No," I said firmly. "Your witness died because someone leaked their name‑"

"I leaked it," he said, finally looking up at me.

That caught me off guard.

"I'm sorry?" I asked.

"I was the one who told the journalist who our witness was," he said.

Even with all of the other conversations in the bar and the music playing over top of it, I could still hear the sound of Evan's heart rapidly pounding.

"Why?" I asked.

I wasn't sure if I should have asked. I didn't know what answer to expect. There definitely wasn't a good answer to this question.

"Because we were having an affair," he finally said.

There was a long pause.

"Ah," was all I managed to say.

"I thought I could trust her," he said. "Turns out I couldn't. So our witness dies, I go to jail for retaliating, my wife leaves me, and finally I get sent out to wherever the fuck this town is," he said.

I didn't know what to say. I didn't usually have people open up to me like this, especially not people in our line of work... people who understood what it was like to make these sorts of decisions.

"Do you regret it?" I asked him after a moment.

"Do I regret what?"

"How you handled the journalist afterwards."

I immediately knew the answer even though he didn't say it out loud. He wasn't sure what to do. Should he admit the truth, or give me the 'right' answer?

"No," he said. "But I should, right? Like... there's a process for this kind of thing, she would have gone to prison-"

"Would she?" I asked. "Would she have been punished for causing a man's death in order to further her own career, or would she have cried about freedom of press?"

Evan didn't answer.

"You did what you had to do," I told him. "Sure, you made a poor judgement call, you trusted the wrong person, and that led to a man's death, but that wasn't your fault. And more so, you took matters into your own hands to rectify those mistakes. There was no way you would bring that man back from the dead, but you showed that these kinds of acts don't go unpunished."

Evan gave me a strange look. He seemed grateful that I was supportive of him, but it almost seemed to be surprising.

"You seem oddly okay with all of this," he said.

"I've been doing this for a long time. You think this is the last time you'll see someone die who didn't deserve it? No, you'll see it again, and again, to the point where it barely bothers you. I might not have burst out laughing when I saw Vanessa's crucified body, but I wasn't shocked or horrified by it. I've gotten used to it. And I've also gotten used to the idea that the person who did that will never be caught. You know, when I first joined the force, during my very first year, we found out that a psychiatrist who lived in Appleton had been convincing his patients to commit suicide."

"Jesus..." said Evan.

"It was subtle, he took his time, and he did it infrequently enough so that we wouldn't see an obvious connection. But four people died because of him across ten years. When we finally figured out he was behind it he vanished. Just packed up and left before we got to him. Hasn't been seen since."

"You never found him?" Evan asked.

"No one did. Now, maybe he jumped off a bridge in his shame and we've just never found the body. But I think he's out there somewhere, maybe in a different country. Maybe he's now a life coach so he doesn't need a medical license and he's back to doing what he does best. This man will likely never face consequences for what he did. It's not fair, it doesn't make sense, but that's how the world works."

"Then why even bother with any of this?" Evan asked. "Why do we have cops or lawyers or judges? Why do we have prisons, why do we have a justice system?"

"Justice isn't real, Evan," I told him. "It's something we made up to convince ourselves that somehow things will work themselves out in the end and everyone will get what they deserve. If you want justice you have to take it."

Evan didn't say anything for a while. He stared at the now empty glass, twirling it around and tilting it so the few drops that clung to the bottom would race towards the edge.

"Can I ask you something kind of fucked up?" he asked.

"Sure," I said.

He might as well, this conversation had already gone further than what would be professional.

"People like Martin, Benjamin, Moses from back where I lived before. People who are like real pieces of shit. People who you know are criminals even if you can't link them to a specific crime. Do you ever think like... what if we just killed them?"

"Of course," I said.

I answered him immediately. There was no sense in stalling or pretending I had to really think about it. Evan seemed surprised with how blunt I was.

"But you have to ask why. Why are you killing them? Because they're bad people? There are plenty of those, we can't just go around executing all of them. If you're going to play judge, jury, and executioner, you're going to need a crime."

"But you understand what I mean," Evan said. "Martin's going to get away with all of this and I... I don't know if I can just stand by and let that happen. Not again."

Suddenly there was a loud yell from the bar. Someone was arguing with the bartender about whether they had had enough drinks that night. I peered out of the booth to see what was happening, in case Evan and I needed to intervene. To my annoyance I saw that the person yelling at the bartender was McKinnley.

"Jesus..." I said, shaking my head.

Evan turned around to see what I was looking at.

"Oh, what the fuck is he doing here? His wife's been dead for less than a day."

"I'm going out for a smoke," I told Evan. "Need to clear my head."

When I walked back into the bar a few minutes later I looked and saw Evan still sitting where I had left him. Instead, I approached McKinnley. When he felt someone standing next to him, he looked up and groaned.

"What do you want?" he asked.

"What are you doing here, McKinnley?" I asked.

"I am in mourning," he said. "I..." he lifted his glass and stirred it, causing the ice cubes to clang against the glass. "am drinking my pain away."

I leaned onto the bar and whispered so as to not cause a scene.

"You shouldn't be here, she's been dead for less than a day, this isn't a good look for you."

"The fuck do you care?" he said rather loudly.

"Why don't we get you home?" I asked.

McKinnley scoffed.

"What are you, my wife?" he asked condescendingly.

"No," I said.

I was tempted to say that he killed her, just to see what reaction that would get, but I feared that he might actually try to kill me in response. He wouldn't succeed, but I didn't want this kind of attention, not now.

"Different people..." he said and then paused to gulp down the rest of his drink. "grieve in different ways. I don't judge you for how you process it, so why don't you just leave me the fuck alone?" he said.

He turned to me and I tried to ignore the drops of foam that were splattered all over his beard. I wondered whether his wife truly was in a better place now that she didn't have to live with this bum every day.

"Another one!" McKinnley yelled at Tanner.

The bartender looked at me first, as if he wanted to know whether I thought giving McKinnley more alcohol was a wise decision.

"It's fine," I nodded.

When Tanner brought over yet another beer he ended up placing it out of McKinnley's reach. I placed my hand over it and slid it over to him.

"There," I said. "Sorry for your loss."

And without another word I returned to Evan.

"Any problems?" Evan asked, who by now had noticed where I had been.

"He's drinking his pain away," I said.

Evan scoffed.

"Maybe I should try that."

***

We didn't end up staying much longer. Once we finished what was in our glasses we left the bar and I drove Evan home. He didn't say much on the trip there. I wondered whether I had opened up too him to much. Maybe he was thinking the same.

"Don't worry about Martin," I said finally. "We're going to figure this out."

"How?" Evan asked.

"We wait. We wait and see if he still tries to start selling here. We know that Benjamin won't stand for that. He might give his son up on his own."

"You think he'd do that?" Evan asked.

"At this point nothing would surprise me."

When we arrived outside Evan's house I was debating whether to share one last thing.

"Well... thanks for the ride," he said.

"Not a problem," I said.

Evan undid his seatbelt and reached for the door handle.

"Hey listen," I said. "Not that it's my business but... is that why you're separated, because of the journalist situation?"

He sighed.

"I mean... there were a lot of problems already, it was a long time coming. But I guess that was the thing that pushed her over the edge."

"You shouldn't be so hard on yourself," I said. "About your wife, I mean."

Evan raised an eyebrow.

"I shouldn't be hard on myself for cheating on my wife? No, George, I think I should be very hard on myself for that."

"No, no, it's just..." I paused, but it was too late, I had to commit to the decision. "it happens to the best of us."

Evan furrowed his brow, clearly not understanding what I meant.

"What are you talking about?" he asked.

I didn't respond.

"Nothing," I said finally. "Have a good night."

Then his eyes widened.

"Wait! You? You... no, that's not possible!"

"Isn't it?" I asked calmly.

Evan burst out laughing but after a few seconds he composed himself.

"I'm so sorry, I shouldn't be laughing at that, that's horrible."

He took a few deep breaths.

"But like... really? You? But you're so..."

"So what?" I asked.

"Boring?"

I smiled lightly.

"I'm not boring, Evan. That's just what I want you to think."

Evan shook his head in disbelief and finally opened the car door. Before he closed it he turned around and peered back into the car.

"Does she know?" he asked curiously.

"What do you think will happen if you tell her?" I asked.

Evan didn't answer but he nodded and closed the door. I watched him walk down the driveway and disappear into his house.

INTERLUDE

"I don't want to phrase this the wrong way, so I hope you understand the angle I'm coming from," Xander said. "But did you ever feel at least a little responsible for what happened to Mr. McKinnley?"

I raised my eyebrows.

"Do I feel responsible?" I asked.

"I mean in the sense that, you did see him there at that bar, right?" Xander said hurriedly.

I knew what he was trying to say but I wanted to see him panic as he got the meaning of his question all tangled up.

"Did you ever think that maybe if you had driven him home he wouldn't have ended up-"

"Sure," I said. "I could have driven him home. So could any of the other people who were at the bar that night. McKinnley was a regular, everyone knew him, they could have offered him a ride. And even if he hadn't drank to the point where he could barely stand up straight, his wife had just died. Someone in that kind of emotional distress shouldn't be driving a car so soon. Maybe the bartender also feels guilty for letting him drink that much. But I think at the end of the day, the only person we can blame for McKinnley's death is himself. Maybe if he hadn't been such a terrible

234

husband, his wife would have been alive, and so would he."

"So you believe that?" Julie interjected. "You think McKinnley killed his wife?"

I paused. I had to be very careful. Even though this had happened a long time ago, I was still officially a police officer and I had to be very clear about the fact that this was just speculation.

"Evan's original theory seemed peculiar, but the forensics did confirm later that there was something odd about the angle," I explained. "See, we know where the point of impact was, Mrs. McKinnley's head hit the wall at a certain height and then she slid all the way down. Now, to hit the door frame that high she would have had to begin her fall from a certain step."

I raised my hands, one pointing straight up to indicate the door, the other horizontal to indicate the stair at roughly the same height.

"But the other thing you have to consider is length. From that stair if she had simply tripped, she would have likely just landed at the base of the stairs, in order to actually reach the door and hit it that hard it would almost have to be... like a running jump from a few stairs above."

"Like someone pushed her?" Julie said.

"Exactly. But I do have to be very clear that this is just speculation. At the end of the day we don't know. Is it possible that she launched herself off the stairs? Possible. But I doubt it. I can't back that up with any reports of any domestic violence because we never received any. I also don't think that McKinnley would kill his wife on purpose, not in a premeditated way, but the idea of him shoving her a little too hard in one of his drunken episodes... well that's not the most far-fetched scenario, I'm afraid."

"In one of his drunken episodes," Xander repeated.

"That's right," I said. "Especially if he mixed his drinks with something else."

SIXTEEN

On the morning of New Year's Eve I woke up in my own bed for once. Martha wasn't next to me. She was likely off on her run. I tossed over and saw that the first streaks of sunlight were piercing through the trees in our backyard. I slowly got up and stumbled into the kitchen. Martha was making breakfast, she was already back from her run.

"You look like you slept well," she said without looking up.

"I did," I said. "For once."

"My parents called," she said, finally turning to me. "They asked if we wanted to visit them tonight."

I sighed. I knew she wanted me to go with them and spend time together, but I knew that until this mess with Martin was resolved I should expect shifts to suddenly go late into the day.

"I'm sorry, I can't," I said. "You should take the kids and go, I just... I don't know how things are going to be with work."

"Yeah, that's what I told them," she said. "So we're going to go."

I didn't know if I should be disappointed that she had made plans without me and had correctly guessed that I wouldn't be available. But at the same time part of me was relieved. If things with Martin were to go south, at least my family was far away.

***

I arrived at the office to find Dennis pacing up and down near my desk.

"There you are," he said when he saw me walk in.

I could see by his expression that something had happened.

"What is it?" I asked.

Dennis raised his arms in exasperation.

"McKinnley's dead."

For some reason I didn't find this surprising. I felt nothing. Was that strange? Shouldn't I feel upset at the death of another human being?

"What happened?" I asked.

"He got behind the wheel when he shouldn't have."

"Fuck," I said.

I collapsed into my chair and tried to process this. I didn't know what convinced me to try and be funny.

"Man, I really thought we had peacekeeper pub crawl down for this year and all of a sudden we're up to, what, four?"

Dennis frowned.

"I'm glad at least one of us finds something amusing about this."

"I'm sorry," I said.

"I see that spending too much time with Evan has started to rub off on you."

"What has spending too much time with me done?"

Evan's voice echoed through the office as he walked in.

"McKinnley's dead," Dennis told him.

Evan stopped in his tracks.

"Fuck," he whispered.

He looked at me.

"What happened?"

***

Later on in the day McKinnley's body was brought to the morgue. I didn't get a chance to look at it but Dennis had mentioned that his car had swerved off the road and crashed into the trees at the edge of the forest. It was possible that McKinnley had seen a deer and tried to avoid it, but we would never know for sure.

"Are you doing anything exciting tonight?" Evan asked me as we passed the time.

"Me? No. Martha's taking the kids to see her parents."

Evan frowned.

"You're not going with them?"

"Nope," I said.

Evan spun around in his chair, not saying anything. I knew he was probably thinking of how to ask me if I was having marital problems without being too blunt about it.

"Do you want to come over for a drink?" he asked eventually.

"And spend time looking at your crime board?" I asked with a laugh.

"Hey, you don't have to come if you don't want to," he said casually. "Stay home by yourself and do... whatever it is you do in your spare time."

Evan lifted his feet up onto the desk but immediately put them back on the floor when he saw Dennis approaching.

"You guys are going to want to see this," he said.

He looked angry.

"What is it?" I asked as we walked after him.

"You'll see," he said.

Dennis led us to the morgue where creepy Joel was waiting for us.

"Santa's been really busy this year!" he exclaimed with a wide smile as he stood over the remains of McKinnley's body. His face and torso were littered with cuts from his broken windshield. The parts of his skin that weren't pale were a deep purple. There was a large gash at the bottom of his neck where I assumed a piece of metal, or perhaps a branch had gone through him.

"So this is what killed him," Joel said, pointing to said gash. "Windshield wiper. Went right through his neck. I imagine it would have been quite painful, but luckily for him he probably didn't feel a thing, thanks to the wonderful concoction he had in his system."

"Meaning he was that drunk?" Evan asked.

"Not just that," Joel said, shaking his head. "There was something else in his system."

He turned to Dennis.

"Do you want to tell them, or should I?" he asked.

But I already knew the answer.

"Tell me it wasn't Insomniak," I said.

"We don't know for sure," Joel explained. "Insomniak is just the brand, so it could be a knockoff version, but it is the same chemicals."

"Thank you Joel," said Dennis. "Could you give us a minute?"

He nodded and left the room.

"Please don't touch any of the bodies," he said on his way out.

"Before you jump to any conclusions," Dennis said to Evan once we were alone. "remember that this could just be a series of coincidences."

"Oh, bullshit," said Evan. "You told us based on how the car swerved he might have hit a deer, no, he might have hallucinated a deer."

"Insomniak is legal," Dennis said firmly. "McKinnley could have bought it, that's not a crime."

"Had you even heard of this stuff a week ago?" Evan asked. "No. And suddenly we have one person dead by overdose, another by impaired driving, and I had a feeling there was something off about how the wife tripped down the stairs. Now I'm starting to become convinced that wasn't an accident."

"But that's all it is," said Dennis. "A feeling!"

"Then how do we prove it?" Evan asked. "We need to figure out a way to prove whether he's responsible or not. Let's not forget that we still have a crucified woman whose killer we have not found, and that was like almost two weeks ago."

Dennis scratched his head.

"Okay. Here's what we do, we bring in the doctor, see if he's sold anything to McKinnley. If not, then we know Martin might be expanding.

George, go to the pharmacy, Evan, you try his house."

***

We left the station and went our separate ways. It was already mid afternoon and the sun was beginning to disappear behind the trees, casting long shadows across the road as I drove. Not long after I reached the road leading to the drug store. The parking lot was empty except for one car, the exact same black one I had seen parked there the last time I had visited. I walked over to it. It was parked in the second closest spot to the front door (the closest one was the handicapped spot), with a sign in front of it that read 'Reserved for Dr. Rah.' I wasn't sure why he needed to reserve a spot if this place always seemed empty. That's when I noticed that the front door to the building was wide open. Strange. I remembered those annoying bells that had rung the last time I was here when I entered the building. I cautiously walked over to the entrance and peered inside.

"Hello?" I said.

There was no answer. I walked into the building, one hand hovering over my hip in case I needed to pull my gun out. The store was completely empty. I peered down one aisle towards the back counter. Slowly I made my way down the aisle and as I got closer I noticed what had happened behind the counter. It looked as though someone had ransacked the whole place. The floor was covered in loose sheets of paper and open pill bottles, the capsules inside scattered everywhere. Several drawers had been pulled out all the way, some were lying on the floor upside down. The back door to the building was also wide open.

"Shit," I said.

Someone had gotten to Dr. Rah before we did. I pulled out my phone and called Evan.

"He's not here," Evan said when he picked up.

"No, he's not here either," I said. "But someone was."

A minute later I called Dennis to give him the bad news.

"Is anyone else there, any witnesses?" he asked.

"No. Nothing," I said.

"Okay, close all of the doors and get back to the station now."

INTERLUDE

"Did it occur to you that Dr. Rah might have skipped town?" Xander asked me. "You had mentioned that he was terrified of Martin."

"True, but this didn't look like him skipping town," I said. "You could have made the argument that he was faking his own death or kidnapping, but he wouldn't be fooling Martin, so that defeated the whole purpose. We didn't know what happened to Dr. Rah, but the amount of coincidences surrounding Martin Nero were now too much to ignore. The fact was that two of his accomplices were dead, and the third one was missing."

I took a sip of water. I knew which part of the story came next. The night of New Year's Eve was a complete mess. I tried to ignore the flashes in my mind. The looks on everyone's faces. Evan lying in the snow, Martin knowing he was caught, Dennis arriving at the scene and realizing what had happened. I took a deep breath. I had to ignore those images. I had to remember our story.

"One idea I had went back to McKinnley. I thought that maybe Martin had gone ahead and started selling locally. We had no way of knowing for sure now, since we couldn't ask the doctor about it. But remember that Benjamin was very firm that this would not be tolerated in his town. It was entirely possible that Martin had nothing to do with Dr. Rah's disappearance, his father might have been the one who decided to straighten things out."

"Interesting," said Xander. "So you get back to the station and what?"

"Well, Dennis agreed with me. There were too many coincidences. It was time we brought Martin and Benjamin in for questioning."

"He wanted the father there too?" Xander asked.

"Yes, he specifically came up with that idea," I said. "So it was New Year's Eve, and we knew where both of them would be. Martin would be at Hellhole with his posse, because it's not like there was anywhere else to party in Appleton, and Benjamin would be having his own celebration at their house with his friends and associates. Dennis told us to go to Hellhole and arrest Martin, while he would take care of Benjamin personally. And then everything went to shit from there."

SEVENTEEN

By the time Evan and I got to Hellhole it was dark. And it was raining. There was a line of people from the front door all the way to the street and down the sidewalk.

"I'm guessing the parking lot will be full," said Evan.

"We can park wherever we want," I said.

We drove by the line of people slowly, trying not to attract too much attention. Several people glanced over at us and shifted uncomfortably, the way people do when they see the police, even if they haven't done anything wrong. We drove around the corner and parked on the side of the road behind Hellhole.

"How crowded do you think this place will be?" Evan asked as we got out of the car.

"Pretty packed," I said. "Everyone under thirty will probably be here."

We made our way around the corner and to the front entrance of Hellhole.

"Now remember, we're just arresting him," I said. "Don't do anything reckless."

"Why are you acting like this is my first day?" Evan asked.

I spun around to face him.

"The last time you saw Martin you almost killed him. I don't want that happening again. Especially not with this many witnesses."

Evan raised his eyebrows.

"Not when there's witnesses. Got it," he said.

He smiled for a moment but his smile vanished when he saw that I didn't find this amusing.

"Okay. I'll be serious," he said.

I turned back around and headed towards the main entrance. We walked to the front of the line.

"Evening," I said to the bouncer.

I didn't even have to pull out any ID, the bouncer knew who we were. Perks of living in a small town. Already from outside of the building we could hear a fast, steady beat but when the door opened the sounds engulfed everything and I began feeling them vibrate in my chest. When we entered Hellhole there was pitch darkness. The hallway that led to the main room had no lights, except from a small crack coming from under the door that led to the coat check room. We walked down the hallway and entered the main room. Strobe lights immediately shone in my eyes before shifting off to the side. The room was filled with dark shapes moving erratically on the floor.

"How are we supposed to find him?" Evan yelled in my ear.

Even like that I could barely hear him. But I already knew where he would be. Martin wouldn't be dancing in the middle of the floor with all of the normal people, he'd have his own secluded place.

"There," I said, pointing across the room.

At the far end of the floor there was the VIP booth that was elevated over the rest of the floor. Through the windows I could see several people sitting together and drinking. One of them was Martin.

"Let's go," I said. "You go around left, I'll meet you at the door," I explained, motioning with my hands.

Evan nodded and headed to the side of the room. I went in the opposite direction, I didn't feel like pushing through this crowd so it was better to go around them. I edged my way down the far wall, trying not to think of how sticky the floor was under each step. Several times one of the rotating lights would shine across my eyes, momentarily blinding me. Finally I got a good shot of the VIP booth. It was blocked off from the rest of the room by a pair of glass doors. There was a tall man with a ponytail standing in front of the doors. He wasn't one of the employees here. He must have been working for Benjamin. As I approached I saw Evan coming towards the guard from the other side. We met up a few feet in front of him. He peered down at us as we approached. I pulled out my badge and lifted it in front of his face. The guard was confused, he apparently hadn't been expecting anything like this to happen tonight and didn't get instructions on how to act. So he did the smart thing, and moved out of the way. We walked up the handful of stairs leading to the doors. Martin didn't notice us until we were opening them.

Martin looked even more insufferable than usual. He was wearing a white shirt that was unbuttoned so that the enormous gold chains he was wearing underneath were visible. I wasn't sure who this was meant to impress, maybe the two girls who were sitting on the couch next to him, one of whom definitely looked too young to be in a place like this. The only other person in the room was a skinny man at the end of the couch who was hunched over and muttering to himself. He didn't even seem to have realized we were in the room. There was a tall champagne bottle on the table, as well as several glasses and a credit card that definitely hadn't been used to divide up cocaine before we arrived.

"Happy New Year," Martin said with a forced smile. "This area is by invite only. I'm going to have to ask you two to leave."

"You're coming with us," I said.

I wasn't in the mood to humour him, I wanted to be out of here as soon as possible.

"Fellas, we've been over this. You kept me in a room over night, me, a perfectly innocent man. And then this piece of shit," he pointed with one finger at Evan. "tried to kill me," he told the girl to his left.

"He'll do a lot worse if we don't find out what you did to Dr. Rah," I said.

Any amusement in Martin's mood vanished the moment he heard that name.

"Alright," he said.

His arms had been around the girls, but he lifted them over their heads and slowly stretched as high as he could.

"I give up," he said.

But then he lowered his gaze. I noticed too late that he was no longer making eye contact with us. Then he quickly nodded.

Even above the obnoxiously loud music there was no mistaking the sound of gun shots. Evan and I both spun around and saw the guard at the bottom of the stairs holding his gun high in the air. The dance floor was already chaotic. Half of the people had immediately ducked onto the floor, which caused them to get trampled by the other half who were already running to the exit. Before Evan or I could do anything, something shoved me into one of the doors. As I collided into the thick glass I saw Martin sprinting down the stairs and onto the dance floor. By the time I got to my feet Evan had already jumped to the bottom of the stairs and was running through the crowd. I ran after him, shoving past the swarm of people piling onto each other, stuffing the dark hallway that led out of the building. I tried yelling 'police,' but the screams and the still-present music drowned out what I was saying. After what seemed like an eternity, I finally managed to squeeze through and burst through the front door into the cold night.

My eyes darted across the street, trying to see Martin or Evan anywhere. There were people running down the sidewalk. Some were crouching behind parked cars in an attempt to hide from whoever had been shooting.

"George!"

I looked over and saw Evan standing by my car.

"He drove off, come on!" he yelled.

I sprinted down the sidewalk, my shoes filling up with water as I ran through the puddles that had begun forming. We finally got into the car and sped off.

"Did you see where he went?" I asked.

"There!" Evan pointed forward.

Far off in the distance were two red lights that were shifting side to side. Poor weather conditions, plus the fact that Martin had been drinking, meant that his driving was erratic. That would be helpful for us. Hopefully he didn't crash into anyone before we caught him.

"Motherfucker," Evan whispered. "I can't believe that guy started firing. What was he thinking?"

"Panicking," I said. "You saw how he reacted when I mentioned Dr. Rah. He fucked up, and he knows it."

Ahead of us Martin's car swerved to the left. I breathed a sigh of relief. The road we were on had houses on either side, but Martin had just turned onto a road that headed into the woods. There wouldn't be any bystanders there. But if he ran into the woods we wouldn't be able to find him.

"Hold on!" I said as we approached the side road.

I turned sharply to the left without slowing down, causing the back of the car to slide violently across the road.

"Jesus, be careful!" Evan said, gripping the door handle in panic.

"Relax," I said.

The windshield wipers started moving faster as rain began to pour down. I could barely see anything a few feet in front of the car, so I had no idea how Martin was able to drive. The backlights of Martin's car were getting larger, I noticed too late that he was slowing down.

"We're going to crash!" Evan said as I began to feel my heart pounding.

I hit the brakes but then I saw Martin's car violently swerve to the left, then to the right, and I realized there was no way to avoid him.

"Get ready!" Evan said.

And we drove straight into the back right of Martin's car.

I felt the back of my head aggressively thump against the headrest as the airbag punched me in the heart. I began to breathe heavily. The cold winter air blew through the now cracked windshield and the sound of rain drops pelting the hood got louder. I blinked and remembered what was happening. Martin. We had just crashed into him. We had to stop him from escaping. I reached down to undue my seatbelt and my shoulder cried out as I moved it.

"You alright?" I asked, turning my head to Evan.

He nodded. There were a few cuts on his face and shards of glass were sprinkled in his hair.

"Fuck, that was a stupid idea," he muttered.

Then we heard a loud bang as the door of Martin's car flew open. There was a splash. He must have fallen out of the car. Then he stood up. There was no way of seeing anything except for what was illuminated from his headlights. As Martin stumbled to the front of his car he turned in our direction. Blood was trickling from his forehead and he looked like he was in a state of shock. And he was scared.

"Come on," said Evan, and he opened his door.

The moment Evan stepped out of the car, Martin looked as though he had just seen a ghost. He began hobbling off to the side of the road and into the woods. Evan ran after him. I managed to finally open the door and I got out, grabbing a flashlight I kept in the door pocket. As I straightened up I felt a sharp stab in my chest. I reached down. There was no blood, and nothing seemed to be poking out of me, so that was good.

"Martin!" I heard Evan's voice from the woods. "Give up!"

I began running after them. As I ran I shone the flashlight. There was no other way of seeing anything out here. It was pitch black, the sky was covered by rain clouds so even the moonlight wouldn't be helpful. All I could see was the slightly darker trees standing out from the rest of the night.

"Evan!" I yelled.

I had no idea where either of them were. I shone my flashlight out into the darkness but there was just rain and trees. Then I heard a gunshot not too far in front of me. I kept running forward.

"Evan!" I yelled again.

And then as I passed a tree, I felt something smash into my face. Immediately my nose felt like it was on fire as I stumbled backwards and fell onto the ground. And Martin was kneeling overtop of me, wrenching my gun from my hands.

"You just couldn't let this go, could you?" he asked me as he stood up.

Before I could say anything I heard a branch snap somewhere close by. Martin spun around and fired two shots. I heard Evan yell. No, no, this wasn't happening. Martin took a step away from me. I felt something warm in my mouth, blood had begun trickling down from my nose.

"Not so tough now, are you Evan?" Martin said. "I bet you didn't think you'd end up like this."

I heard Evan groan in pain.

"I know that you're used to just being able to kill whoever you want and get away with it, but that's not how things work in my town."

"Fuck you," I heard Evan say weakly.

"Yeah... you think we didn't know who you were? We know everything that happens here."

I tried to sit up and immediately felt a pain in my ribs, which helped me momentarily forget about my nose. Martin was standing just a foot away from me. I could see something moving on the ground in the distance near a tree. That had to be Evan.

"Tell me, what were you going to do when you charged into that room? Would you have actually killed me if they hadn't pulled you off? Too many fucking pigs like you who think they can just do whatever they-"

And I kicked him in the back of his knee. Martin's scream was drowned out by the sound of another gunshot. I had no idea if he had hit Evan again or if it had gone wide, but I didn't have time. In half a second he would turn around and kill me, so I had to stop him. I planted my feet on the ground and raised myself into a crouching position before tumbling forward right into Martin, pushing him onto the ground.

"Get the fuck off me!" he yelled.

I pushed one hand into his face as I pinned his wrist down. I yanked his arm up and slammed it against the ground repeatedly until he let go of my gun. I quickly grabbed it and got off him. I stood up, pointing the gun directly at his head. Martin was wheezing heavily, in complete shock and out of breath. His eyes looked funny as they fixated at the gun pointed directly between them.

"Okay," he said, nodding quickly. "Okay, let's talk about this."

"Stand up," I said. "Evan!" I yelled, not taking my eyes off Martin as he stood up. "Are you alright?"

"No, he shot me," Evan groaned.

"I give up," Martin said, slowly standing up and raising his hands.

And then I made a sound. Martin looked confused for a moment, until he realized that I was laughing. I wiped the blood from my face.

"I have been waiting so long for you to give me an excuse," I said.

Martin's eyes widened. I wasn't lowering the gun.

"No. Now listen, I'm a civilian, I'm surrendering to you, I-"

"You shot a police officer, Martin. I can execute you right now and say it was self-defence, and everyone will believe me."

"Not my father," he said. "My father will know you did this on purpose. You shoot me, he'll fuck you up."

If Martin thought that bringing up his father would deter me, he was mistaken. But I had to be fast. Evan was shot, and I had no idea how long he had. I had to get him to a hospital.

"I'm not scared of your father," I said.

"But you have a family," Martin said. "A wife, kids. You don't think he can get to them?"

"I will deal with your father soon, don't you worry," I said.

Martin took a step back. Now he was beginning to panic.

"Look, just... put handcuffs on me, take me back, yell at me all you want, throw me in jail. Whatever. Just..."

"You're right, Martin," I said. "If I shoot you in the head, they'll know it wasn't an accident."

Martin exhaled. He lowered his arms just slightly. They must have been getting tired.

"So I'll have to make it look messier."

I lowered the gun an inch and shot him in the side of the neck.

INTERLUDE

I reached up and touched my nose.

"Do you know I've spent the last six years afraid to sneeze?" I asked Xander.

I laughed when I saw his stunned expression, I admitted it was a sharp segue from what we had just been talking about.

"Yeah," I said. "Every time it happens I feel this sharp pinch, right here."

I squeezed the top, right between my eyes.

"You know, the doctors said that it probably would have healed properly if it hadn't been broken a second time just a few days later," I said with a smile. "But we'll get to that."

It was brief, but I saw the concerned glance that Xander and Julie gave each other. Yes, they already had suspicions about me before they had even met me, but now they were beginning to think that maybe I really was insane. But that was okay, if they wanted to think that I was a liar, I would scare them a little. It would be fun.

"How did you get your gun back?" Julie asked me.

"Sorry?" I asked.

"Martin attacked you and got your gun, but then he runs away and leaves it?" she asked.

For a moment I wondered if anyone had ever broken her nose. No, it was too symmetrical, there had been no damage there. Maybe someone should try.

"I don't know," I said, and I closed my eyes for effect as I sighed. "I've tried so many time to really remember what happened in those moments, but it's all such a blur. I remember Martin hit me, hence this," I pointed to my nose. "I remember falling and him taking my gun. There were shots, but there had already been shots before I was hit. I think once Martin realized he had shot a cop he knew there was no getting out of this. He would be going to prison for a very long time. So I think he panicked and ran."

"But why not take your gun with him?" Julie persisted.

"Why don't you ask him?" I said, a little more sternly than I wanted to.

"I can't," she said.

There was a long pause and then Xander decided to try and defuse the tension.

"Did you try to chase after him?" Xander asked me.

"No," I said, turning my gaze away from Julie, who still looked suspicious. "It was dark, and raining, and even if I could see what was happening, Martin was maybe 20 years younger than me, I wouldn't have been able to catch up to him. No, when I saw the state Evan was in, I decided I had to help him first."

EIGHTEEN

One of the physically hardest things I had ever done was helping move Evan back to the road where our car was.

"Where are you hit?" I asked as I kneeled down next to him.

"Leg," he managed to wince.

I shone my flashlight down and saw a hole in his pants where his thigh was.

"Shit," I said.

I knew it would be horrible walking through this cold rain without a coat, but I took mine off and crudely wrapped it around Evan's leg. He groaned through gritted teeth as I pulled the coat sleeves, tightening it.

"Come on," I said, and I slowly lifted him to his feet.

I put Evan's arm around my shoulder and we began to hobble slowly back towards the road. Faintly in the distance I could see several strips of light, where both our and Martin's cars were still shining their headlights. With my free hand I pulled my phone out of my pocket. I saw that Dennis had already tried calling me twice. I called the ambulance first.

"I need an ambulance for a gunshot victim," I said once I had finished dialling. "Regional Road 43, off of Smithson."

The operator asked me if we were really out in the middle of the woods.

"Yes, in the woods. You'll find two cars crashed into each other."

Then I called Dennis back.

"I tried calling you, where are you?" Dennis asked.

"We're in the woods," I said. "We have a problem."

After I finished my call with Dennis we continued hobbling through the forest, mud splashing onto our shoes and pants. The cold rain was causing my shirt to stick to my body and send piercing shivers down my spine every few seconds. As cold as the air was, it was sharply contrasted by the pain in my nose, which felt like someone was repeatedly opening an oven right in front of my face.

"You killed him," Evan finally spoke up.

I said nothing. What was strange was that I felt nothing. I should at least be afraid. I knew the next few hours would be critical. But no, I couldn't let Evan see how little I was bothered by this.

"I did what I had to," I finally managed to say.

"But... you didn't have to," he whispered.

The lights were getting bigger and soon after we reached the road. All things considered our police car was still in good shape due to having a reinforced bumper, while the entire trunk of Martin's car had caved in.

"I'm going to put you down for a second," I said.

I gently lay Evan on the ground and then walked over to our car. I got into the driver's seat and put the keys in the ignition. It coughed a few times, but I was able to get the engine running and I pulled back out of Martin's car and onto the edge of the road. Soon after I saw lights in the distance.

"I think the ambulance is here," I said, walking over to Evan.

As I lifted him up he groaned again.

"Listen," I said. "Don't say anything about Martin, let me take care of that."

"Why?" Evan asked. "If they ask-"

"I will handle this," I said sharply. "They need to focus on keeping you alive."

As the lights got closer I realized it wasn't an ambulance, it was too small. Within seconds a police car emerged out of the darkness. It stopped a few feet in front of us and Dennis stepped out.

"Fuck," he said when he saw my blood-stained face and the fact that I was helping Evan stand up straight. "What happened?" he asked.

"We went to the club and Martin's bodyguard fired a few shots. Martin manage to run out of the club and we chased him. Crashed into him here."

"Where is he?" Dennis asked.

He was walking over to our car and peering into the backseat, which was empty.

"He..." I said.

I didn't know what to say. But there was no hiding it.

"He's dead," I said.

In all the years I had known Dennis I had never once seen him scared. But now I did.

"Oh fuck," he said, grabbing his head with his hands. "Oh fuck, fuck. No, this is bad. Where is he? What happened?"

I gulped.

"I-"

"I shot him," Evan said.

I turned to him in disbelief, but Evan's face was completely calm, or as calm as it could be given that he had been shot. There was nothing in his expression that gave away he had just lied for me. Dennis tilted his head and stared at Evan. For a moment he looked like he wanted to push his finger into Evan's bullet wound to see how much pain he would cause.

"Jesus Christ," was all he managed to say. "Jesus, Evan, do you have any idea what you've done?"

"Don't blame him," I said suddenly, trying to salvage this. "It was my fault."

Dennis raised an eyebrow.

"Your fault?" he asked.

I wasn't going to let Evan take the fall, not for this.

"He means Martin took his gun," Evan said before I could explain.

He was going to keep going with this.

"He took George's gun, he started shooting in my direction, I shot back. It was self-defence."

"Yeah..." Dennis said. "Self-defence."

He was beginning to pace back and forth. Martin's last words came back to me. Everyone would believe it was self-defence. But not Benjamin. He would know it was intentional.

"How did it go with Benjamin?" I asked.

Dennis scowled.

"He's in the interrogation room. He's probably wondering where I went, I had just begun talking to him. Fuck."

And then we heard a faint screeching noise in the distance. After a moment it became clearer. The sirens told us the ambulance was on its way.

"Shit," said Dennis, as he turned in the direction of the sound. "Okay, are you hit anywhere? Do you need to go to the hospital?" he asked me.

"Well, Martin fucked up my nose, so I should probably have someone take a look at it," I said as I gingerly touched it and immediately felt pain. "And my ribs are pretty sore."

"But do you need to go to the hospital right away?" he asked.

"No," I said, unsure why he was asking.

"Okay, right now the official story is Martin escaped on foot. No one other than the three of us knows what actually happened. We're going to get you to the hospital," he said, pointing at Evan. "George, once the ambulance leaves I need you to do something with the body."

"Like what?" I asked.

Dennis raised his hands in despair.

"I don't fucking know! I didn't tell you guys to kill him! Jesus Christ. Hide the body, I don't know, bury it, we can't pretend he died by accident cause there's a bullet in him."

By now Dennis was yelling so we could hear him over the sound of the sirens. The ambulance's headlights were shining from behind Dennis, illuminating his body in the darkness.

"Deal with the body, get a doctor to fix your nose, come back to the station. No one hears about this, understand?" he yelled.

When the ambulance arrived they immediately put Evan on a gurney. Dennis made a quick call to have someone set up a roadblock on either end of the road we were on, as well as to have someone tow Martin's demolished car. He explained that there was no point in trying to find Martin out in the woods now.

"Are you sure you don't want to ride with us?" the paramedic said as he looked at my face. "That needs to be taken care of."

"I'll come by the hospital," I said, nodding my head. "I'm going to take the car."

The paramedic looked at the damaged police cruiser.

"Is that thing still driveable?" he asked.

I nodded.

"I'll be there soon after you," I told the paramedic, who still looked skeptical. "I just need a moment to myself. Please, just focus on him, I can't lose him. Not now."

I looked at Evan, who was lying in the ambulance. He managed to look up at me and give a shaky thumbs up.

"Alright," the paramedic said.

The ambulance left a minute later, leaving me alone with Dennis.

"Is there anything you want to tell me?" he asked.

"What do you mean?" I asked.

"Was this actually self-defence?" he asked. "Or was Evan just trigger-happy?"

I didn't know why he was asking this. But then I remembered what Martin had yelled in his final moments.

'I know that you're used to being able to kill whoever you want and get away with it.'

What did that mean? Who was Evan, exactly? And what did Dennis know that I didn't?

"He had my gun," I said. "We're both alive right now because Evan took that shot."

Dennis stared at me silently for a moment but then he nodded. It seemed he believed me. He turned and walked back to his car.

"I don't suppose I can ask for your help in moving the body?" I yelled.

"The moment I walk back into the interrogation room, Benjamin's going to ask me which part of our operation went wrong that I was gone for so long," he said angrily. "We can no longer interrogate Martin, so our only hope now is to break Benjamin. We have a very long night ahead of us."

He got into his car and drove off.

***

It took me several minutes to make my way back to where Martin's body was. At least once the ambulance had arrived they had given me back my coat. It was drenched in Evan's blood, but I still put it on, as the last thing I wanted to do was freeze to death out here. When I found Martin I saw that he had died with his hands around his neck, desperately trying to stop blood from seeping out of it. Not that it did much good. I thought back to my conversation with Evan not long ago, when he had asked me why we didn't just execute criminals. This was why. This was a mess, and now I had to clean it up. I was already angry at myself for shooting Martin. Not for killing him, but for shooting. He had been right, there was no way to make this look like an accident. It was messier than a clean shot to the head, I had wanted to be able to tell the lie that I had shot blindly into the darkness to defend myself, but now Evan would have to use the same excuse.

Why had he though? Why had he taken the fall for this? He had seen the look on Dennis' face, this was bad, why would he want to shield me from the repercussions? Evan didn't owe me any favours. In fact, I didn't think he particularly liked me too much. What had Martin said? Evan had killed someone... Maybe he had understood. Maybe he knew what would happen next, and he wanted to take the burden off me. I remembered that Evan had told me we were more similar than I thought. He had no idea how right he was.

"You had to run, didn't you?" I said as I began dragging Martin's body.

I pulled him by his hands towards the car. At first I had tried actually lifting him and carrying him like I did Evan, but Evan had one working leg which he had used to help me even out the load. Martin was too heavy for me to carry on my own.

"You could have been sitting in a cell right now. We'd all be indoors. We'd all be warm. What was your plan anyway? Run? Hide in your house? What happens when you get to your house and find out your father's not there to protect you?"

The body obviously didn't answer me. I tried to ignore the sensation of his lifeless fingers occasionally brushing against my wrists. Part of me expected him to suddenly come back to life and dig his nails into my veins. But he didn't.

Eventually we reached the road again. I didn't know what I was going to do next. I couldn't just leave Martin's body out in the woods and I had no way of burying him. But I had to get to the hospital and have them do something about the disaster on my face. Maybe by the time they let me out I would have come up with a plan. As I got into the car I checked my phone and saw that I had missed a text from Martha.

'Happy New Year.' it read.

NINETEEN

I arrived at the hospital not long after. I knew I should have resolved the body issue first, but the pain in my face was making it difficult to think. So I parked just outside the emergency room, and hoped that no one would steal the car in the time I was gone. I tried not to think about Martin lying in the trunk. He had already lost a lot of blood by the time I had dragged him out of the woods, but there was still some pouring out, so I had to carefully wrap him in the large blanket I kept in the trunk. Thankfully the emergency room wasn't too busy tonight and the doctors managed to look at me right away. They quickly confirmed none of my ribs were broken.

"Looks like you took quite the tumble," the doctor said as he felt my nose and I did my best not to squeeze my eyes shut from the pain.

"You could say that," I said.

Shortly after my nose was in a splint, but before I left, I asked him about Evan.

"Ah, the cop with the gunshot wound," the doctor said. "Yeah, he's just down at the end of the hallway. He was asking about you too."

He handed me some pills to take for the pain and left me alone. I walked to the end of the hallway and found Evan's room.

Evan was sitting on a tall bed. His pants were off and I could see the thick white bandages that were wrapped around his right thigh. There was a small red dot in the middle where blood had begun to seep through.

"Oh you're alive," he said when he saw me.

I didn't know what to say. I turned and peered out the hallway, which was deserted.

"Anyone in there?" I asked, pointing to the door in the corner, which I assumed led to a bathroom.

"Nope," said Evan. "Just us."

I closed the door behind me.

"Listen," I said, staring down at my feet. "I don't know why you did what you did but... thanks, I guess."

I managed to look up and saw that Evan was extremely pale. For a second I thought it was from the blood he had lost, but there was something about him that suggested he was uneasy being in the same room as me.

"Why?" he asked.

"Why what?"

"Why did you kill him?"

There was a long pause. My heart was pounding. I knew I was safe, there was no way Evan was going to retract his story now that he had already told Dennis that he was the one who had pulled the trigger.

"Is there a good answer to that question?" I asked finally. "Or are there just excuses?"

"I was thinking about what you said the other night," he said. "About justice not being a real thing, and how the system doesn't punish people like Martin. You said you couldn't just kill someone without a reason, but at the very end you thanked Martin for giving you an excuse. You've been waiting for this opportunity, haven't you?" he said.

My jaw tightened.

"I'd appreciate if you kept your voice down," I said. "And I wouldn't be so quick to judge, Evan. Because I also heard things out there in the woods. Things about you. I'm not going to ask what Martin meant, because frankly it's not my business. I don't care who you were before you came here, all that matters is what you're doing now. But when you told Dennis that you had killed Martin he believed it immediately... which means that what Martin said was probably true."

It wasn't possible for Evan to grow even paler than he already was, but he started shaking, as if me reminding him of what Martin said was bringing back memories that he had buried.

"Speaking of which, why did you lie to Dennis?" I asked.

"Because of what Martin said," he replied. "When Benjamin finds out his son is dead he will go after the person responsible. Them and their families. I did what I had to do to protect yours."

I immediately felt bad for chastising him.

"I... thank you," I said.

I remembered Martin's threats, remembered how I knew he was right, and that Benjamin would soon become a problem that I would have to deal with. Evan had bought me some time, at least for now.

"But what about you?" I asked. "You have a family."

Evan stared down at his knees. He began to awkwardly swing his feet back and forth.

"If Martin knew about my past, that means his father did too. He won't think of touching my family."

Evan looked me in the eyes.

"He's probably scared of me."

I didn't know whether that was true or just projection. Benjamin had never been scared of anyone, or at least hadn't ever shown it. And if Evan really was dangerous, would Benjamin have approached him that first day and implied he could turn him? I wasn't sure, but tonight wasn't the time to think of these things.

"Did you take care of..." Evan started to ask but he saw my eyes widen.

I doubted that anyone was listening in, but I didn't want them to hear that Martin's body was in my car.

"Not yet," I said. "Once I leave here, I'll handle it. I needed something for the pain, my nose is fucking bothering me."

Evan nodded, and then he almost smiled. He leaned in.

"Is it in the car?" he said, his voice barely above a whisper.

"Yeah," I said.

Evan looked stunned at the idea of me just leaving a car with a dead body in the parking lot.

"Jesus..." he whispered. "How are you not panicking right now?" he asked.

"I am," I said. "Like I said, I came here to get my nose fixed, and I wanted to check on you. Now I have to go."

"Okay," Evan said. "Thanks for dropping by. But yes, deal with that right away, he's probably starting to smell already."

I was confused.

"No, he won't. Not for a while, it hasn't been that long yet."

Evan's mouth was shaking. I realized he was barely containing laughter.

"But he's been in the trunk since last year."

***

By the time I was outside the hospital I was still groaning internally at the stupid joke Evan had made. I wondered at what point in the night he had come up with it and how long he had been waiting to use it. As I approached the car, I glanced around the parking lot. There were a few cars here and there, but I didn't see any people. I stared at the trunk of my car. I knew he was still in there, but there was a part of me that was wondering if he wasn't. I couldn't open the trunk fully, in case someone happened to walk by, or God forbid, any of the cars nearby had dashcams. I unlocked the trunk and put my hand on it. I half expected to hear a scream and see Martin lunge out at me. I lifted the trunk door just an inch and shone my phone into the corner where Martin's legs were, as I was too scared to shine on his face. He was still there. I closed the trunk and called Father Bertrand.

"George! Happy New Year," he said.

"You as well," I said. "Listen... I have a problem. I'm going to need your help with something."

TWENTY

When I arrived at the church not long afterwards, I could see the light on in front of Bertrand's house. The door opened momentarily and he came walking out. I drove over to the house and parked my car next to his shed. When I got out of the car, I saw a concerned look on his face.

"What happened to your car?" he asked in shock as he gazed at the numerous dents in the hood.

"Long story," I said. "Are we alone?"

"Yes, of course," Bertrand said, glancing around the front yard.

"Your housekeeper's gone?" I asked.

"Yes, she doesn't stay here overnight. She's with her family," Bertrand said.

I wanted to ask him if he had any married women staying over, but I decided not to anger him. Like it or not, I needed his help.

"Where do you have cameras?" I asked.

"Cameras?"

"Yes, security cameras. I don't believe that you're passing me confessional gossip just by the sounds of people's voices. You have cameras somewhere so you know who's coming and going."

Bertrand frowned. He seemed disappointed, as if I were accusing him of a crime.

"One at the front door of the house," he said. "One in the corner." he added, pointing to a small white box just under the roof of the house. "It gets a wide angle of the yard and the door leading to the church."

"Can it see us from here?" I asked.

"No, not this angle," he said. "It's pointed away from us, towards the chapel. And there's one on the back of the house which covers the yard."

"Are there any that see us now?" I asked.

"No. George, what's going on?"

I sighed.

"I understand the risks you take for me, Father. What you provide me is valuable, and I know I don't always show my appreciation. But now I really need your help."

Bertrand was starting to get scared.

"What happened?" he said slowly.

I looked over at the light in front of his house. It was far enough away that when I popped open the trunk it wouldn't illuminate Martin's body.

"I have something in my trunk, and I need to keep it here for a while until I figure out what to do with it."

Bertrand's eyes slowly went to the trunk. He took a step back.

"What is in there?"

I didn't answer. I just opened it. He couldn't see what was inside from where he was standing.

"I must ask you not to scream," I said.

Bertrand looked even whiter than Evan had back at the hospital. He took a few steps forward until he saw the large, human-sized shape wrapped tightly in a blanket.

"Is that-" he began as his eyes widened.

He knew it was a body. Now to tell him who it was.

"That's Martin Nero."

There was probably nothing I could have said that he would have found more shocking.

Bertrand staggered back.

"Oh, Jesus Christ," he whispered.

"Hey, that's blasphemy."

Bertrand turned in my direction, incredulous that I could have just made a joke.

"What the fuck did you do?" he gasped.

"I'm not going to bother trying to justify my actions to you, Father. There's nothing I could say that would convince you this was necessary. But right now I need your help. I need to keep this somewhere while I figure out how we're going to spin this story in a way that Benjamin won't murder all of us."

Bertrand made a weird sound that almost resembled choking.

"You want to leave him here?!"

"Yes. I can't do it at home, or at the station. I need to keep him somewhere absolutely no one will find him."

"No," Bertrand said, and he turned around, beginning to walk away. "Absolutely not, you get that thing out of here, and don't ever come-"

"Bertrand," I said sternly.

I didn't yell, but I wanted my voice to carry some weight with it. The priest stopped in his tracks, but he didn't turn. He was too scared to face me.

"Think about everything we have been through together," I said.

I didn't like this. I didn't want to threaten him. I'd rather he'd go along with this willingly, but I guessed I had to squeeze him a little.

"Think about all of the things you know. Things you could never prove, but you know. And now think about whether I'm about to take no for an answer."

Bertrand eventually brought out a key which he used to unlock the shed by the side of the house. He walked in and turned on the lights. There was a lightbulb which had to be turned on by pulling a string, the rest of the shed was similarly crude. There was a single window high up, there were a few tables covered in saw dust, and the various tools hanging from the walls were beginning to rust.

"Does your housekeeper have a key for this place?" I asked.

"No, she'd have to use this one," Bertrand said quietly. "And she's off tomorrow so she won't be here anyway."

I spotted a large blanket folded on one of the tables.

"I'm going to put him there," I said, pointing to the table that was underneath the only window.

If someone were to peer from the outside the table would block the body.

"And then cover that whole table with the blanket," I said.

I went back to the car and pulled Martin out of the trunk. I slowly dragged him into the shed and rolled him under the table. Once we covered the table with the blanket we went back outside. That's when Bertrand turned to me.

"I will let you keep him here for one day," he said. "When the sun goes back down, I want you to come back and take him away and do whatever you have to. And then you and I are done."

I had half-expected him to make demands.

"Done?" I asked.

"Yes. We're done. I'm not passing along any other information to you."

I gave a quiet laugh.

"Bertrand, your information is valuable-"

"Oh, is it?" he asked, raising his voice. "Because I told you that McKinnley was abusing his wife, and what did you do about it? Nothing! He killed her! You knew he was going to, and you stood by and did nothing! Why do you have me pass on information if you just choose to ignore it?"

"I don't ignore it," I hissed. "And keep your voice down."

But Bertrand wasn't backing down.

"Come back tomorrow night, take him, and never come back."

He turned around and began walking away.

"Bertrand," I said. "The key."

He stopped and looked at me.

"What?"

"I need the key," I said, stretching my hand out. "I can't have you getting a guilty conscience and showing what's in the shed to anyone."

Bertrand hesitated, but after a few seconds he walked over and handed it to me.

"Tomorrow night," he repeated. "I want him gone."

And then he began to walk away again.

"The work you do for me has made this town a safer place, Bertrand. Whether you believe that or not, I don't care."

All I wanted to do now was sleep, but I knew that Dennis had already started interrogating Benjamin on his own. I owed it to him to go back to the station and try to help salvage the mess I had created. As I started the car I saw that Martha had called me twice, I had forgotten to reply to her Happy New Year text. I figured I would call her back now as I drove.

"Happy New Year," I said.

There was silence on the other end, aside from her breathing.

"You there?" I asked.

"I'm here," she said. "Where have you been all night?"

"Working," I said.

I could already feel an argument about to start but tonight was not the night to push me.

"Working," Martha repeated. "So you've been at the station the whole time?"

"No, I've had to drive around a bit," I said.

I wondered what would happen if I sent her a picture of my broken nose and then turned my phone off for the rest of the night.

"How are the kids?"

"They're asleep now," she said. "They were asking about you earlier."

Now came the difficult part.

"Listen... I think you should all stay there for a few days," I said.

"Why?"

Instantly Martha's annoyed tone vanished. The moment I was telling her to stay away instead of trying to convince her to come back, she knew something was wrong.

"Just... things here might get a little messy. So just stay with your parents. I'm sure they'll be happy to spend time with the kids a bit more."

"Is everything alright?" Martha asked.

"I can't talk-"

"About it over the phone," she finished. "Right. Well, I guess we'll stay here until we're given permission to come back."

"Martha," I said sternly. "You have no fucking idea the night I've just had."

And I hung up. She could sit with that last sentence for a while, I didn't have time for this. As I pulled into the station I leaned up and looked at myself in the rearview mirror and saw just how terrible I looked. But that was good. Benjamin would ask what happened to my face and I would tell him-

TWENTY-ONE

"Your son did that."

I was sitting in the interrogation room across from Benjamin. He was wearing a baby blue suit that he had obviously been in at his house party when Dennis came to arrest him. Benjamin had actually combed his hair, which he seemed to only do on special occasions. Now it made him look like a medieval peasant, which was still an improvement from before. He looked tired, but he was still doing his best to look as though all of this amused him.

"What have you told him?" I had asked Dennis when I arrived at the station.

"Just that he's under arrest for the disappearance of Dr. Rah," Dennis replied. "He says the name sounds familiar, but he doesn't know the doctor. When he asked why, I told him this is in connection to Martin, who would be arriving at the station shortly."

I sighed.

"So what, do we say he got away?"

"Well we certainly don't tell him the truth," said Dennis.

I scratched my head, trying to think of what to do. I was still trying to figure out how I would dispose of Martin's body, and now I needed to tell Benjamin a lie that would match with that.

"Let me take a crack at him," I said.

Dennis hesitated.

"That's not a good idea."

"You need to rest," I said. "I know you, I can tell when you're stressed and can barely hold it together."

Dennis had been tapping his fingers together rapidly, something I noticed he did when he needed a cigarette.

"Go grab yourself a coffee," I said. "Grab me one too, while you're at it."

"No, I want to see what he says," said Dennis.

"When I walk into that room, the first thing he will ask is what happened to my face. When I say that Martin did this, he'll laugh in disbelief. You can go and bring those two coffees and he'll still be laughing when you get back."

And sure enough I was right. As soon as I said the words Benjamin sat quietly for a second, then his face twisted as he struggled to contain the air in his mouth. And then he burst out laughing. I did nothing. I sat, waiting for him to finish. Let him have this. Let him have this moment. Let him imagine the sight of his son hitting me in the face and not realizing that it cost him his life.

"I'm sorry," he said.

By now he was already pressing his face into the table, gently knocking his head on it repeatedly as he tried to contain his joy.

"Wow!" Benjamin said as he straightened up. "I'm sorry. I'm sure he had his reasons, you know, kids will be kids, right?"

He giggled a bit longer before finally taking a few deep breaths.

"So, George... maybe you want to tell me what's going on here. Dennis seems to think my son was involved with some doctor who magically disappeared, and somehow this is my fault? Because everything Martin gets up to always ends up being my fault."

I didn't answer him at first. I stared at Benjamin's face, wondering how to make him crack. I knew I would only have one shot at this, and I had to work quickly before many people knew that Martin was missing.

"Do you know what Insomniak is?" I asked.

"Insomniac? That's... that's like when a person can't sleep, right?" Benjamin said, using all of the power in his brain to figure out what the big word meant.

"Yes, but I'm referring to the brand. It's a sleeping pill, well, that's what it's supposed to be. See, if you mix it with alcohol it can cause vivid hallucinations, if that's you're idea of a party."

"Can't say it is," Benjamin said. "Never know what goes into that stuff. Same with alcohol, which was why I liked making mine at home until you boys had to ruin the fun."

I smiled.

"Be that as it may, abusing Insomniak can lead to death. It's not something I would like to see plaguing my town."

"Neither would I," said Benjamin.

"We have it on good authority that your son was involved in trafficking it."

Benjamin blinked.

"You're saying our town's been having a drug epidemic? Cause I haven't seen anything."

"No, they weren't selling it here," I said. "They knew you wouldn't stand for it, so they were smuggling it out of town. By 'they' I mean your son, Vanessa, who is now dead, Jane, who is now dead, and their supplier, Dr. Rah, who is now missing, and let's face it, probably dead too."

Benjamin rolled his eyes and groaned.

"This is about that suicide, isn't it?" he asked.

"Suicide?" I asked. "You came up to me at the funeral and said it was a staged murder, you laughed at me for apparently not being able to figure that out."

Benjamin's mouth slowly dropped open in disbelief as I spoke.

"Jesus Christ, THAT'S why I'm here? George, I was joking! I was saying that to fuck with your head, because that's my idea of fun."

"Yeah well, trying to sabotage a police investigation isn't something I find funny," I told him. "So here's where we are. We have a dead girl whose killer we still have not found. We have another girl dead by suicide who implicated your son as the killer, and as the ringleader of a trafficking operation, and we have a doctor who confirmed this and then vanished into thin air."

"All circumstantial evidence," said Benjamin, who was no longer smiling. "The doctor could have told you the sky was green, we couldn't confirm whether he said that now, because he's gone."

"But see, here's the thing Benjamin," I said, leaning forward. "I know you. I've known you for a long time. I've arrested you and your son countless times, and you have never, ever stepped in to save him when you knew he fucked up. You let him lay in the bed he made. And despite our disagreements, I do respect that, really."

Benjamin seemed uneasy, as if he were unsure if I was mocking him.

"My point is you seem to have no problem with your son being a criminal, just as long as he's smart enough not to get caught."

There was a long pause as I waited for Benjamin to say something, but he didn't.

"You can nod your head in agreement, that's not incriminating," I said.

"Sure," said Benjamin, still weary of any tricks. "Let's go with that, not the worst assessment."

"And it's not like this is the first time Martin has been involved in trafficking, he's done this before. But you put a stop to it, because you didn't want this happening in Appleton."

Benjamin smiled oddly.

"I put a stop to it..." he said slowly. "because it was wrong. It didn't matter whether it was happening here or somewhere else."

He spoke in a weird tone, as if he wanted to indicate that while I was right, he didn't want to admit that was the reason.

"Fair enough," I said. "But the fact remains that Martin got involved in trafficking again, except now they were exporting it to some far away city so the hookers and homeless people could all get fucked up together. However, according to the recently-deceased Jane's note, Martin wanted to start selling here. And apparently the girl had a problem with this. But Martin's not one to be deterred by someone telling him 'no.' Because we've already found our first victim of Insomniak overdose here in Appleton."

That seemed to surprise him.

"What are you talking about?" he asked.

"McKinnley. They found him in the woods, he had this shit in his system. I don't blame him though, he must have been really upset after his wife died just days earlier. A death which, I will let you in on a secret, is starting to look more and more suspicious. So the question is... did you know about Martin's operation and did you know he was starting to sell here?"

Nothing. He said nothing for the longest time.

"I don't know what you're talking about," Benjamin said after a minute. "My son's not involved in any illegal activities."

"Okay," I said politely.

And I stood up.

"Where are you going?" Benjamin asked, his tone suddenly changing.

"This is boring," I said. "I told Dennis it doesn't matter what you knew or didn't know, in fact, we just arrested you as a precaution. We have Martin in the next room and I'm sure he'll start singing whatever I want him to."

Benjamin scoffed.

"You think you can sway me that easily? Play me against my son by implying he's about to do the same? Come on, George. You'll have to do better than that."

I smiled. He wanted me to do better? Then I would.

"I imagine it must have been embarrassing for you to get arrested at your party in front of all of your friends," I said. "Or maybe it wasn't. Maybe you enjoyed the show, you could appear as the harassed victim, oh poor Benjamin, the police just won't leave him alone. Either way, I appreciate that you made it easy. Your son was a bit more challenging. First, his bodyguard opened fire in a night club, which is already a crime, does he work for Martin, or for you? Hopefully not for you. But anyway, then your son gave us a little chase."

I reached into my pocket and pulled out my phone. I swiped a few times until I reached the picture I had taken of the remains of Martin's car. I turned my phone and watched in satisfaction as Benjamin's eyes widened.

"My car got pretty beat up too, but it's still driveable. This one? Not sure. Then we had to chase him on foot, which at my age is a bit difficult. That's when your son gave me this," I said, pointing to my nose.

Benjamin's face was a mixture of emotions. Anger at us for crashing into his son's car. Annoyance at Martin for running from the cops instead of just giving up. Fear as he realized that Martin was really in a lot of trouble. But there was one emotion that he wasn't showing.

"I've noticed you no longer think my broken nose is funny. I appreciate that, because this fucking hurts. A lot. But you know who's in more pain than me? Evan."

Benjamin blinked. He seemed to have completely forgotten about Evan until I said his name.

"Do you want to see his bullet wound? I have a picture of that too," I said.

I was doing my best not to smile. I had never seen this look of hopelessness in Benjamin's eyes. All the times we had been in this room together, it had always been a joke to him. Now for the first time it was serious.

"So your son is in the next room probably shitting his pants knowing that he's going to prison for shooting a cop. Or maybe he's still in denial and yelling 'my father, my father,'" I raised my voice to an obnoxiously high pitch as I imitated Martin. "hoping that you will get him out of this. But you can't. Martin evaded arrest and assaulted two police officers and he's going to prison for a very, very long time."

I turned and walked over to the door. I grabbed the handle and waited a few seconds.

This was the dramatic effect I needed. I looked back at Benjamin. There was a look of intense concentration on his face. He was already trying to figure out how he would weasel his way out of this one.

"Unless of course, we agreed to drop the charges," I said. "But why would we do that? Why, unless he agreed to plead guilty to the lesser charge of drug trafficking. I think we could work that out. Maybe throw in a few conditions, like a written testimony where he names all his co-conspirators, both living and deceased. That does leave the unanswered question of who killed Vanessa and nailed her to a sign. Why would Martin want assault charges dropped and then admit to a murder? Well, it's possible that Martin himself didn't commit the act. He instead asked his well-connected father to clean up the mess for him."

It wouldn't have surprised me if Benjamin had started throwing up on the table as I said this.

"Come to think of it, didn't that same father tell me that Martin's other accomplice didn't commit suicide, instead she was murdered? Well, now we have consistency. Maybe once his father was finished dealing with Vanessa, he dealt with Jane too. I mean, there's no way Martin could have killed her, he was actually in this very room when she died."

And I walked out of the room. Dennis was standing there, holding the two coffees, his hands shaking. I quickly grabbed mine before he dropped it.

"That was..." he blurted out. "I don't even know what to say."

I drank the entire coffee in one go. And then I smiled.

"I feel really alive right now."

INTERLUDE

"It was a beautiful night, all things considered," I told Xander, trying to contain my smile. "When Dennis told me a few minutes later that Benjamin had asked for a lawyer, something that had never, ever happened before... that's when I knew we had him."

"I mean... it's impressive," Xander said, looking completely stunned. "But when you were saying that to Benjamin, did you realize how many different ways that could have gone wrong? You didn't know where Martin was, he could have gotten to the lawyer already."

"You're right," I said. "We had no idea what happened to Martin, but I liked to imagine that he was walking through their house yelling 'Dad help!,' not realizing that we had gotten to him already."

I laughed.

"Sorry," I said. "It's... if you knew him, you would know how satisfying this was. But forget Martin finding the lawyer, the lawyer could have shown up at the station to advise Benjamin and could have said 'I'd like to see my other client first,' and we'd have to admit we were bluffing about Martin being in the other room."

"And the lawyer didn't think to do that?" Xander asked incredulously.

"To his credit, Benjamin realized immediately that I was trying to play him and his son against each other, but that was before I told him that Evan had been shot. I made it really clear that one of the Neros was going to prison. Now, as for this lawyer, Werner, I think his name was. Well, we had only met him the one time, a few days earlier when Evan tried to assault Martin. But I figured if anything, he was employed by Benjamin. Martin probably wasn't paying the lawyer anything. So... I gambled that in order to save his own ass, Benjamin would tell his lawyer not to represent Martin. If the lawyer talks to Martin first then Martin might be able to negotiate a deal first. Benjamin was in a hurry to save himself, and because of that he failed to cover all the bases."

"I just can't believe that someone would give up their own kid like that," Xander said, shaking his head.

"I know," I said. "It sounds messed up, and it is. But you have to understand that Benjamin was a proud man. Now, you might wonder, what is there to be proud of when you're a petty criminal? Well, the thing is, he got to where he was all on his own. No one helped him, no one saved him. And he raised his son to be the same way. As I said earlier, Benjamin would defend his son from bullshit charges, but if Martin legitimately fucked up, then he was on his own. And that's what happened here."

TWENTY-TWO

"State your name for the camera."

Dennis wanted this filmed. I guessed he was as happy that we had finally outmaneuvered Benjamin as I was.

"Benjamin Nero," Benjamin said.

I wondered if the camera would pick up the sound of his lawyer sighing just out of frame. Werner was a small man in an expensive suit. He wasn't old, but all of his hair was gone, and he looked like the type of person who would buy a new sports car every year because that was the only way he could impress women.

"Do you swear to tell the truth, the whole truth, and nothing but the truth, so help you God?"

"Yes, yes, let's get on with it," Benjamin snapped.

He wanted to be out of this room. He probably wanted to smack his son a few times for the mess he had created. He began telling us of how Martin's operation had first started.

"Martin had come to me with the idea of trafficking narcotics in order to gain extra money. The reason he told me was because he wanted to know whether this would interfere with any of my own business operations in Appleton. Of course, I have no idea what he was talking about."

Benjamin gave an odd smile. He obviously wasn't going to implicate himself in anything.

"Martin apparently took that to mean that he could do this, just not in Appleton. So he used some of his connections to smuggle them out of town."

"So you were aware that he was doing this?" Dennis asked.

"I was," said Benjamin. "And you want to know why I didn't report this to the police. Fair question. I was curious to see how long he could keep this going until he inevitably fucked up and was caught. Let's face it, even if he hadn't told me he was doing something illegal, I could easily figure it out. His friends come over in the middle of the night, secretly bringing large amounts of money, they talk about this shit in my house, loud enough so the neighbours can hear because they think it's a safe place. If I turned my own kid in this wouldn't be fun."

I clenched my fist. One of the conditions had been that we couldn't charge Benjamin with knowing about any of Martin's activities, but still, the idea of him sitting by and letting all of this happen and now facing no repercussions was infuriating.

"You say his friends, who would that be referring to?" Dennis asked.

Benjamin scrunched up his face. I didn't know if he actually couldn't remember the victim's names or if he was just trying to be funny.

"The dead girl," he said. "The one on the sign, what was her name?"

"Vanessa Miles?" Dennis asked.

Benjamin snapped his fingers.

"Yes! That's the one," he said with a smile, as if he were remembering an old acquaintance. "The girl on the sign. So she's from out of town, but she was friends with our deceased Jane, as I recall, and Jane knew Martin from school. So Vanessa visits us periodically and Martin gives her the supply which she takes back to her town and asks the local crackheads if they want to have a good time."

"And where were they getting this supply from?" Dennis asked.

Benjamin shrugged.

"Some guy they called 'Genre.' Think he ran a store somewhere nearby."

Dennis looked at me confused. I didn't know what to think either. That was the first time I had heard that name. Then it clicked.

"Dr. Rah's first name was John," I told Dennis.

"Oh fuck, that's what they were saying?" Benjamin asked. "John Rah. Shit, that makes way more sense, I never understood it, who calls themself Genre?" he laughed.

"What can you tell us about Vanessa's death?" Dennis asked.

Benjamin shrugged again.

"No idea who did it," he said.

"Martin didn't mention that he was going to kill her?"

"You don't know that Martin is the murderer," the lawyer piped in. "That's just speculation."

"I can speak for myself, Werner, thank you," Benjamin snapped.

He turned back to the camera.

"If my son was planning on killing anyone, and that is a huge if, he would not consult me on that. That's not the type of activity I engage in."

Dennis scratched his head.

"Was anything going on between them in the weeks leading up to her death? Did they have some disagreements? Were there any changes in the business?"

Benjamin did that face again where he was thinking hard.

"The only thing I can think of is around the start of December, Martin asked me again if he could sell in Appleton. I told him my opinion hadn't changed."

Dennis nodded. That was something we could use.

"And you don't know where he was the night before we found the body? Did he go out anywhere?"

"My son's always going somewhere, can't keep track of him, can barely get him to stay home," said Benjamin. "Fact, the only time he's home is when he needs something from me. And you checked the cameras yourself, we didn't have footage from that night. So I can't help you there."

"And what about yesterday morning?" Dennis asked.

That would have been when Dr. Rah went missing.

"He was gone all day," said Benjamin. "Figured he was out with friends."

"So you don't know anything about Dr. Rah's disappearance?" Dennis asked. "Martin didn't ask you to help him?"

"Help him kidnap someone?" Benjamin asked. "No. And if he had, do you really think I would have done such a poor job? Come on."

Dennis turned to me.

"Talk to you outside for a second?"

We left the room but kept the camera rolling.

"What are you thinking?" I asked.

Dennis stifled a yawn.

"We go public. Martin was part of a drug operation that went south. His own father testified. One of his accomplices was murdered. Another is missing, probably dead. And when Martin was confronted he shot a police officer and ran away. What are you planning to do about..."

Even here he didn't want to say the word 'body.'

"I think I have an idea," I said. "I'm going to leave it somewhere not far. And then I will let someone find it."

Dennis nodded. He seemed to approve, or at least he thought this was the least shitty way to resolve this.

"So in a few hours we issue a search warrant for Martin. And then when someone finds him the case is closed."

"Yeah," I said.

Now that he said it I realized he was right. This was almost over.

"You don't seem too happy," I noticed.

Dennis rubbed his eyes.

"Guess I'm just tired. And there's also the fact that soon Benjamin will find out the truth. And his anger is something we're going to have to deal with. I suppose you don't want to just destroy the evidence and have Martin be a missing person forever?" he asked.

I shook my head.

"That already happened once with that psychiatrist. He escaped and to this day people look over their shoulders wondering if he'll be there. I don't want people to be scared of Martin's shadow too."

Dennis nodded.

"Makes sense."

He opened the door and went back inside. He turned the camera off.

"Okay Benjamin, you're a free man."

Benjamin smiled and let out a sigh of relief. Dennis left the interrogation room with the camera.

"Come on," he said.

As we reached the end of the hallway and were about to turn into the main office space, we heard Benjamin's voice behind us.

"I'd like to see my son," he said.

I turned around. And finally I let myself smile.

"He's not here," I said.

Benjamin looked puzzled.

"What do you mean, he's not here?"

"I mean we never arrested him," I said. "He managed to escape. He's probably in your house right now looking for you so you can help fix his mistakes. Thanks for the testimony though, we'll put it to good use."

Just minutes ago I had been angry that Benjamin was never going to see the inside of a prison cell. But right now, when I saw the look on his face as he slowly realized that we had completely outplayed him, I felt that this was even better.

TWENTY-THREE

I was awoken on New Year's Day by my phone ringing. I lifted my head off my pillow and saw that it was just before noon. I looked around and saw that the bedroom was empty and remembered that Martha and our kids were staying at her parents' house. My phone showed that she was calling.

"Hello?" I mumbled, straining my eyes from the sunlight shining through the window.

"Is everything alright?" she asked in a worried tone.

"Everything's fine," I said. "Why?"

"I'm watching Dennis on the news."

And then it all came back to me. The shooting in the club. The chase through the woods. Me killing Martin. Hiding his body at the Church. Interrogating Benjamin. Outplaying Benjamin.

"Oh," I said. "Sorry, I was asleep."

"Are you alright?" she asked again.

"I'm okay. I told you it was a rough night. I needed to get some sleep."

I stood up and walked over to the living room and turned the TV on.

"Do you want us to come home?" she asked.

I did want that. But I still had to properly deal with Martin's body. And then there was the looming danger of what Benjamin would do when they found the bullet in his son.

"I do," I said. "But maybe stay there another day until this all cools down," I told her.

I had the volume down so I couldn't hear what Dennis was saying, but as he spoke his head kept doing a brief tilt downwards as if he were falling asleep mid-sentence.

"Are you worried about Martin?" she asked.

"We'll find him soon enough," I said as I sat down on the couch, my eyes closing again. "He's a lost puppy without his father's help, he'll turn up soon."

There was a long pause.

"I'm sorry," she said.

"For what?"

"I know I've been... difficult lately-"

"No," I said immediately. "No, you're right, I don't pay attention to Carrie and Hope enough. I don't spend time with them, but it's not that I don't want to. This... this was a mess, I didn't want to talk about it but... when we found that first body, just the idea that that happened here..."

"Did Martin Nero do that?" Martha asked, sounding shocked.

"We don't know for sure," I said. "But probably, yes."

There was another pause. Martha was likely reconsidering her offer to bring the kids back to town.

"We'll find him," I said, trying to reassure her. "And when this is all over I'm going to talk to Dennis about maybe reassigning me. Maybe something lighter."

"You don't have to do that," Martha said.

She didn't want me to do this just because I thought it would please her.

"No, I'm getting old. I can't keep chasing murderers for much longer. Or maybe I'll just leave the force altogether."

"I think you're too young to retire," she said.

"Not by much," I laughed. "I don't know. Private investigator sounds fun. I would have scoffed at it a few years ago, but now I think maybe a change will be good."

On the TV Dennis nodded his head and turned away, indicating that the statement was over. I turned it off.

"Just promise me you'll be safe," she said.

I wondered whether I should mention what happened to my nose, but I figured that if I did that now her head would be filled with horrifying ideas of what else Martin could do to me. So I decided I wouldn't tell her until Martin's body was found and we knew the danger was over.

"You don't have to worry about me," I said.

***

When the sun went down I made my way to the church. I parked in front of the shed, where I knew I was safe from any cameras. A light went on in one of the windows in the house and I could see the shadow of Father Bertrand staring down at me. He disappeared a few seconds later and I waited for him to come outside.

"A promise is a promise," I said. "Thank you again for your help."

"Just take him and leave," Bertrand said, not even pretending to be happy to see me.

I took out the key to the shed that I had taken with me and went inside. Thankfully the cold winter weather had more or less preserved Martin's body, but there was a slight smell in the air, faint enough that maybe no one would have noticed unless they already knew there was a body here. As I approached the table under the window and reached for the blanket covering it, I once again had the silly notion in my head that Martin would be alive underneath it. But of course, he wasn't. He was still wrapped in the second blanket, the one from my car. Thankfully he had already lost the majority of his blood in the forest, and what was left had been absorbed by the blanket so none of it had gotten on the floor of the shed. Otherwise I probably would have had to burn it to the ground and the priest would have been angry about that. I dragged Martin back into the trunk of my car one last time.

"So I guess this is it," Father Bertrand said.

"I'm sorry?" I asked as I closed the trunk.

"This is it," he repeated. "We're done."

Then I remembered. He had said this last night. He had put his foot down and thrown a fit and was now trying to back out of our arrangement. He actually thought he had any say in the matter.

"No," I said.

"What?" Bertrand asked, not expecting me to argue.

"We're not done. Our arrangement will continue as it has until now."

His mouth dropped open.

"No, we agreed-"

"We didn't agree to a goddamn thing," I said. "You announced some demands yesterday, but they didn't mean anything."

I was tired and the last thing I needed right now was Bertrand being difficult.

"You're going to continue giving me any relevant information that comes through your confessional booth."

"No," he said, shaking his head. "I'm out."

I took a step towards him. Impressively, Bertrand stood his ground and didn't back away.

"I think you're forgetting that I know you were sleeping around with parishioner's wives. I don't think they would be too happy to hear about it."

"You think you can bully me with threats?" Bertrand asked. "I know things about you too!"

"Like?"

Bertrand hesitated.

"That you've known about crimes that were going to happen. You knew McKinnley was abusing his wife-"

"All hearsay," I said. "I heard it from you, who heard it from her. Was there any evidence? Not that I saw."

"You could have saved her!"

"Based on what?" I asked. "Should I have barged into their house and arrested McKinnley because someone told me his wife was scared of him? And if you did tell someone any of this, remember that implicates you as well. You would be admitting that you've been sharing things you heard in confession. First the church will excommunicate you, and then the people of this town will nail you to a cross for spilling their secrets, not to mention fucking their wives."

Bertrand pointed at the shed.

"I'll tell them about the body!"

"No you won't," I said. "You're complicit in this now. You let me keep a dead body on your property for almost 24 hours."

"You didn't give me a choice!" he yelled incredulously.

"Sure I did. You could have called the police, had me arrested," I said calmly.

"But they already knew about this, didn't they?" he asked. "They wouldn't have done anything!"

"Is that a question?" I asked. "See, you don't even know. I asked for your help and you agreed. Now you're a part of this."

"You put him in the shed!" Bertrand yelled. "You put him there and you took the-"

"I took the key?" I asked and smiled. "You think that padlock and a wooden door would have stopped the police if they knew there was a body there?"

Bertrand said nothing.

"I understand you've been stressed about this, and I do apologize for that. But our arrangement will continue as normal until I decide that I don't want it to anymore."

I got into my car and drove away before he could continue arguing.

***

The area in the woods where Martin had died was not too far from the cave where he had met with Vanessa the day before her death, the cave that the locals called the Hole. I decided that was where I would leave his body. After he was shot Martin would have ran and sought shelter there. Shelter from the cold, from us, but there would be nothing he could do to stop all of his blood draining out of him. The Hole was a deep cave, with many uneven surfaces. Some parts of the ground were smooth patches of dirt, others were piles of stones that made it easy for people to break their ankles. Even during the day it was wise to bring flashlights, and Martin wouldn't have had that with him. Deeper into the cave there were several openings in the rock formations. A step in the wrong spot would result in a several foot drop. Now that I thought back, shooting Martin was a bad idea. I could have broken his neck and then dragged him to the Hole and dropped him into one of these openings, said that he had ran in here and slipped. Benjamin probably still wouldn't believe that it was an accident, but it would have looked more natural than what actually happened.

As I walked through the woods, I kept my ears open for any sounds that would indicate someone else was out here. It was unlikely that there would be anyone, as it was freezing cold out and pitch black, but I imagined that Benjamin might have had people out looking for his son during the day. I had to keep my own flashlight off just in case there was anyone and they noticed the single beam of light in the woods. What worried me the most was that I had to leave my car by the side of the road. If anyone happened to be driving by they might wonder why the police were back out here the night after the incident. But there ended up being nothing to worry about. I reached the Hole and put Martin's body down, immediately feeling a sense of gratitude from my back. Dragging him out all the way here almost seemed counterproductive if I was hoping for him to be found soon, but it had to be done. I shone my flashlight into the cave to see if anyone was there.

"Hello?" I said.

But there was no response. Just a series of 'hello's growing fainter and fainter until they disappeared. So I picked Martin back up and carried him into the cave. About a minute into the cave I finally saw what I was looking for. There was a literal hole in the ground where the rock had split open, likely before I was even alive. I shone my flashlight down and saw that it was about an eight foot drop. I lowered Martin down into the opening headfirst and then dropped him. Finally my work here was done.

TWENTY-FOUR

Two days later a pair of hikers stumbled upon Martin's body and called the police.

I had woken up normally, no phone calls, no alarms, just naturally opening my eyes when I was rested. It was a nice change, and I wondered whether I should live my life like this more. I heard a bang in the kitchen as Martha opened and closed a drawer. They had ended up coming home yesterday, despite still believing that Martin was out there somewhere. I stood up and walked out of the bedroom. Martha winced when she saw me, which she had done yesterday several times. I had warned her about my nose over the phone and she had seemed primarily worried about whether it would have scared our children, which I assured her it wouldn't.

"Was I being too loud?" she asked.

I noticed she was doing her best to maintain eye contact and not focus on what was between them.

"No, no," I said. "It's fine."

I turned and saw Carrie sitting at the dining room table. She was reading, as she usually was, but she had been staring at me and immediately looked back down at her book when I turned in her direction. She thought she was being subtle, but she wasn't.

The three of us sat down for breakfast (Hope was still asleep), and everything seemed to be going fine until Dennis called.

"I have to take this," I said.

For once Martha didn't seem annoyed that I was prioritizing work. It seemed that an actual physical injury helped her understand that I was never being distant or secretive for fun, but rather these were the types of situations I was dealing with.

"Yeah," I said when I answered Dennis' call.

"They found Martin," Dennis said.

I hadn't told him what I had done with the body. I figured he probably didn't want to know. But now he did.

"He's dead," Dennis told me.

He was saying things I already knew, but in the unlikely event that someone was listening in on our call, all of this information had to appear new to me.

"Oh," I said, trying to think of a natural response to this news. "How?"

I could almost hear Dennis angrily exhaling. He knew exactly how, and he knew I knew.

"He was at the Hole, as the kids call it. It looks like he had stumbled into it when he ran from you and then fell through an actual hole and broke his neck."

"Oh my God!" I exclaimed.

"Yeah..." said Dennis. "Although if the fall didn't kill him the bullet in his neck likely would have."

"Bullet?" I asked.

"Mhm," said Dennis. "It would appear that one of Evan's bullets hit him. I imagine it wasn't intentional. After all, Evan had already been shot, it was dark and raining, and he was just defending himself."

"Absolutely," I said firmly. "Evan would never have done this intentionally."

"I agree."

I waited to see if he would say anything else.

"Have you told the family yet?" I asked finally.

"I have," Dennis said. "Benjamin is very upset, as you can imagine."

"Is he going to be a problem?" I asked.

"I don't think so," Dennis said.

But he had hesitated for just a second before he said that. And that was all of the confirmation I needed. Benjamin was going to be a problem. I turned and looked at my family at the table and remembered Martin's last words.

"And if he does become a problem," Dennis added. "you have nothing to worry about. Evan is the one who killed Martin."

INTERLUDE

"That last sentence," I said as I recalled that phone call to Xander. "It just bothered me. I didn't think too much of it at the time, but a few days later it made perfect sense."

"Were you relieved, though?" Xander asked. "That it was over?"

I nodded slowly.

"My hope was that Benjamin would realize he had just avoided a prison sentence by giving up his own son, and he would consider himself lucky and not do anything rash like try and avenge his son by killing the cop responsible. And there were still some loose ends. At that point I figured that Dr. Rah was probably dead, but we still needed to actually find him. If Martin had killed him the body would probably be somewhere in town."

"Here's what I don't understand though," Julie said. "The first victim was a grand display. If Martin killed the doctor too, why not do something similarly stylish?"

"I imagine at that point he was panicking," I said. "And he had known we were onto him, he was just hoping that no one would stop by Rah's workplace that day. We would have to ask Martin what his thought process was, but we can't."

"Do you think it was an accident?" Xander asked.

My hands were under the table so he couldn't see how hard I was clenching my fists. I knew what he was asking, but I wanted to hear him say the words.

"Was what an accident?" I asked as calmly as I could.

"Do you think that Evan accidentally shot Martin, or was he intentionally trying to kill him?"

I sighed and put my head down.

"I know that you researched me and this entire series of events extensively before you asked me to come on your show," I said a moment later when I lifted my head back. "So I know that you know that I have been asked this question countless times by countless people just like you, as well as journalists, and judges, and lawyers, and other police officers. I have been through all of this before, and I don't know why you think that I would suddenly change my opinion on this show."

The entire time I had been here we had been having a polite conversation. Despite how grim the subject was, I tried to make the story at least somewhat entertaining. But now the facade was dropped. They were fools if they thought they could catch me off guard with any of their questions.

"So you stand by your statement from before?" Xander asked, his eyes narrowing in curiosity.

"Evan was lying on the ground, already shot, and Martin was pointing a gun at him, intending on killing him. Evan firing back was a primal instinct of self-defence. Did he intend on firing a bullet into Martin's neck? No, I don't think so."

"But given Evan's prior history-" Xander began.

It took all of my strength not to slam my fist on the table.

"His history is irrelevant. In fact, now you're starting to sound just like Dennis, who took Evan's history as an excuse and ran with it. And look where that got him."

TWENTY-FIVE

Dennis had advised me to stay home that day. He doubted that anything would happen, but he was planning for a worst case scenario. Benjamin might try to get revenge on either of the two cops who tried to arrest his son the night he died. Dennis had first tried to convince me to bring my whole family to the station, where we would all be safest, but I told him that bringing them all there would only scare them. They would know something was happening. So instead I stayed home with them. Evan had been discharged from the hospital the day before, and he came to the station. He lived alone and didn't have a family to protect, so the safest place for him would be with the rest of the cops.

I spent the whole day doing regular tasks, trying not to think about any horrifying scenarios that could happen. I imagined Benjamin coming to our house and me having to execute him in front of my family. I tried to imagine the looks on their faces and decided to never try to picture that again. First I took down our Christmas lights, later I built a snowman in the backyard with Hope. I tried to bake something with Martha until she got annoyed that I wasn't following her instructions and I left her to finish it alone. In the late afternoon I got a call from Dennis. I anticipated the worst.

"Anything happen?" I asked.

"Everything was fine," he said. "But we need to talk about something."

"Oh? What is it?" I asked.

"It's... it's better if we discuss in person. Do you mind if I drop by?"

I was a little surprised. Dennis hadn't visited my home in years, not that I didn't invite him. But I was suddenly worried about what he needed to talk about. Maybe this was the real reason he had wanted all of us at the station today.

***

Dennis arrived in front of our house about half an hour later, and to my surprise he brought Ross with him. Ross remained sitting in the passenger seat of the car as Dennis got out. He looked like he had finally gotten a good night's sleep after all the time he spent outside of Jane's house, but he seemed just as puzzled as I was about why he was here.

"Everything okay?" I asked.

Suddenly my heart began thumping. Something was definitely off.

"I told you we needed to talk, but I'd rather not do it in your house. Or anywhere there are people," he said quietly. "But I didn't want your family left alone, so Ross is going to stay here. That okay?" he asked.

"I... sure," I said.

I walked back into the house to grab my coat and assure Martha that the police car in our driveway was nothing to worry about. A minute later I was back outside.

"Come, let's walk," Dennis said.

I followed him onto the street and we walked past several houses before we finally started talking.

"Are you going to tell me what's wrong?" I asked.

Dennis looked past his shoulder. There was nobody there.

"Your... arrangement with Father Bertrand..."

Oh Christ, the priest had talked. Dennis had never once brought Father Bertrand up since I first told him about the arrangement. He had preferred to never know the details.

"What about it?" I asked, trying to remain calm.

"It's not illegal," said Dennis. "But it is unethical."

"For him, not for me," I said.

And that was the truth.

"I'm just gathering information from a source," I said.

Dennis exhaled.

"Yeah, you can tell yourself that, but the fact remains that the people trust you and you are manipulating someone to give up their secrets."

I was about to argue but Dennis raised a hand.

"The ethics of it isn't what I want to discuss. My point is that, even though it's wrong, you have a justification for it, that one day you might potentially save lives due to something Bertrand told you that you otherwise wouldn't have known."

I nodded, even though this 'some day' had already happened. But Dennis didn't need to know that.

"We..." he paused and looked over his shoulder again.

Dennis looked scared.

"We make sacrifices. Sometimes we have to break our own moral codes for the greater good."

"I suppose," I said slowly. "I only use Bertrand's information to help people, I would never spread secrets out of malice-"

"I don't think you would," Dennis said quickly. "Again, whether it's right or wrong isn't the point. I'm coming to you now because I think you are the only one at the station who will understand why I've done the things I've done."

"What are you talking about?" I asked.

Suddenly I wished I had brought my gun. It was silly to think I would need it, but I got a strange feeling Dennis was about to tell me something that I wouldn't like.

"I..." he stopped and turned to me, and his eyes showed something that might almost resemble shame. "I have a similar arrangement with someone," he said.

"Who?" I asked.

I hated that I guessed who it was a second before he told me.

"Benjamin," he said.

I stopped in my tracks. I didn't know why he was telling me this.

"What do you mean?" I asked.

I tried to maintain eye contact with him but I was tempted to glance around. I was sure that from here I could still see our house. I could run back if I needed to.

"Why do you think there are so few murders in Appleton?" he asked.

I thought for a moment.

"Because it's a boring town with boring people?"

"No, I'm being serious," he said.

"I don't know," I said, shrugging. "I guess the people here are content and don't feel the need to kill each other?"

Dennis continued walking further down the street and I followed him, still unsure where this conversation was heading.

"Benjamin believes that people should be allowed to have vices that don't harm others. So if someone wants to drink till they can't stand or gamble their life savings away or fuck a hooker, who's consenting, of course, then why shouldn't they be able to? There's not much to do here, so you have to find a way to have fun, it's the only way to stop yourself from going crazy. At least that's how he described it. He said that since most of the losers in the town tend to gravitate towards him they tend to listen to what he says. So he can keep them in line. And that's how our town stays safe."

I was confused.

"Is this you talking, or him?"

"Him. But he's right," said Dennis. "He came to me and said we could work together. He can control the more unstable people in town, like his son and his friends."

"And what does he get out of all of this?" I asked.

"We leave him alone," said Dennis. "We let him and his friends have their fun and turn a blind eye to any of their mischief, since they won't actually be harming anyone."

I stopped.

"I'm sorry, so you're saying this whole time the reason we never threw Benjamin in jail for anything was because he's been paying you off?"

"He has not been paying me off," Dennis snapped, stopping in his tracks. "He has been transparent with me to make my job easier."

I didn't know what to think of that.

"You realize what you're admitting to right now?" I asked him quietly. "Benjamin is a known criminal, and you're telling me you've had a working relationship together, you've been scratching each other's backs?"

"I did what I had to!" Dennis hissed quietly. "I've been keeping this town safe!"

"Is this why Benjamin never asks for a lawyer?" I asked, suddenly connecting everything in my head. "Because he knows you'll just pull some strings?"

Dennis looked disappointed.

"I thought you'd be more understanding," he said. "I'm not proud of what I've had to do, I wish there was a way for me to keep Appleton safe the proper way, but if I have to sacrifice my integrity to keep people alive, then that is a fair sacrifice."

Right now I didn't know what I was supposed to do. I could have just been honest and told him the truth. Told him that I had made sacrifices too, sacrifices that would have horrified him, all in the name of the greater good, but I couldn't tell him that. I still needed to know what this was headed towards.

"Why?" I asked.

"Why what?"

"Why are you telling me this? Why now?"

Dennis looked down at the ground and gently kicked some of the gravel on the road.

"I trust Benjamin," he said.

I rolled my eyes.

"No, not trust," he said quickly. "Trust is the wrong word. But... I believe him. We've had this relationship for years now and it has been beneficial. So when he tells me something I believe him. It would be detrimental for him to lie."

"Okay..." I said.

Believing a word that Benjamin said was a terrible idea, but I wanted to see where Dennis was going with this. There was suddenly a bang and we both turned towards the nearest house. The owner had just stepped out for a smoke.

"Come," Dennis said, gently grabbing me by the elbow and pulling me away.

My street eventually sloped downwards, leading to an intersection at the edge of the forest. We kept walking until we got near the intersection. There were actually streetlights here, so now I could get a better look at the guilt in Dennis' eyes. Or was it something else?

"Do you remember when I visited Jane's parents after she died?" he asked.

There was a weariness in his expression, which was strange. I got the feeling like he was afraid to tell me something. But what? What could be worse than what he had already admitted?

"Yeah," I said.

"I gave them the letter. The one we found by her body," he said. "I wasn't going to... imagine finding out your child had taken their own life... and imagine having their final words written down and having to read them and understand the thoughts that went through their mind at the end. But the worst part was that in that letter she admitted to being a criminal. I didn't know if I could put them through that, it would destroy them."

I didn't want to imagine what they had gone through. I thought of my own children but quickly put them out of my mind. That wasn't a scenario I even wanted to imagine.

"And?" I asked.

Dennis sighed.

"I went back and forth but I eventually decided it would be wrong of me to withhold this from them. They deserved the truth, as much as it might hurt. And when I gave it to them they said..."

He paused and sighed.

"What?" I asked.

I didn't know why he kept stopping. What could they have said that was scaring him so much? And then Dennis turned to me and said the worst thing he could have said.

"They said it wasn't her handwriting."

My heart sank.

"What are you talking about?" I asked.

"It's wrong," he said. "They even showed me some other things she had written. They brought out her diary, and it was different."

That wasn't possible.

"But... how?" I asked. "You're saying the note was fake? Like, someone else wrote it?"

Dennis shook his head.

"No... it wasn't completely different, but just off enough that someone who was familiar could notice. Except the signature, that was as different as you could imagine."

"I'm confused," I said. "So... did she write it or didn't she?"

Dennis looked around the intersection. We were still alone.

"Okay, imagine someone breaks into your house and tells you that they're going to kill you."

I didn't know what to think now.

"Okay?" I said.

"Now, they force you to write a suicide note, and you know that there's no way out of this, you can't escape, you can't convince them to show mercy. You're going to die, and it's going to look like you offed yourself, and this person is going to get away with it. Unless..."

"Unless what?" I asked.

"Unless you make the note look slightly off... I suppose you could try to put some code word or something, but if the killer is smart they'll be looking out for that. So the only thing left to do is alter your handwriting so that someone who was close to you would notice that something didn't add up."

"You're saying that-"

"Jane was murdered," he said.

I blinked a few times. I didn't know how to react. What did he expect me to do? Do I agree with him? Do I tell him it's insane? Do I ask who he thinks did it? And then I remembered something.

"Oh God," I sighed. "He said it."

"What?"

"Benjamin. He came up to us at the funeral and said it wasn't suicide and he laughed that we hadn't figured it out."

I turned around and screamed into the darkness.

"He fucking said it right to our faces!" I said, spinning back around to Dennis. "He-"

"George," Dennis interrupted. "It wasn't him."

"What?"

"As I've explained to you, Benjamin and I don't keep secrets from each other," he said. "When I realized Jane was murdered my first thought was Benjamin was cleaning up his son's mistakes. But he told me it wasn't him."

I shook my head.

"Oh, it wasn't him, then it was one of his people-"

"No," Dennis said firmly. "And it wasn't Martin, because he was at the station that whole night."

I blinked.

"Then I'm lost," I said.

Dennis sighed.

"Who else suggested that there was something off about Jane's death?" he asked.

I had no idea what he was talking about. Then after a few seconds it all fell into place. My eyes widened and Dennis nodded, realizing I had figured it out.

"Wait, that makes no sense."

"I know it sounds ludicrous," said Dennis.

"Are you actually suggesting that Evan killed Jane?"

Dennis frowned, realizing that it was going to take some work to convince me.

"Do you know why Evan was moved to our town?" he asked.

"I do. He told me."

"What did he tell you, exactly?"

I blinked. Did Dennis actually know the story himself? Was he trying to get it out of me?

"He said they were going after some guy... had a Biblical name, I think?"

It was Moses.

"Abraham, maybe?" I said out loud. "And they managed to flip one of his people. But he died right before the trial."

Dennis nodded.

"The name was Moses, not Abraham," he said.

So he knew that part.

"Did Evan tell you how Moses knew this person was ratting on them?"

I sighed.

"Evan told a journalist that he thought he could trust."

Dennis stared at me, trying to figure out whether this was really all I knew or if I was withholding something.

"And why would he share this information?" he asked.

I hesitated.

"He told you," Dennis said. "So I don't know why you're being so evasive-"

"Because he was cheating on his wife with her," I said.

I didn't know why I felt embarrassed. This was Evan's secret, not mine.

"And then when he found out his witness was dead because of her, he beat the shit out of her, went to jail, and then Moses pulled some strings to have him released and transferred here."

I paused, waiting to see if Dennis had any more remarks to make.

"And what's your point?" I asked.

Dennis narrowed his eyes.

"Beat the shit out of her? Is that how he described it?"

I frowned. Actually, now that I thought about it, Evan hadn't mentioned exactly what he had done.

"No... he just said..."

I tried to remember what he had said. And then it all clicked.

"He-" Dennis began.

"Killed her," I finished.

My heart dropped.

"That's what Martin was talking about. He called Evan a murderer right before..."

"Right before he got murdered," Dennis said.

He smiled grimly as he realized I was beginning to piece it together.

"'Beat the shit out of her' is technically correct, but I'm guessing he didn't mention that she died from her injuries. Whether he intended on killing her or not is debatable. It was only thanks to Moses that he managed to escape prison time. Evan inadvertently kept Moses out of prison by revealing who the source was, so Moses returned the favour by destroying evidence, paying off the right people, and getting the charges reduced to manslaughter. The official story stressed the fact that this journalist had mob connections, and left out the part that she and Evan were having an affair. 'Cop Kills Journalist' is a bad story, 'Cop Kills Journalist Who Was His Mistress' is worse.

But their chief of police still thought it was risky keeping Evan around, so he called me about a favour I owed him. Have you noticed that this pile of bodies only started appearing when Evan came to our town?" he asked.

"That doesn't mean anything," I said. "That could just be convenient timing."

"Convenient timing," Dennis repeated. "Yeah. I suppose it could. Tell me something, now that we're here all alone with no one around. Did Evan have to pull that trigger when you were out in the woods?"

I didn't know what to say. Do I just admit that I was the one who killed him? No, I couldn't do that, not now that Dennis had already admitted that he was working with Benjamin. If I told him the truth, and he told Benjamin, my family could now be in danger, and Evan's sacrifice would have been for nothing.

"Yes," I said. "There was no other way. He would have killed both of us. He shot first, let me remind you."

"I believe you," Dennis said. "But it doesn't negate the fact that there is a trail of bodies wherever Evan goes."

"No," I said, shaking my head. "I don't believe he killed Jane."

"The note is fake, George," said Dennis. "Her parents said so, the handwriting was off. And I think they'd be a pretty good judge of that. I believe them."

"You believe them," I said. "You also seem to believe that Benjamin didn't kill her because you two are apparently buddies and buddies don't lie to each other."

I could almost hear Dennis' teeth grinding against each other. This conversation clearly wasn't going the way he expected.

"You're going to judge me for the decisions I've made?" he asked. "Cause I don't judge you. I wonder how Martin's body ended up in the Hole? You threw him in there like he was a piece of trash. Forget the type of person he was, that was still someone's kid."

"Yeah well that 'kid' caused nothing but misery in this town," I said.

He wasn't going to make me feel guilty about Martin.

"Or are you saying that wasn't his fault either?" I asked. "Maybe Evan's responsible for everything. Maybe he killed Vanessa and Dr. Rah, too?"

Dennis scowled.

"I appreciate that you're taking this seriously," he said.

"How can I take this seriously?" I asked. "You're telling me that the person we've been chasing this whole time is one of us, based on what? The word of a known criminal, and the fact that someone's handwriting was slightly off when they were in the middle of overdosing on pills. This is nothing, you have nothing!"

I realized I was yelling. I had to catch my breath. I needed to figure something out. There obviously wasn't anything I could do to convince Dennis that he was wrong.

"Listen to me very carefully," said Dennis. "Benjamin doesn't believe that his son's death was an accident. I've already told him what you both told me, it was dark, raining, he had a gun, both of you were injured, but he won't listen. He is convinced one of you chose to just shoot him instead of taking him into custody. He asked me which one of you shot him, I told him I didn't know."

So that's where this was heading. Now Dennis had my life in his hands.

"When I tell him, there will be retribution. He will go after Evan, he will try to kill him, get revenge. And he won't even try to hide it, he'll expect me to pull strings and get him out."

"That's not my problem," I said. "You made your bed with Benjamin. You should do the right thing now. He's told you he wants to kill a police officer, it's your job to prevent that from happening."

"If I do that, he goes public with our arrangement," Dennis said.

I was stunned.

"So you're going to let him kill Evan just to salvage your own career?" I asked.

"No," he said. "There are a few ways out of this. One is you tell Benjamin that you killed his son. Lie to protect Evan."

I let the implications of that sit for a moment. Dennis was actually suggesting that I put my own family in danger to save Evan by lying, no, not lying, I would ironically be telling the truth.

"But you're obviously not going to do that," said Dennis. "So there is one other option. We make a deal with Benjamin."

"We?" I asked.

"Yes," he said. "We arrest Evan. He came to our town, discovered a drug ring and started systematically killing all of them. You testify that he executed Martin, we have the suicide note pinning him to Jane, and he probably got the rest of them too-"

"Do you actually believe that?" I asked. "Do you really believe that he's responsible for all of this?"

"He's a killer," Dennis said. "He comes here for a fresh start, a disgraced cop, and he can be the hero. And look how conveniently we stumble upon this operation. Tell me, do you really believe that Martin Nero could crucify someone?"

I wanted to say yes, just to argue his point. But I couldn't.

"No," I said quietly. "No, it seems like more work than he would be willing to do. But I can't believe that Evan would do this."

"Do you even know him that well?" Dennis asked. "We've only worked with him for a few weeks."

A few weeks, but we had almost died together out in those woods.

"I... I don't know what to say to any of this."

Dennis nodded and stepped closer, clapping me on the arm.

"Here's what I need you to do," he said. "Take the night to digest all of this. And we will discuss it tomorrow when you come in. Just know that Benjamin is angry, and he wants justice for his son. I keep telling him I don't know the details about what happened out in the woods, but I can only stall for so long."

The fact that Dennis was painting himself as the real victim in this scenario made me angry. We walked back to my house in silence, I didn't even want to speak to him. When we reached our driveway Ross was still sitting in the car where we had left him. I walked past the car and over to the front door.

"George!" Dennis yelled just as I was about to reach for the door handle.

I turned back and looked at him, trying not to appear angry so that Ross wouldn't start asking questions. And for the first time Dennis looked afraid.

"I'm putting a lot of faith in you," he said. "My life is in your hands now."

INTERLUDE

I sighed.

"You know... of all the twists and turns I experienced over that three week period, that was probably the thing that caught me off guard the most. Not the first body, not our encounter with Martin on New Year's Eve... and not the part that we'll get to in a bit. But this, finding out that someone I looked up to was cozying up to this... this waste of space, that was something I had never expected."

I looked at both Xander and Julie.

"How long have you two been working together?" I asked.

"We started the show almost four years ago, but we've known each other longer," Xander said.

"I worked with Dennis for 10 years," I said and laughed, still in disbelief after all this time. "It's... I had difficulty trusting anyone for a long time after that."

"And when he came to you and admitted all of this, did you think to turn him in?" Xander asked. "Or were you maybe worried that he was expecting you to do that?"

"Well that thought must have crossed his mind," I said. "And I was worried about what kind of contingency he might have. If I rat out Dennis, does Benjamin come after me? Possibly. I imagine he would be angry that I had burned his source. Mainly it was my family I was worried about. If I lived alone and didn't have anyone in my life and only had to worry about myself then maybe I would have done more. The other outcome I saw was that I could have just warned Evan that Benjamin was planning to avenge his son."

"That was honestly my first thought," said Xander. "But... I would say there's problems there."

"Oh, there's problems," I agreed. "First we have the fact that I knew Dennis was corrupt and instead of doing things by the books, just told Evan to wait and act in 'self-defence.' But more importantly, if I did go along with this, one of two things happens. One is that Benjamin goes to Evan's house and kills him, and my warning wasn't enough. The other scenario, what I would technically call the preferred outcome, is Benjamin goes to Evan's house and Evan... defends himself. But I worried that if this happened, Dennis would just use that to add fuel to the fire. He would point to this and say 'See? Look how easily he killed another person! It had to have been him the whole time!'"

"Was there any part of you that thought maybe Dennis was on to something when he said that Evan was the one behind all of it?"

"No," I said immediately. "Never."

It looked like Xander wanted to raise his eyebrows in surprise but he stopped himself after a second, resulting in what just looked like his face twitching.

"And when you found out about what he had done before Appleton, the fact that he murdered-"

"He was never convicted of that," I said.

I saw Xander's jaw fall open.

"I'm not defending his actions," I said calmly. "But as this is being recorded, we should clarify that the charges had been dropped."

Xander composed himself. I could almost feel Julie's smugness from across the room. They were going to take that clip and use it to further justify that I was hiding something.

"You're right," Xander said. "Not a convicted murderer, but the fact remains that he killed the journalist."

"Yes. He did," I said. "I'm not going to speak for him or try to justify what he did or give excuses. When this story, that is, what happened in Appleton, first became public, Evan told me that this would happen, that people would try to get my opinion on his... prior work history. And he made it very clear to me that he could speak for himself."

Xander nodded.

"I can respect that."

"Thank you," I said. "But even if you looked at the situation with the journalist and assumed the worst about Evan, there was still a huge stretch between that and what happened in Appleton. There were things that weren't adding up, sure. Like Dennis said, the idea of Martin crucifying someone, when we really thought about it, seemed far-fetched."

"But weren't you previously going on the assumption that Martin was a terrible person, and he might be responsible for this?" Julie asked.

"Oh, he was a garbage human being," I agreed. "But... have you ever tried hanging a painting in your house?" I asked.

They both nodded.

"By yourself?" I asked.

Xander nodded.

"No," said Julie. "I'm a little too small."

I smiled.

"Okay, so you had trouble doing it. Now imagine the painting was maybe 100 pounds heavier. And imagine you're doing this at night, outside, it's fucking freezing cold outside, and the whole time the painting is crying, screaming, and begging you to stop."

Julie went pale again.

"Yeah," I said. "If she had just been shot then I'd say 'yeah Martin could do that,' but... again I thought back to when we first found it, Evan had been telling me that the person who did this wanted her to be found."

"Evan seemed to be really good at figuring out how the person behind this was thinking," Xander said.

"Dennis would agree," I said. "Just like how Evan had immediately felt that Jane's suicide seemed suspicious. So you could force pieces to fit. Evan was really good at his job. Evan was unprofessional and seemed to find humour in fucked up situations. Evan had a history of violence. But at the end of the day, there was another suspect, one that made so much more sense. But Dennis dismissed it because he thought he and Benjamin were pals and had each others' backs, and he never for one second thought that Benjamin might be playing him. And he paid for that mistake dearly."

TWENTY-SIX

I barely slept that night. I lay awake next to Martha thinking about what I was going to do. I ran through every scenario for how I was going to handle it. In the middle of the night I thought about waking Martha and telling her everything and asking for her advice. Then I had to do my best not to laugh, because that would definitely wake her up and I would have to explain what a stupid idea I had just had. I remember seeing 3:30 on my alarm clock, so I must have fallen asleep sometime after that. When I heard the alarm go off a few hours later I thought about just taking my family and leaving. But I couldn't do that. I couldn't leave Evan alone to fend for himself. Not after he had lied for me, to protect all of us.

"Listen," I said when I walked into the kitchen. "I think today's going to be a long day at work," I said.

Martha turned to me and looked concerned. If I had said this a month ago she would have just rolled her eyes, but now that the full story of Martin had come out she was concerned.

"Is something happening?" she asked.

"Just some loose ends we have to tie up," I said. "But I think after today it's going to be safe."

354

Safe, yes. But not quiet. I knew that if things went according to plan this would probably be a huge news story, we'd be hounded by the press. And things at the office would be really tense. But we would be safe.

"Look, about what we talked about yesterday-"

I broke off when Carrie let out a yell in the dining room. I walked over and saw that Hope had taken her book and was now running with it. I sighed and turned back to Martha.

"I'll take care of them," she said. "You have to be off soon."

"I meant what I said about maybe retiring," I said. "I... I think I can kind of start to feel it taking its toll. Waking up almost feels like a workout."

Carrie stomped back into the dining room, having gotten her book back. She huffed as she took each step.

"Do you know what she keeps reading?" I asked.

I should have known the answer. All it would take would be for me to sit down beside my child and actually ask them a question for once.

"She was telling me about it yesterday," Martha said, and her tone seemed to indicate that she was having the same thought that I was.

"I know I can do better," I sighed. "I can try."

Martha smiled, something I had been seeing less and less of lately.

"Thanks," she said.

***

When I arrived at the station I was just hoping that Evan wasn't there. I didn't know if I would be able to look him in the eye and pretend that his life wasn't going to completely change in a few hours. My stomach turned when I saw him sitting at his desk. He looked cheerful and that just made it worse.

"Morning!" he said when he saw me.

"Hey," I said, already planning to say that I was tired when he asked me what was wrong.

"Sleep well?" he asked.

"Absolutely not," I said.

Just as I was about to sit down I saw Dennis standing in the doorway of his office, staring right at me.

"Uh-oh. Looks like the boss wants you," Evan said.

I sighed and walked over to Dennis. He sat down in his chair as I entered the office and shut the door behind me.

"Have you given any thought to what we discussed yesterday?" he asked.

"You want to arrest him?" I asked.

"You're still hesitating," Dennis said.

He chuckled.

"It's amazing how close you've gotten to him. Remember that first day? Him laughing out by the side of the road when we found the girl? We were both so sick of him, and now you're defending him."

"I don't think he's a killer," I said.

"Except he literally is," said Dennis. "Evan has killed two people that we know of. And you know what, I think you're covering for him."

I felt a choking sensation in my throat.

"What?"

"I don't think him shooting Martin was as much of an accident as you're saying. I think that you two had the situation relatively under control, but Evan couldn't help himself."

I opened my mouth to argue.

"I don't blame you," he said quickly. "You're loyal, George, perhaps a little too much, and I respect that. But we know he's killed two people. And he was really quick to point out that Jane's suicide was suspicious. Maybe he did that so when we inevitably found out it was staged we wouldn't suspect him."

"You know who else said her death was suspicious?" I asked.

Dennis' tone soured.

"I know you think I shouldn't trust him," Dennis said. "It makes sense. But the reason you say this is because you've only known about my arrangement with him for a few hours. I've built up years of trust with him, and he hasn't deceived me a single time before."

"That you know of."

"Look, you have to understand, this personality he shows off, where he just comes over and tries to be a shit disturber, it's all just him having fun. He's a character, sure, but he's not a murderer."

I didn't know what to think. There was no changing Dennis' mind. I had hoped there was another way out of this, but it looked like I had to go with my original plan.

"So you want to arrest him?" I asked.

"I do. We arrest him for the murders, the public will probably be disturbed that a cop was behind it, but he's from out of town, he wasn't really one of us. And Benjamin will not seek retribution for Martin's death. Justice will be enough."

I sighed.

"I want to talk to him first," I said.

Dennis' eyes widened.

"You're going to-"

"I want to ask him about the journalist," I said. "I need to understand his thought process, what he went through. Everything you're saying, these accusations, they all stand on the foundation that he already killed someone before he moved to Appleton. I need to hear it from him... because I don't believe that he could be behind all of this."

Dennis crossed his arms.

"Okay, here's what we do," I said. "I'll go visit Evan at home after work. I don't want him arrested here, I think that would be a fucking disaster for team morale. So I go to his house, and you follow me. Just... park around the corner or something. I'll talk to him, and if I'm convinced that he was capable of all of this, then I call you, you come in and arrest him."

Dennis clearly didn't think it was ideal, but after a moment he nodded.

"Fine," he said. "If that's what it takes to bring you on board."

***

I delayed talking to Evan about this all day. Finally, an hour before I was supposed to leave, I approached him.

"Hey, listen," I said, leaning on his desk. "Do you have any plans after work?"

"Nope," he said. "Probably just going to stay home."

"Do you mind if I swing by?" I asked. "There's something I wanted to discuss."

Evan looked puzzled.

"Sure? Something we can't talk about here?" he asked.

"No. Definitely not here," I said.

"Okay, not a problem."

Several minutes later Dennis called me back to his office again.

"We're set for tonight," I said.

"One more thing," he said. "I talked to Benjamin, let him know what the plan was."

I didn't like the idea of Benjamin knowing too much.

"He wants to be there," said Dennis.

"No. Absolutely not," I said.

Dennis raised his hands to calm me down.

"George, listen. Evan killed Benjamin's son. Now, whether it was justified or not, we can argue that all day, but in Benjamin's eyes it makes no difference. His son is dead, and Evan pulled the trigger."

I sighed. I couldn't argue with that.

"Benjamin wants nothing more than to beat Evan to death with his bare hands. He is settling for Evan going to prison."

"Settling," I repeated. "Like he's doing us a favour. We're doing this properly, going through the legal system, not that Benjamin has much respect for that."

"He wants to be there, he wants to witness Evan being put in handcuffs," said Dennis. "And I'm allowing it."

Dennis was reminding me that he was the boss, even if he wouldn't say it out loud. I had been up all night thinking of how to manage this situation, and I thought I had a solution, but now Benjamin being there was putting a wrench in my plans. I may have to improvise.

"Fine," I said. "You can bring your friend. But I have one condition."

Dennis sighed.

"Okay, let's hear it."

"Benjamin doesn't bring a gun," I said.

Dennis blinked. That clearly hadn't been what he was expecting.

"You might trust him. But I don't. If I find out that he has a gun, I will assume he's planning on shooting Evan, who, I may remind you, is still officially a police officer. You want to arrest him? We do this properly. If Benjamin tries to take control of the situation, I will react accordingly. Do you understand?"

Dennis didn't like the idea of me giving him orders, but he knew he needed me to go along with his plan.

"Fine," he said. "We do it your way."

TWENTY-SEVEN

Evan left work and then Dennis left work and finally I left work. I checked my phone just in case Martha had forgotten I would be out late and was looking for me. But there was nothing. I wondered whether I should call her just in case everything went south. But then I decided against it. I wouldn't think that way. I was going to come out of this on top. I parked my car outside of Evan's house and called Dennis.

"Just wanted to check where you are," I said.

"We're just down the street," he said.

And then I saw a pair of headlights flash for a second at the end of the road.

"See?" he asked.

"Yeah, I see," I said.

"Are you sure this is how you want to do this?" he asked.

"I need to hear it from him," I said.

I hung up and stared at my phone screen. Once I was in Evan's house there was no turning back. Bridges would be burned, but I didn't see any other way out of this. I got out of the car and walked over to Evan's front door. Evan was dressed like he had just gone out for a run, head to toe in a black tracksuit.

"Come on in," he said.

The last time I had been here his living room had been completely empty, but since then Evan had actually purchased two red armchairs and a round wooden table which was placed between them. I imagined Evan could probably go months without even requiring a second chair, and could have just bought one, but it would have been weird for only one of us to be sitting during this conversation.

"Thanks for seeing me," I said.

"Of course."

Evan turned around and headed towards his kitchen.

"Do you want water or something?" he asked.

"No. Thanks," I said.

Evan returned a moment later with a single glass for himself and noticed that I was still standing.

"You can sit, you know," he said, motioning to one of the chairs in the room.

I walked over and sat down. As I settled into the surprisingly comfy chair, I slowly brushed my thumb against my coat pocket. I could feel my phone through the layer of fabric. I knew it was there because I had just put it there, but I still had a paranoid feeling like it would suddenly vanish into thin air. And then I would have nothing.

"So what did you need to talk to me about?" he asked as he sat down across from me.

I had thought about every single thing I could say to him, every angle I could approach this. I still had no idea how this was going to play out. I took a deep breath and started.

"When we were out in the woods and Martin had my gun pointed at you he said something. He asked you if you thought you could just come to our town and kill anyone and get away with it."

Evan flushed.

"Why did he say that?" I asked.

Evan sighed and put his glass down.

"On the day we first met I asked you if you had ever killed anyone," Evan said.

I remembered.

"You said no. I also said no. But I lied," he said.

He looked down at his glass and picked it up, swishing it around as if he wasn't sure how he should act in this situation. He was probably waiting for me to say something, to criticize him, ask him how he could have done this? But nothing. I just waited.

"It was the journalist," he said finally, and he managed to gather the strength to look me in the eye. "The one I told who our witness was. When I found out what she had done, that the witness was dead because of her... I went to her apartment. I didn't mean to kill her, I didn't know what I was going to do, I think I just... I needed to understand why. She must have known what would happen if she leaked that name. And when I confronted her she just laughed. She was surprised that I was upset! She told me that the witness didn't deserve sympathy, he was a criminal just like the rest of them, and he shouldn't be forgiven for everything he had done because he had a change of heart at the last minute. And I told her, that this one person could have helped us put Moses and a dozen others like him away for years. And she just shrugged it off. Like it was nothing. She couldn't understand what the big deal was. And I thought back to the last conversation I had with him. We were in his cell, and he told me he was afraid someone would find out, and he made me promise that I would protect him. I told her this story and she laughed again. She said I was weak for having my heart strings pulled by some thug. And then something inside me snapped. I got up, I walked over to her and I hit her."

I hadn't moved this entire time. I sat across from Evan, wondering if he had ever actually told this story in full to someone. Something glistened on his face and I realized that he was doing his best not to cry.

"Do you remember your first crime scene?" he asked me. "The first time you saw a dead body?"

"I do," I said.

"People might say Appleton is quiet, but the place I came from, not so much," he said, and he wiped his eye. "I saw bodies all the time. And I realized really quickly that I had to find a way to handle this emotionally, cause otherwise this was going to fuck me up. So every time we were called to a crime scene I just always told myself 'this is some guy.' It's not someone I knew or cared about, it was just a job, a mystery I had to solve. If I didn't connect emotionally then I wouldn't stay up all night thinking about them, and I know that sounds-"

"You don't have to explain to me," I said. "I understand."

Evan swallowed hard and wiped his eye again.

"But... this only worked cause every victim was a stranger. But our witness, that was the first time the body was someone I knew. And all of this... emotion that I had buried inside me for years just came out."

He hung his head down in shame.

"I didn't mean to kill her. It... it just happened."

For a while neither of us said anything.

"What did you feel?" I asked.

Evan finally lifted his head.

"What do you mean?"

"What did you feel when it happened?"

Evan blinked.

"I..." he said. "I don't-"

"I felt nothing," I said.

And in that moment I felt as though I had suddenly gotten several hundred pounds lighter.

"When we were out in the woods," I said. "I was worried about you bleeding to death, I was panicking over how I would explain everything that happened, but the actual act of putting Martin down... I felt nothing. Not remorse, not shock, not... joy, not relief, nothing."

Evan almost looked sorry for me.

"And I didn't know, is that normal? Shouldn't I be feeling something?"

"I'm not sure," Evan said. "I suppose maybe it's different for everyone. Have you... have you tried talking to someone about this?"

I let out a laugh.

"Like whom? My wife? My kids? Can you imagine that? I can't even tell Dennis, cause he thinks I didn't do it."

"Right," said Evan.

"I don't know... maybe cause of the situation we were in, maybe that's why I don't feel bad?" I asked. "Knowing it was either him or us-"

"But it wasn't," Evan interrupted.

He stood up.

"He gave up. We could have just arrested him, even if we couldn't prove the trafficking or the murders, he had just evaded arrest and shot me. We had him. You didn't have to."

Evan was raising his voice. I could see he had been holding this in for a few days now and was letting it all out.

"Do you resent me for what I did?" I asked quietly.

"I..." he started. "No. No, I don't. I wish you hadn't, but I understand why. I guess it takes one to know one."

"Okay," I said.

Then I pulled my phone out and called Dennis.

"Who are you calling?" Evan asked.

But I ignored him.

"So?" Dennis asked when he answered the phone.

"You were right," I said.

And I hung up.

"What's going on?" Evan asked.

"There's another reason I came here tonight," I said.

"What do you mean?"

"I had an interesting conversation with Dennis the other day. I... learned some things about him."

"Like what?" Evan asked.

He was starting to get concerned.

"I think it's better if he explains," I said.

A few seconds later there was a knock on the front door.

"You should probably get that," I said, my phone still in my hand.

Evan looked alarmed but he stood up and walked over to the door. When he opened it, I knew that Dennis and Benjamin were both there. None of them could see me from where they were standing, so they didn't see me press one more button on my phone as I put it back in my pocket.

"Evening, Evan," Dennis said.

"What's going on?" Evan asked.

"Why don't we come inside and discuss this?"

"What the fuck is he doing here?" Evan asked, likely referring to Benjamin.

I stood up and crossed the room just in case Evan decided to run.

"I'm just here to talk to the man who killed my son."

There was silence by the front door.

"Evan..." Dennis said. "This will be easier if you cooperate."

A moment later Evan walked back into the living room. If Martin had come back to life Evan would not have looked more shocked than he did right now. Dennis followed him into the room, and finally came Benjamin, who was wearing a white suit, which for once was actually fitted properly.

"George!" he smiled. "So good of you to join us."

"First thing's first," I said as I approached him. "Spread your arms."

Benjamin rolled his eyes.

"Really?" he asked.

"He's unarmed," said Dennis. "I already-"

"I'm sure you told him," I said. "But as you can imagine, trust is something I'm light on right now. Spread your arms."

Benjamin gave an exaggerated sigh and then lifted his arms. I felt across his arms, then down his sides, his pockets and his legs.

"I hope your wife doesn't hear about this," Benjamin said when my hands were at his thighs.

I didn't bother responding. If he wanted to make jokes, fine. He wouldn't be laughing for long.

"Are we good?" Dennis asked when I straightened back up.

"Does someone want to tell me what the fuck is going on?" Evan yelled.

Dennis looked at me.

"Did you fill him in?" he asked.

"No," I said. "This was your idea, so you can tell him."

"Why don't you have a seat, Evan?" he asked.

"I think I'll stay standing," Evan said loudly.

He was beginning to panic. He wasn't showing it, but I saw his eyes dart to the doorway leading to the kitchen. I imagined there might be a back entrance to the house there.

"I'd like you to look at something for me," Dennis said as he pulled out his phone.

He swiped a few times and then handed it to Evan, who looked down and appeared confused.

"What is this?" he said.

"On the left is Jane's suicide note, which you might recognize. On the right is the last entry in her journal, courtesy of her parents. As you may have noticed the handwriting looks a little different."

"Yeah..." he said. "A little, yeah, it's off."

"Very observant," said Dennis. "Now why do you think that is?"

Evan looked back at the picture. And I saw it. I saw the moment when he pieced it together. He looked up at me and made a strange face that would have been a smile, had the situation not been so tense.

"I told you there was something off about how she died," he said.

"Well..." Benjamin said with a laugh. "Looks like we've got a detective here."

Evan turned to him.

"Your son was locked up when she died. You did this."

"That would be easiest, wouldn't it?" Benjamin said. "Just blame everything on me, as you always do. But unfortunately it wasn't me," he said.

"Then who?" Evan asked.

None of us answered. Evan looked from Benjamin to Dennis to me, and when he made eye contact with me and I looked away, he groaned.

"Wait..." he said. "You don't actually think-"

"Remember the first time we met?" Benjamin asked. "Do you remember when I told you I was looking forward to working with you? I knew exactly who you were. I knew before you even arrived. I saw the pictures of what you did to that girl."

He laughed.

"Now that's a crime of passion."

"That was a mistake," Evan said darkly.

"But I could use someone with that kind of drive," said Benjamin. "Now imagine my surprise when you move to our quiet little town and suddenly people start dropping like flies. You know, my son was initially scared to come to me for help."

"Sorry, we're talking about Martin?" I asked. "The kid ran to you for help at the first sign of trouble."

"When he heard one of his girls got nailed to that sign he was terrified," Benjamin continued. "Someone was coming after him, he was convinced. But I told him to just wait. The cops might spin in circles for a bit, but eventually they'd figure out who was doing this. You didn't actually think my boy was capable of doing that?"

"Are you listening to this?" Evan asked Dennis. "Tell me you don't buy into this-"

"Unfortunately I do," said Dennis. "See, Benjamin here's a real piece of shit," he said, clapping Benjamin on the shoulder. "No offense," he added hastily.

"It's fine," Benjamin smiled. "I am what I am."

"But he's not a murderer," Dennis continued. "Not in the many years I've known him. You on the other hand, you are."

"I-"

"Yes, yes, it was an accident, she deserved it, charges were dropped," Dennis waved his hand. "The fact of the matter is there is only one person in this room who we know has killed someone."

I supposed that I should have been grateful for the fact that at this moment Evan did not look in my direction.

"When I went to see Jane's parents, when I realized that the note had been coerced, that someone had killed her and in her last moments she had left a clue to point us in the right direction, I immediately thought you were behind it," Dennis said to Benjamin.

"Typical. Always using me as a scapegoat."

"I was surprised," Dennis said. "For all of your talk about letting your son face consequences for his mistakes, here you were cleaning up after him."

"Why are you guys talking like you're friends?" Evan asked, noting Dennis' weird tone.

Dennis turned to me.

"You owe him this explanation," I said.

I reached into my pocket and felt my phone, as if I were afraid it wasn't there. But it was. I hoped Dennis didn't notice the motion, but he was too engaged in telling his story.

"Benjamin and I have been... scratching each other's backs for years now," Dennis said. "That's how we keep our town safe, I let him and his friends have their harmless fun, as long as it stays that way, harmless. It's so much easier when we're all getting along."

"Wait, wait," Evan said, his jaw close to hitting the floor. "You're a dirty cop?"

"I wouldn't use that word," Dennis said. "I've had to make sacrifices, but it's all in the name of the greater good."

Evan turned to me.

"You knew about this?" he asked, genuinely sounding hurt.

"Only since yesterday," I said.

"We've built up trust over the years," Dennis continued. "So when Benjamin told me that he wasn't responsible for the Jane incident, I was at a loss as to who it could be. And then you shot Martin and it's like a lightbulb went off in my brain."

"That dipshit almost killed both of us!" Evan yelled.

He turned to me.

"Are you buying into this?"

"Do not talk about my son that way," Benjamin said angrily before I could respond. "He was a good kid. Sure, he misbehaved, but he wasn't a bad person. But you... you just couldn't help yourself, you put him down like a rabid dog because you could. You had gotten a taste of what it was like to take a life, and you enjoyed it."

"If your son had just given up he would still be alive," Evan said.

Benjamin took a step forward and I immediately moved to get in the way.

"Understand something, boy," Benjamin said. "The only reason you're still alive right now is because of him," he said, pointing at me. "The moment I knew you were the one who pulled the trigger I was ready to come here and beat you to death myself, but he insisted that we arrest you instead. I'm going to enjoy watching you get dragged away in chains and thrown in a cell for the rest of your life. It won't bring my son back, but your suffering might bring me some peace."

"This is insane," Evan whispered as he took a step back. "I had nothing to do with Jane's death. He's lying to you Dennis, he's been cleaning up his son's mess. He kidnapped that doctor too, probably killed him."

"You can blame me all you want, I have an alibi for all of it. What do you have?" Benjamin asked.

He looked around the sparse room.

"No one to back up where you were. You'll say you were at home the whole time, but you're here by yourself. No one can confirm anything. Good thing, too. I imagine having a wife would make all this murdering difficult. She'd start asking all those nagging questions about where you've been."

"Alright," Dennis said. "Enough speeches."

He looked at me and nodded. I sighed. I reached into my pocket, not the one with my phone, but my other one, and produced handcuffs.

"Oh, fuck you," said Evan.

He took another step back. His eyes darted to the kitchen again. Suddenly Dennis pulled out his gun.

"Don't even think about running," he said.

"No, this is bullshit," Evan said. "You can't actually do this!"

He looked to me, pleading silently. He had to know that I wouldn't believe any of this. Even if Dennis did, I knew the truth about what happened to Martin.

"Evan Doherty," said Dennis. "you're under arrest for the murders of Vanessa Miles, Jane Brown, and Martin Nero, as well as the disappearance of Dr. John Rah."

"No, fuck you. This isn't happening, you know I didn't do this!"

His eyes darted to me and then back to Dennis. I slowly walked over to him with the handcuffs.

"Hands in the air," Dennis said, lifting his gun a little higher.

"How can you believe him? How can you not see that he's lying to you! He's trying to frame me to get revenge for what happened to his kid."

"Hands," Dennis repeated.

By now I was standing next to him.

"Do what he says," I said quietly. "Make this easier."

Evan was stunned.

"How can you do this to me?" he asked.

Out of everything that was happening, that seemed to hurt him the most.

"I'm sorry," I said.

I closed the handcuffs around his left wrist and brought his arms down.

"You're going to let me take the fall?" he asked. "After I saved you?"

"Don't," I said.

And just as I was about to close the handcuffs around his other wrist, Evan threw his head back, slamming the back of his skull into my nose. I felt it burst open a second time. I toppled back to the ground and Evan began to move forward but just as I hit the floor I moved my foot to the side, colliding right into his shin and sending him flying forward. I turned my head just in time to see Dennis raising his gun, his eyes widening.

"No!" I screamed, raising my hand.

Dennis froze just in time.

"No," I repeated as blood began to fill my mouth. "Don't."

I clamored to my feet and climbed onto Evan, who was lying on the ground. I secured the handcuffs around his right wrist and lifted him to his feet. That's when I noticed Benjamin was laughing.

"Wow..." he said. "You look fucking terrible."

I could barely inhale without feeling my nose fill up with blood. I wiped my face with my free hand, but instantly regretted it as my thumb flicked the tip of my nose.

"Are you okay?" Dennis asked as he lowered his gun slightly, to where it was now pointed at Evan's knees.

"Fine," I said. "Don't try anything like that again," I snapped at Evan.

"Fuck you," he said. "I put myself in danger for you, and now you're going to let them put me away?"

"Stop talking," I said. "Please."

I tried not to sound desperate, but I couldn't have Evan telling them we lied about Martin, not now. We were so close.

"What's he talking about?" Dennis said.

"Nothing," I said angrily, but deep down I knew what was about to happen.

"You're taking your anger out on an innocent man," Evan said, looking at Benjamin.

"Evan, don't do this," I whispered. "Don't force my hand."

"Innocent?" Benjamin asked.

"Yeah," Evan said.

"Please-" I said.

"No, fuck you," he said. "I'm not going to prison because of you. I didn't kill Martin. He did," Evan announced.

There was silence. I had perfectly planned out tonight, and now it was about to completely fall apart.

"What's he talking about?" Dennis asked.

"Yeah," Evan said. "Martin had his gun but he had to gloat about how he had beaten us. He should have talked less and just finished the job, but he gave George enough time to get his gun back. Martin begged and tried to convince him that if George killed him you'd come after his family, so George tried to make it look like an accident, like a shit happens stray bullet, right here," he tilted his neck up since he couldn't point to the spot.

I closed my eyes and lowered my head in frustration.

"He had told Martin he had been waiting for years to do this and now shooting a cop gave him the perfect excuse."

"Don't," I said.

"And then the next night he placed the body in the cave. Where did you have it for that first night?" he asked me. "You couldn't have taken it home. So where did you hide it?"

And then he laughed.

"Oh fuck, tell me you didn't hide it with the priest."

"Priest?" Benjamin asked curiously.

"Oh, you didn't know? George has been blackmailing Father Bertrand for years. I guess that's why he went along with this charade tonight, corrupt cops have to stick together."

"Is this true?" Dennis asked.

For the first time he was looking hesitant.

"Did you kill Martin?"

I opened my mouth but Evan spoke faster.

"Yes. And I took the fall for it to protect his family."

I sighed. Benjamin looked as though veins in his forehead were about to burst.

"I want them both arrested," he said to Dennis.

"No," said Dennis. "There's no evidence to support-"

As Dennis said those words he turned his head in Benjamin's direction. And that ended up being a horrible mistake.

I quickly pulled my gun out and pointed it at Dennis.

"Drop the gun," I said.

Dennis and Benjamin both turned towards me. Even Evan tried to tilt his head away from the gun that was now right next to his face.

"What are you doing?" Dennis asked.

His gun was still pointed towards our feet. He had lowered his guard.

"I said 'drop it,'" I said.

Dennis looked confused. Benjamin shook his head and laughed in disbelief.

"George-" Dennis began.

"No, I don't want to hear it," I said. "You've been lying to me for years, letting this piece of shit run loose in our town and letting him feed you lies. You're blind if you don't see that he's behind all of this."

"What the fuck," I heard Evan whisper beside me.

I wondered whether he was regretting breaking my nose.

"George, what do you think you're doing? You're not going to shoot me," Dennis said.

I moved my hand an inch and fired a single shot between Dennis and Benjamin, which sent them both ducking to the ground and yelling in disbelief. Evan also dropped down, wincing in pain as the barrel had fired right beside his head.

"I'm not fucking around, Dennis. Now drop it!"

Dennis' eyes widened as he realized what was happening. But finally he placed his gun on the ground.

"Slide it over," I said.

He did so, the gun ending up a foot away from mine and Evan's feet.

"You really think you can get away with this?" Benjamin asked. "My son-"

"You shut the fuck up, I will deal with you in a second," I said, not taking my eyes off Dennis.

With my free hand I reached into my pocket and pulled out my phone. It had been recording from the moment they walked into Evan's house.

"Thanks for reiterating your entire plan," I said as I tapped the screen and ended the recording. "I knew if I reported you for being in bed with a known criminal you would just deny it. Good to have these things on tape."

Dennis' eyes went wide.

"You motherfucker..." he said.

I put my phone back in my pocket.

"So what?" Dennis asked. "This is blackmail?"

"Blackmail?" I repeated. "No, there's nothing you have that I want. I was just going to arrest both of you and then use this as evidence. But then you..." I brushed the gun against Evan's head. "Just had to spill the big secret, didn't you?"

"I'm sorry," said Evan, who was still recovering from the sound of the gunshot. "I thought-"

"You thought I was actually going to arrest you? You thought I believed this stupid theory that you were secretly behind all of the murders here? A theory that hinged on you killing Martin, something I knew you didn't do?"

I shook my head in disappointment.

"This was supposed to go so smoothly. But unfortunately now I have to go into damage control."

I looked at Benjamin.

"Everything he said was true," I said. "I killed your son. And Evan took the fall for me. To protect me. To protect my family. But now the jig's up."

Benjamin was now as pale as his suit. He seemed to know where this was going.

"We can discuss this," he said, slowly lifting his hands. "We can come to an understanding. My son was problematic, I know, but I'm willing to forgive and forget-"

"Dennis might believe every word you say," I said. "But I don't. I told your son I would deal with you soon."

And I shot Benjamin three times.

Dennis stumbled back towards the wall in shock as Benjamin toppled over, blood exploding all over his white suit. I stepped around Evan and picked up Dennis' gun.

"Now that that problem is solved," I said.

I walked over to Benjamin's body as he continued twitching on the ground.

"George..." Dennis said over the sound of Benjamin gasping for air. "We can talk about this."

"Can we?" I asked.

"Yes," he said, nodding. "Listen, you want to take me in, okay. I give up. But you don't have to, we can all walk away from this."

"Walk away?" I asked. "After you had me arrest Evan?"

"If you show that recording to anyone, all of the work we've done over the years goes to waste," said Dennis. "They'll comb through everything, anyone we've arrested could be set free, they'll work on the assumption that we've just been doing what Benjamin told us!"

"We?" I repeated. "No, this is your problem. I'm not going to answer for your mistakes."

"So what's your plan?" Dennis asked. "You're going to arrest me and let this maniac go free?"

I shook my head. Dennis hadn't figured it out.

"You still think Evan did all of this. You still believe Benjamin's word on blind faith?"

Dennis pointed at Evan, who was still seated on the floor, arms behind his back.

"He's the guy we're looking for, George!" Dennis said frantically.

"No, he's not," I said.

"George-"

"No," I repeated, more firmly this time. "He's not."

Neither of us said anything for a few seconds. Then Dennis furrowed his brow, deep in thought. And then a look of horror dawned on his face.

"Wait..." he said.

I shook my head and sighed.

"All because of that fucking letter. Wow."

"No, that's not possible," said Dennis.

"You were really close," I said. "So I guess congratulations are in order."

Then I raised Dennis' gun and shot him.

Evan began screaming as he squirmed away frantically on the floor, which was difficult for him as he was still handcuffed.

"What the fuck?!" he screamed.

I noticed that Benjamin's phone was in his front pocket, so I pulled it out and looked at it. Thankfully he hadn't had the same idea I had and wasn't recording any of this.

"What the fuck did you just do?" Evan continued yelling.

I straightened up and looked at him. Evan's eyes widened as he saw me in between the two bodies and wondered whether he was about to be next.

"I need you to be quiet," I said.

I pulled out my phone and called 911.

"I need an ambulance at 14 Everest Drive. My partner and I have been shot, our boss is dead. Please hurry."

And I hung up. I walked over to Dennis and checked his phone. No recording either. Mine had gone on a bit too long, I would have to fix that later.

"George..." Evan said wearily. "George, what the fuck is going on, what are you doing?"

I walked over to Evan and crouched down in front of him. By now he had backed up into the wall and looked like he was still trying to get further away from me.

"Jesus Christ, please you don't have to do this, we can-"

"Shh," I said, calming him down. "Now listen to me very carefully," I said. "Once I handcuffed you, Dennis let his guard down, he lowered his gun for just a second and Benjamin lunged at him. Benjamin grabbed Dennis' gun and killed him.

Then he turned the gun towards us to try and kill us too, and he managed to get one shot off before I got him. Do you understand?"

Evan's chin was wobbling frantically, I could hear his breathing getting more rapid.

"Do you understand?" I repeated.

"Yeah..." he managed to wheeze.

"So repeat it back to me."

"Benjamin grabbed Dennis' gun, killed him, tried to kill us, but you were faster," he whispered.

"Good," I said and allowed a faint smile. "Now let's get you up."

I pulled Evan to his feet and walked him back to roughly the same spot we had been standing in before I had first pulled my gun out. I stood behind Evan and then took Dennis' gun and pressed it against the front of Evan's shoulder.

"Wait, what are you doing?!" he asked.

"We have to make it believable," I said.

"No, please, I've already been shot once, I-"

"Evan," I said loudly. "I already told the operator we've been shot, I can't undo that."

"Oh fuck," Evan gasped, realizing there was only one way out of this.

"Don't worry," I said. "Ambulance will be here in a few minutes. We're going to be fine. We're in this together now."

And I pulled the trigger.

The bullet exploded into Evan's shoulder, before bursting out through the back and lodging itself halfway through mine. Before I knew what was happening I was falling to the ground, the weight of Evan's body pressing down on mine. The air was filled with our screams, and I felt my head begin to spin. But no, I couldn't close my eyes, I couldn't lie back and slowly accept death. I was still holding Dennis' gun.

"Easy," I said. "I need to push you off me."

Evan grunted in pain as I rolled his body off to the side. As I tried to sit up I made the mistake of pressing my right hand on the ground to support myself, which sent a wave of pulsating pain into my shoulder.

"Fuck!" I yelled, grabbing my shoulder with my other hand.

I had never been shot before. I slowly got to my feet and walked over to Benjamin's body. The whole time I had my left hand pressed against my wound. I didn't want a trail of my blood going to Benjamin's body and back, so I tried to soak up as much of it as I could in my hand. I knelt down and placed Dennis' gun in Benjamin's hand before stumbling back over to Evan and collapsing on the floor.

INTERLUDE

"You're a much braver man than I am," Xander said.

"How so?"

"If Evan had broken my nose I would have just said fuck it, they can arrest him."

I laughed.

"Yeah. I won't lie there was a part of me that thought that for a few seconds. But I get it. From his perspective we were about to throw him away for life for something he didn't do. So him acting that way made sense."

"So can you just go over what your plan was from the moment you walked into the house?" Xander asked. "Did anything change along the way, did anyone sway your opinion?"

"Dennis' theory was already far-fetched," I said. "First I needed to hear the story of what happened to the journalist. I didn't think Dennis was making it up, but I wanted to hear it from Evan himself. And what really got to me was that last conversation he had with her, where she said that he shouldn't feel bad about the witness being killed in his cell, because he was a criminal just like the rest of them. The fact that this was what set Evan off to... act the way he did, I couldn't believe that same person then went on a murder spree through our town. It just didn't make sense. So my plan at that point was simple, I needed to have a record of Dennis admitting he was compromised. Like I told you earlier, I didn't know if this went further up, or if he had some contingency plan. So I needed to have something concrete."

Xander nodded.

"Do you think that Dennis really believed it? That he really thought Evan was the killer, or was this just a convenient way for him to wrap everything up, Evan goes to jail and Benjamin is kept happy?"

I sighed.

"The note was doctored. We know that for a fact now. So even if Martin was behind everything else, he couldn't have done that."

"But why would Benjamin have her write a note that implicates his own son?" Julie asked.

"At this point we don't know how much Benjamin knew about their operation, but I'm guessing he must have realized that Martin was planning on selling in Appleton, and that was something he wouldn't stand for. Maybe he felt that Martin had gone too far and a few years in a cell would do him good. I don't know. We can't ask him."

"So the recording stops just before Evan headbutts you," Xander said.

"Yeah, I guess when I was pulling out the handcuffs I must have brushed against it and made it stop," I said. "But fortunately we already had all the information we needed."

"Do you wish you had recorded the whole incident?" Xander asked. "Would that have made the investigation easier?"

"No," I said. "Let me ask you, you've heard that recording, haven't you?"

He nodded.

"Can I ask how?"

"It's floating around on the internet, pretty easy to find actually," he said.

"Yes, I know," I said. "I didn't post that recording online, I gave it to the investigators as evidence, and somewhere along the way someone didn't do their job properly and leaked it. And I'm glad that this clip which is now circulating on the internet forever did not include Dennis' last moments, because that's not fair to him or his loved ones."

"What's your opinion on Dennis after all these years, now that you've had time to think about it?" Xander asked.

I sighed.

"I think he was a good person who made one terrible mistake. I think he genuinely believed that he could control Benjamin and keep him on a leash. And maybe to an extent that was true, but because of that he eventually developed a blind spot and Benjamin took advantage of that."

We sat in silence for a moment as Xander processed everything he had heard and he finally exhaled.

"Wow. It's a fucked up story," he said.

"Yeah, you're telling me. I lived through it," I said.

"Alright," said Xander. "We're almost done here, folks, but a few loose ends before we wrap up. How was your relationship with Evan after this?" he asked.

"Evan took a leave of absence after this incident. He was gone for several weeks, then he came back, but he didn't last long. He ended up moving out of Appleton in April, I think?"

"Did you ever see him after that?"

"Yes. We periodically bump into each other. He's doing well."

"And what about you, you stayed on the force after, right?"

"Yeah, unfortunately when your boss turns out to be compromised and then dies that kind of creates a bit of a mess in your office. The Feds ended up getting involved, they turned our station upside down to make sure that everything and everyone were squeaky clean. They offered me Dennis' job, but I said no. I had just promised Martha that I would try to be more active in our children's lives, and being chief of police would have done the exact opposite. So the Feds ended up bringing in someone from out of town to be the new boss."

"Well I admire that," Xander said. "And if you don't mind me asking, how is your family?"

"We're good," I said and smiled. "Yeah, I ended up finding ways to balance work and home a lot better after that. And to be honest, a case like that, with so many fucked up things happening, that can be draining, it's enough adrenaline and trauma to last you a lifetime."

"Can't imagine," said Xander. "Now what about Dr. Rah?"

I sighed.

"About a month after all of this a couple of guys were out ice fishing and they found his body at the bottom of the lake."

"Jesus..." Julie said.

"Yeah. Now, whether Martin or Benjamin put him there, we have no idea. My guess would be Martin, because the state that Rah's store was in indicated that this was hastily done."

"Fuck," said Xander. "That's... wow. Alright everyone, this has been our interview with Detective George Hoffman, it's been a pleasure having you on the show."

He reached out to shake my hand. I smiled and shook it but just as I was letting go Julie asked one final question.

"Can I just squeeze one more thing in?" she asked.

"Of course," I said.

"How did you end up finding out Father Bertrand was leaking information to Dennis?"

"Oh, thank you for reminding me!" Xander said. "I had forgotten about that."

"Right," I said. "So Father Bertrand passed away several years after all of this happened. I don't want to go into details, but he had been ill for some time. Now, when he died he left a will and in it he included a statement where he admitted to passing on potentially incriminating information he heard in confessions to the police force. He also confirmed that he had confessed this himself on his deathbed, but ironically the priest who took his confession kept this information to himself. Who would have thought?"

Xander chuckled.

"Anyway, Bertrand didn't list his police contact by name, just referring to them as 'a police officer,' and he said that this went on between 2002 to 2009. We did an internal investigation, but obviously there's the problem that if one of us is guilty, we might hinder the investigation, so an outside body was brought in, and they combed through everything. It was like what the Feds did after Dennis died all over again. Now, I remind you that gathering intel from the priest wasn't illegal, and even the ethics from our side were gray, at best. But after what happened with Dennis, we had to do a lot to rehabilitate our image with the public, so we didn't need this kind of scandal. So they investigated the handful of officers who had been on the force from 2002 to 2009, myself included, but they found nothing linking any of us to the priest. The conclusion that was drawn was that Father Bertrand's contact was the one other officer who had been there at that time, one who had a known history of corruption, and one who died at the start of 2010, which would explain why Bertrand had stopped."

"Wow," was all Xander managed to say.

"Yeah, it's crazy," I said, shaking my head. "Dennis had been dead for years and was still finding ways of surprising us. You know someone for years and it turns out you didn't know them at all."

EPILOGUE

"Can you pass the salt, Martha?" I asked.

The four of us were sitting and eating breakfast, something I was now insisting we all do together every day. The salt wasn't actually that far away from me, but Martha realized that if I reached for it that would strain my shoulder, and I didn't want to remind our children that I had been shot a few days ago.

"You don't have to go to work?" Hope asked.

She was still processing the idea of me being home all the time, something she wasn't used to.

"No, I get to stay home and rest for a little," I said.

"But then who catches the bad guys?" she asked.

I smiled.

"There's plenty of other people there who can do that."

Carrie was old enough that she had pieced together what had happened. According to the news report there had been a violent altercation that left one cop dead and several more injured. For now they weren't mentioning the fact that Dennis had been working with a local criminal.

"Here," Martha said, finally passing the salt over.

I looked at her and noticed how we had seemingly switched places over the last few days. Now Martha was the one who was barely getting any sleep. She kept blinking as she stood hunched over, holding the salt out, and she looked like she was about to tip over and fall asleep. Even though I assured her the danger was over, as Martin, Benjamin, and Dennis were now all dead, she didn't believe me. She was beginning to see shadows and death around every corner.

"Thanks," I said.

It was close enough that I could reach for it without triggering my shoulder. Nevertheless, I could feel Carrie watching me, on the look out for the slightest indication that I was in pain. For once she wasn't reading and had found something new to become fixated on. Martha and I hadn't told her that I had been shot, but somehow she had noticed that something was off when I moved my right arm. I had spent the last few days paranoid every time I changed that she would burst into the room and ask about the bandages on my shoulder.

"So," I said, turning to Hope. "I think we might be able to build another snowman today."

"But won't it melt like the last one?" she asked.

The snowman we had built last week had melted while I was recovering from getting shot. That was the first time Hope had experienced something like that and she had cried for almost an hour as her snowman 'died.'

"It will," I said. "But you can't focus on that. We'll have fun building it, and that's what's important. The memories."

"Should you be doing that?" Carrie asked. "Won't it hurt your-"

"Hurt my what?" I asked.

She recognized the look in my eyes and knew what it meant. Whatever Carrie knew or didn't know didn't matter, she wasn't going to say a word about it in front of her sister.

"Actually you're right," I said when she didn't answer. "Since I need to take it easy, why don't you come out and help us?"

Carrie's eyes widened as she walked right into the trap.

"You'll take a break from being locked up in your room all week."

Before Carrie could answer, the doorbell rang. Martha immediately stiffened in fear. I was puzzled. We hadn't been expecting anyone. I stood up and walked over to the window and noticed a familiar car parked outside. I sighed. I knew this moment would come, and it was time to get it out of the way.

"It's just Evan," I said, and Martha relaxed a little.

I opened the door.

"Morning!" Evan said with a huge smile.

I noticed what he was doing. This was the same thing he had done the morning we had found Vanessa's body. Evan was hiding his misery by looking overly cheerful. I knew he wasn't really happy, because I knew why he was here.

"Hi," I said. "You're up and about?"

Evan had been in the hospital for longer than me. I hadn't realized they had let him out.

"Yeah, just wanted to stop by and say hello," he said.

He peered his head in and made eye contact with Martha and the kids.

"Hi!" he waved.

They all waved back.

"Actually I wanted to talk to you about something," he said to me. "Do you want to go for a walk?"

"Sure," I said uneasily, looking back to Martha to see if she was okay with it.

She was clearly nervous.

"You guys are going to be okay?" I asked.

"We'll be fine," Martha said. "You make sure he comes back in one piece this time," she told Evan.

He smiled politely.

"Will do," he said.

I went to get dressed and made sure to grab my gun. I didn't know if I would need it, probably not, and Evan likely expected me to bring it, but I wasn't leaving anything up to chance. I put my coat on and followed Evan outside.

"So where do you want to do this?" I asked.

Evan looked across the road. There were no houses on the other side of our street, just endless trees. The forest sloped down and eventually led to a small lake.

"Might as well go into the woods," he said.

"Lead the way," I said, extending my arm out.

We didn't speak as we walked down the street and onto a small dirt path that led into the woods. Since it was winter the trees were bare, so we had to go deep into the woods before we were no longer visible from the houses on my street. Suddenly Evan stopped.

"Pad me down," he said, extending his arms.

"What?"

"Pad me down," he repeated. "Like I'm a suspect."

I sighed and went along with it. There was nothing in his pockets, nothing taped to his arms or legs, no wire. Nothing except his phone.

"Should I worry about this?" I asked when I felt his phone.

Evan took it out, removed the battery and the card and placed all three objects on the driest part of ground he could find.

"Now we can speak freely, because you know that no one will ever hear this conversation."

"I don't know why you're being so dramatic," I said.

Evan looked as though part of him just wanted to run as far away from me as possible.

"You saved my life. Twice. I understand that. If it weren't for you, Martin would have shot me, or I'd be in a cell right now for something I didn't do. I owe you my life, George, and I doubt I'll be able to repay that. I hope you're never in a situation where I have to. But I need you to be honest with me."

"Of course," I said, still pretending not to know where this conversation was heading.

Evan took a deep breath.

"Did you kill all of them?"

I figured that he would gently ease into this topic but instead he decided to jump right in.

"All of whom?" I asked.

"Everyone. Jane, Vanessa, Dr. Rah... was it all you?"

I tilted my head.

"And what would give you that idea?" I asked mildly.

"Yes or no, was it you?" he asked, not wanting to play around.

"No, no. You need to show me how you got to this conclusion," I said. "Is there a picture of me on that cute little board in your room with string connecting me to everyone else?"

I smiled and reached my arm out. Evan instinctively flinched away, but I didn't stop. I clapped him playfully on the shoulder, the one that I had shot through.

"Come on, Detective," I said cheerfully. "Walk me through your thought process."

Horror was appearing on Evan's face as he saw how casually I was approaching this.

"Oh my God..." he whispered.

"Don't even think about running," I said. "You knew the risk in coming here and asking me these things. You could have just stayed home and kept your theories to yourself. But you couldn't help yourself, could you?"

Evan took a step back.

"What are you afraid is going to happen?" I asked. "I'm being serious, talk me through how you got here."

Evan straightened up, trying to not look afraid.

"The suicide note. We know it was fake, which means someone forced her to write it and killed her."

"Okay," I said.

"All signs point to Benjamin, but Dennis said he wasn't-"

"All just words," I said.

"Benjamin wouldn't rat out his own son like that, he enjoyed watching us run in circles. That note became the only evidence we had of Martin's involvement."

"Not exactly true," I said. "Jane had already told us he was involved, hence why we had him interrogated in the first place."

"Yeah... Jane told us," Evan said in a strange tone. "Jane told us that she and Vanessa had gone to Hellhole that weekend, Jane told us she went to church the morning after, all we had was what Jane told us. You know what Jane didn't tell us? Which Church she goes to. She didn't mention that. There's several in this town. And yet you immediately went to Father Bertrand to confirm her story."

He paused, waiting for me to contradict him.

"A lucky guess," I said. "Or perhaps I remembered seeing her there myself," I pointed out.

"Perhaps..." Evan nodded. "Except you couldn't have, because when Father Bertrand came by your house for Christmas he mentioned that he hadn't seen any of you for a while. Just like Jane hadn't been there for a while. Now, why would she suddenly start going again?"

I smiled lightly. He was getting close.

"Good question," I said. "Why do people go back to a place like that if they've been away for so long?"

Evan pondered for a moment.

"Because she felt guilty about what she had done," he said. "She was a mess when she came to us, she knew that they had been destroying lives. She-"

And then Evan closed his eyes and groaned.

"Jesus Christ," he whispered. "She told Father Bertrand everything, didn't she? And then he told you."

I didn't say anything for a moment, waiting to see if he would add more.

"That's an interesting theory," I said.

Evan's eyes widened and he buried his face in his hands.

"What the fuck?" he whispered. "So you knew about all of this before we even met?" he exclaimed.

"No, not all of it," I said. "Jane didn't mention Martin Nero, but I had my suspicions. And even if it wasn't him, I doubted it was just the two girls running this show, so I needed to find a way to spook the rest of them. Vanessa was from out of town, and I didn't know when, if ever, she'd be back, so I had to deal with her first."

"You did that?" Evan said, completely stunned. "You crucified someone?"

"Let's not get into judging each other," I said. "Sure it was a much slower death than your girlfriend got, but I would argue Vanessa was more deserving."

"Jesus, George!" Evan said. "How could... that was a person, how could you do something like that?"

"It had to be big," I said. "It had to send a message to Jane and anyone else involved that someone knew, and someone was cleaning out the house. I thought it would be enough to make Jane come to us and spill everything, but she kept trying to defend Martin and wouldn't give us details about what they were doing. And I couldn't go to Dennis and tell him I knew about the operation before we had even found the first body.

So I decided we needed this in writing. We get rid of Jane and point all the fingers at Martin."

"Did he even do anything wrong?" Evan asked quietly. "Did Martin actually do anything? Please don't tell me that we killed an innocent man?"

"Innocent?!" I exclaimed. "Evan, have you seen what Insomniak does to a person when they abuse it? Think about Mrs. McKinnley. Think about her blood and brains caking that door frame. Think about how far her teeth and skull were scattered across the floor after her husband got fucked up and launched her down half a flight of stairs. Did you want to see shit like that every few days? Cause that's what was going to happen! Benjamin was right about one thing, we didn't need that here."

"But Martin didn't kill them," Evan said. "We were going to throw him in prison for a murder he didn't commit."

I shrugged.

"Look, these things rarely work out the way you want them to," I said. "By the time the dust was settled Martin was dead, and we only had Jane's testimony that he was running a drug ring, and that he probably killed Vanessa. And Benjamin was about to walk free, imagine how annoyed I was at that. Even when we were at your house I wasn't planning on killing them, I had the recording that proved he and Dennis were working together and I was ready to use that to prove your innocence. But you just had to tell Benjamin that I killed his son. And that left me no choice. He would have come after my family eventually, so I had to get rid of him."

Evan was now as pale as the snow on the ground. He tilted over slightly and stretched his arm out, supporting himself on the closest tree.

"Breathe," I said. "It's over. Everything's fine. You and I made it out."

Evan looked over at me.

"Dennis was your friend," he said. "He trusted you and you shot him for no reason."

"You think I had no reason?" I asked, unphased. "You think he would have let all of that go? He would have eventually realized it was me. He was so fixated on that fake note and the idea that you had written it, but now that he knew I had gotten rid of Martin and Benjamin, he would have noticed the pattern. He would have realized I'm a little too good at getting rid of problems."

Evan managed to straighten up.

"How long have you been doing this?" he asked. "How long have you been murdering criminals who you couldn't handle properly?"

"Criminals here are rare," I said. "I suppose we should thank Dennis for that. But it's like I told you. Justice is something we made up to convince ourselves that everything is going to be okay. Sometimes people who cause problems just have to be dealt with. You asked me about that once, remember? Why don't we just get rid of people like Martin and Benjamin, abuse our power to make the world a safer place?"

"And you said we needed evidence of a crime first," Evan recalled. "We couldn't get rid of them just cause we could."

"Exactly. And after years of not being able to tie either of them to anything, I finally had my crime. And now Appleton is a safe place again," I said. "Now, is there anything else you would like to ask me, or can we head back?"

Evan stared at me as if I were an alien. He was at a loss for words.

"No?" I asked. "Okay, then let's get going."

I turned away and took one step.

"Why are you so calm?" he asked.

I stopped and turned back.

"I could have you arrested right now, you just admitted to everything."

"You could," I said. "But you won't."

"You don't think I will?"

"You won't. Because deep down you agree with me. You told me a while ago that you thought we were more similar than you had originally thought."

Evan shook his head at that.

"I am nothing like you. You're a murderer."

"I'm not the one who was charged with manslaughter," I reminded him.

"That was different."

"How?" I asked. "How was that different? Tell me, did that woman commit any crime? She was a journalist, she was reporting, that was her job. Did she know the witness would suddenly die in his cell after she published his name? Maybe, maybe not. So it's unethical, but not illegal. You told me yourself, you agreed she would never face any repercussions for what she did. She wouldn't have gone to jail, since again, she committed no crimes. And it's not like she's the first reporter to ever sleep with a source. No, the only one of you who had actually done something wrong was you. You killed her, and you also didn't face any prison time except for what, a few days? Tell me, how do you think her parents felt knowing their child was beaten to death by the cop who was fucking her?"

Evan's eyes widened and he lunged at me. But I was ready. When he was a foot away from me I quickly punched him in his wounded shoulder. Evan screamed but I quickly pushed him into the closest tree and covered his mouth with one hand. With the other hand I pulled out my gun.

"Hush," I said quietly. "Don't make too much noise."

I pressed the gun against his stomach.

"I told you the last time I had a gun pointed at you, we're in this together now. So here's what's going to happen. We're going to walk back to my house, and I'm going to invite you to have breakfast with us, and you're going to sit and you're going to smile politely when my children ask you questions about how we saved our town together, and you will avoid giving them detailed answers when my wife shoots you a look that she doesn't want them to hear about this. Then we're going to go to the office together and continue being partners. And you will never, ever, breathe a word about what actually happened out in the woods on New Year's Eve, or what happened at your house a few nights ago. Over the next few weeks, maybe months, maybe even years, you will be asked time and time again by relatives, or other cops, or journalists, or judges, or talk show hosts, about what happened during your first few weeks in Appleton, and every single time you will tell them the same story."

I kept feeling Evan's breath pushing against my palm. I was close enough that I could see my reflection in his eyes. He was probably wondering whether that face was the last thing he was ever going to see.

"Now I'm going to remove my hand from your mouth and you're going to tell me that you understand," I said.

I removed my hand. For a moment Evan said nothing, his mouth was slightly open and no words came out.

"I understand," he said finally.

***

A few minutes later we were back on my street and I could see my house in the distance.

"Can I ask one thing?" Evan said, after not speaking for the whole trip back.

"Of course," I said calmly, my tone completely opposite what it had been in the woods.

"Dr. Rah," said Evan. "What happened to him? Or are you not going to tell me?"

I turned around.

"That wasn't me," I said. "I have no idea where he is. I imagine he's probably dead and we'll find him eventually. Martin or Benjamin, whichever one did it probably didn't take him too far away from Appleton. Like I said, these things rarely work out exactly how you plan them. They panicked and tried to hastily tie up a loose end, and that gave us the opening we needed."

We walked up to the house and I opened the door.

"We're back," I announced.

Everyone was still at the table. I turned to Evan.

"Why don't you come eat with us?" I asked in a tone that suggested this was a spontaneous decision and not something we had rehearsed. "We have enough food, right?" I asked Martha.

"Oh, no. It's okay," said Evan, lifting his hands.

All part of the show.

"No, come, I insist," I said.

I walked back over to the table and sat down in my spot. Evan joined us a moment later.

"Are you alright, Evan?" Martha asked.

"Yeah, I'm fine," he said. "They let me out of the hospital last night-"

"No, it's just... you look like you're worried about something."

She noticed it. And she was wondering whether the danger really was over. Evan looked in my direction and I smiled at him.

"No," he said. "Everything is fine."

Acknowledgements

As always, I have to thank Mom, who has been my biggest supporter over the last few years, and the first to read any project that's done. If she wasn't always asking when the next book is going to be ready, I probably still wouldn't have finished any of them.

And I have to thank S. V., who once again served as my editor and convinced me that my stories were worth telling.

Town of Liars

About the Author

M. B. Whitehill was born in Southern Ontario, where he has lived his entire life. In 2020, after years of starting and stopping, he finally decided to take writing seriously. In 2024, he self-published his first novel, *Sixth Life of the Prophet*.